I0593402

Lies Untold

BROKEN PROMISES
BOOK TWO

LEXIE WINSTON

NEIGHPALM PUBLISHING

About the Author

Lexie Winston has been an astronaut, rock star, princess and time traveller. In her dreams. But none of the dreams have lived up to what becoming an author has been like. She gets to live in a world of pure imagination, and her heroines get to do the things she's always wished she could.

When not writing books, Lexie is a mother of two gorgeous teenagers and the wife to a patient and understanding man. They live in Western Australia and are lorded over by a black toy poodle. She loves camping, reading and if her iPad was stolen, her world would explode. (It has the kindle app on it.)

And check out my website at lexiewinston.com

And you can find all my links at
https://linktr.ee/LexieWinston

Also by Lexie Winston

The Collectors Division

(Paranormal Reverse Harem Series)

Guardian

Guardian's Blood

Guardian Ascending

Collector's Division Omnibus

Neighpalm Industries Collective

(Enemies to Lovers Reverse Harem)

Abandoned Girl

Broken Girl

Tormented Girl

Wanted Girl

Cherished Girl

Loved Girl

Superficial Girl - Jacinta's Story Part 1

Superficial Girl - Jacinta's Story Part 2

Neighpalm Industries Collective 1-3

Neighpalm Industries Collective 4-6

Seductive Sins Collection

(Reverse Harem Series)

Glorious Gluttony

Gangs, Guns, and Glory

Galaxy Circus

(Sci-Fi Reverse Harem Series)

Apprentice

Stagehand

Whisperer

Mama - Galaxy Circus Novella

Performer

A Night Most Wicked - Galaxy Circus Novella

Broken Promises

(Dark Poly Romance Series)

Secrets Kept

Lies Untold

Trust Broken

Love Found

M.I.T.H.O.S

(Contemporary RH)

Spies Like Me

Coming March 2023

First published by Neighpalm Publishing in 2023

Lies Untold - Broken Promises Series 2

Mobi format: 978-0-6453753-0-5
Print: 978-0-6453753-1-2

Cover design by Breakout Designs
Editing by Elemental Editing

 Created with Vellum

Content Warning

This books contains scenes of a sensitive nature and readers are advised to continue at their own risk. These scenes include and are not limited to

Drug Use

Violence

Non Con

Dub Con

Blood and Knife Play

The Broken Promises series will contain MM and FF and is considered a poly romance as opposed to a traditional reverse harem romance.

Chapter One

Beware of the fox in the henhouse.

What the fuck? I turn it over, and there's more.

They are coming for you and Gio next.

The throbbing sound of the club music penetrates the fog of confusion the note causes. On one hand, it's vague as shit and almost juvenile. On the other, can I really afford to ignore it? I mean we're not stupid, we know there are people constantly gunning for us, but why give us this warning now? Balling the piece of paper in my hand, I scan the bar for a clue as to who left it. I know it's probably futile and they are long gone, but I can't help myself.

Nothing stands out in the crowd of beautiful, half naked, intoxicated people. No one is paying any particular attention to me or seems to be suspicious. Blowing out a sigh of frustration, I tuck the piece of paper into the top of my dress to show Gio when I get back to the

VIP area. I'll also need to look at the security footage and see if anyone is recognizable in it.

Now, I just have to make myself return. I'm half tempted to call it a night and head home. To be honest, I'm exhausted. The last six months since Dad's death have been nonstop. I finished high school, plus we managed to keep all the vultures who came after Dad's empire at bay, assuming we were a couple of teenagers who didn't know what we were doing. Suffice it to say, the population of mafia families on the West Coast has dwindled to just us and a handful of others, most notably the Maricuso family, the one Penelope wanted to marry me off to. The damn step-witch would do anything to get rid of me.

I've recently discovered this is the family that Stacey's family belongs to. I didn't put two and two together until it was literally shoved in my face. While we have an uneasy truce with them, Gio says Dad couldn't stand Mario, the head of the family. There's something somewhat sinister and dishonest about him, which is saying a lot considering our line of work, and he has no children, which makes the line of succession unclear. It's one of the things that I need to investigate while Gio is playing college student. We want to make sure that if we have to take him out, we're not, in fact, promoting Stacey to the front of the line. Wouldn't that be something? Not that we don't have plans for her either, but I do like watching her sweat, and that's the real reason I need to return to the VIP section.

I wave my hand at one of the staff, signaling I need

a drink. A little fortification never hurt anyone, and my weed buzz is wearing off. I don't have any handy, so I'll need to return to my office and grab something. Turning my back to the bar, I look out over the dance floor. With the bar sitting slightly higher, it gives me a good view of everyone on it.

Bodies writhe and grind to the pulsing beat of the music. The club is packed tonight, just like it is most nights. We are one of the hottest nightspots in Banebridge and have a line out front for those waiting to get in.

Things are going so well business wise that families from the East Coast have been sniffing around, looking to expand their empire, as have one or two of the Mexican cartels, while the ones we don't have agreements with have been trying to muscle in on our exclusive market. Things are heating up, and I know that I won't be getting any downtime in the near future, especially since Gio has reenrolled in college.

Personally, I think he's crazy, and we had quite an argument over it. He claims that the classes will help him with our businesses, which he's probably not wrong about, but it's also dumping a lot of responsibility on my shoulders while he's off trying to have the normal college experience. Things between us have been tense, what with that and his secretive meetings.

My eyes stop on a couple on the outskirts of the crowd, and I frown. I'd recognize that mop of floppy, curly brown hair anywhere. Although I can't see his face, because he has it nuzzled into the neck of the girl he's dancing with, I also recognize the body whose leg she's grinding on. Sage and I have barely spent any time apart over the last six months, and I think I could identify him blindfolded if I were close enough to smell him. I watch as his hands run up and down the female's curvy ass, and an intense wave of irrational jealousy washes over me. I grit my teeth and try to will away the intense need to put a bullet in her skull. Sage is entitled to his fun. God knows I've made it clear over the last few months that nothing can happen between us. It would complicate things beyond what they already are. I'm still trying to convince myself that I'm not attracted to him because if I give in to my impulses, I could find myself falling for my best friend once again, and I swore that would never happen. Nope, Sage is firmly in the friend zone, and that is where he will stay.

"Ms. Russo?" A voice has me turning my back on the sight, and I smile at the staff member who has my drink. I'm not sure I pulled it off, though, because he blanches and quickly backs away. Damn it, I need to perfect a non-psychotic smile, but it's so hard when the image of what's behind me is flashing in my brain like the neon lights of the Kitty Kat Club. I down half my gin and tonic in one go and take a deep breath before letting it out slowly. Behind the bar is a mirror, and my gaze catches on Sage and his little piece again. *Fuck it.* Grabbing my drink, I turn and march in his direction. They are lost in their own little world, and it's not until I tap him on the shoulder that they realize I'm standing right next to them. Sage startles slightly at the contact, and when his eyes meet mine, I can see he's been indulging in his own product. His eyes are wide, and his pupils are pinpricks, but it's his chick that draws my attention.

"What the fuck do you want?" she snarls, pushing me away with one hand, leaving the rest of her body wrapped around my... Sage. She barely manages to move me, and it's all I can do to hold in my chuckle of amusement. My night is now looking up once more. I relish the thought of a fight and drawing blood. Sage's look of terror as he steps in to stop her hits me hard, but I keep the blank look on my face. I don't want to show him how much it hurts that he would actually care enough about the girl to be worried about what's going to happen to her when she gets on my bad side. I raise an eyebrow at him, and he releases a sigh and stays where he is.

I look her up and down. She's pretty, or she would be without the sneer on her face. Short, black, bobbed hair frames her face, and she's wearing a dress very similar to mine, but instead of being black, hers is white, and under the UV lights, it's practically see through. It's going to look good covered in blood.

"Sage, introduce me to your friend," I say quietly, but we're close enough that he can still hear it over the throb of the music.

"She's no one, Tori, so there's no need to get your panties in a twist," he replies flatly. The girl's face falls, and just like that, I feel better. I'm such a psycho bitch that hearing him dismiss her like that is exactly the thing that makes me feel better. His sidepieces need to know from the get-go that I'm his number one and will always come first for him, no matter how long they are together.

"What the fuck? You were just telling me you've never felt like this about anyone," the girl snaps at him, her hands on her hips.

"I never have. This batch of ecstasy is off the fucking charts." Sage's goofy smile returns, and I laugh out loud as the girl's face falls once more. I should have known she meant nothing to him.

"Run along, sweetie, we've got adult things to deal with." I dismiss the girl, giving her my back, and it's only the widening of Sage's eyes that tells me she's not going to let this one go.

"Who the fuck do you think you are?" she screeches as I sense more than feel her reach for my sleek ponytail.

Before she can grab it, I whirl around and snatch her hand out of the air. She yelps as I squeeze her wrist hard. I'm not strong enough to break it like this, but I do know a quick move that will take care of it. I'm contemplating whether or not to use it when I feel a hand on my shoulder.

"Don't bother, Tori. She's not worth it," Sage says, and again, the pleasure I feel at the disappointment on her face makes a smile creep across my lips. What she sees must make her think twice, because she yanks her hand out of mine and turns before flouncing off without a backward glance.

"Come on," I tell Sage without looking at him. "I have some information to share with you and Gio." I head in the direction of the VIP staircase, not waiting to see if he will follow or not. I don't want him to see the jealousy in my eyes, because he's not the type of person to let it go. He'll question me about it, and I'm not ready to face it. Besides, it's probably at the end of a long list of issues I have to worry about right now.

I push my way through the crowd, my mind whirring over everything that needs to be dealt with and how little time I have to do it. We don't have enough trusted people in our inner circle to delegate at the moment. There have been rumbles that maybe Lorenzo should have been next in line to head the family, and until we figure out where these are coming from, everyone within our organization is suspect. The only ones I'm sure of are Sage and Gio, and even Gio is being shady. He keeps disappearing, and no matter how many people I put on his tail, he manages to lose them.

I feel Sage step up next to me, and neither of us talk as we make our way up the VIP stairs, but then I think of something and put my hand on his arm, stopping him midway up the steps. "The girl I told you about, the one that betrayed me, is in the VIP with a group of friends, all of whom I used to go to school with. Gio and I are going to lull them into a false sense of comfort before I get my revenge, but do me a favor—don't use any of them for your extracurricular activities, please." I bite my lip, not wanting to look him in the eye, but he puts a finger under my chin and lifts it so I can't avoid his eyes.

"You just point them out, love, and I will avoid them like the plague, but I am going to need someone to take care of my little problem since you ran off my sure thing." He adjusts his package with the hand that is not under my chin, and I roll my eyes.

"I saw Gio's friends Tristan and Xavier up there. They like to take extras into their bed, so why don't you ask them?" I knock his finger away. I'm almost tempted to offer him a hand job to relieve the pressure, but that's crossing a line I swore I wouldn't. I already went too far with my sub at the club, but that's not personal. He's no one in the scheme of things, while Sage is so much more than that, but it is getting harder and harder to resist. I must wait too long, because he starts grinning at me and pushes me back against the stair rail, getting up close and personal.

"Or I can give you a lesson on pleasing a man. No one has to know that you went to the dark side for a brief moment." The grin drops as he crowds my space. I feel his breath brush against my lips, and his familiar scent surrounds me, and my determination weakens. I mean, what would it hurt, right? There are no feelings involved, and I would just be helping my best friend who is in need.

Suddenly, a faint peal of familiar laughter reaches my ears, and my head turns. Standing at the top of the stairs are Stacey and Nikki Steel. Neither of them is looking down at us, so the laughter must be about something else, but it breaks me out of the spell of lust that Sage weaved around me.

I stop and think about what I just thought. Fuck, that's what got me in trouble in the first place, caving to the needs and wants of my best friend, and look at how that turned out. I straighten my spine and grit my teeth, pushing Sage out of my personal space.

"Not going to happen." I brush past him and continue up the stairs, heaving out a sigh. I'm not a hundred percent sure if it's from relief or disappointment. Fucking hell, I'm messed up. I don't look back, but I do feel Sage catch up to me once again. With his hand on my back, we present a united front despite the tension between us as the two of us enter the VIP area together. Stacey and Nikki both watch us like hawks as we step around them and make our way back to the ridiculous thrones we'd been seated on previously. Gio is nowhere to be seen, but no one is sitting in our seats since they know better. I sit back in mine, the drink I ordered before a wet mess on the little table between the two chairs. Sage throws himself into Gio's chair and slumps indolently.

"When am I going to get a chair too?" he asks, a small pout on his lips as I wave a waitress over.

I smile at him, reach over, and pat his leg. "I'll order one for you tomorrow. Will that make you happy?" I ask as the waitress gets to us. He grumbles but looks pleased. "Can you take that away and get us both new ones?" I ask her, gesturing at the drink on the table. It's been sitting unattended for too long, and I learned my lesson about how easily I can be drugged through a drink.

The girl quickly gathers the old one and hurries away to get us fresh ones. I'm not concerned about the staff here. They know that they'll end up dead if they allow anyone to slip anything into my or Gio's drinks, but Sage still gets up to trail after her. I feel a rush of warmth, and again, I have to tell myself that he's off-limits. I'm beginning to sound like a broken record.

To distract myself, I look around the VIP area again, studying the group that came in with Stacey and Nikki. Of course, Fiona and Felicity are here too. I can see James Walter and some of the rest of the football team. Finally, my eyes snag on my wayward brother. He's over on the other side of the room talking to Tristan and Xavier, as well as a blond guy who looks somewhat familiar. I bite my lip, trying to figure out where I know him from.

"You know, if you eye fuck my boyfriend any harder, you're going to end up pregnant."

Chapter Two

"I mean, I know he's hot, but you need to be a little more subtle." The voice is husky and sexy, and when I drag my eyes away from the blond guy, I find the gorgeous redhead I noticed before I went downstairs. Oh, right, the blond guy was with her, and I think these are Xavier and Tristan's adopted siblings that I didn't get to meet on the first day of school. I grit my teeth, willing a blush not to appear on my cheeks. The memories of that day still cause me grief, and I don't want anyone to see my weakness. I look the girl up and down. She's smoking hot and wearing black, wide-legged pants with a tight, black sleeveless top that hugs her curves to perfection. All of that black just helps to highlight the shocking red length of her long hair. I itch to run my hands through it before using her locks to pull her head back.

"Oh no, Vienna. Tori's more likely to eye fuck you

than Colton. She's a rug muncher." Stacey steps up next to her, smiling wickedly as she crosses her arms.

Nikki is standing behind her, looking a little cautious. Her eyes swing between me and the two girls confronting me. I can see her little brain ticking over as her gaze slides to Gio. Oh, I think maybe Nikki Steel has been read into the program. I bet her dad told her to stay on our good sides, because she looks like she would rather be anywhere than here at the moment.

"What, Tori, too scared to admit it?" Stacey jeers, and I raise an eyebrow.

"I didn't hear you complaining when my head was between your legs. In fact, it was, 'Oh yeah, Tori,' and 'More,' as far as I remember," I deadpan, not letting her get a rise out of me. "And when I railed you with the strap-on, you asked me to pull your hair and slap your ass. Ah, good times." I pretend to reminisce before standing up and descending the steps toward the two girls. Vienna remains quiet while Stacey and I throw barbs at one another. "But do you remember the noises I made when it was your turn to return the favor?" I stop in front of her, standing slightly taller with my heels on, and she has to look up at me. I lean in and drop my voice. "Oh no, that's right, there weren't any because I was unconscious when you raped me." The last words are said on a quiet growl, and it's all I can do to stop myself from putting a bullet in her brain when she smirks at me unrepentantly, but no, that would be too quick. I want to torment her and drag this game out for a while until she's shaking in her boots and always looking over her shoulder.

"You always thought you were better than me," she snaps, "and I proved that wasn't the case."

"What, because I wouldn't pimp my brother out to you? I'm a big believer of free will, Stacey, but obviously that's not an issue you have." I turn to the redhead. "So the blond is your boyfriend? I'd be careful with this one. She's not opposed to sleeping her way to the top." I smirk, looking back at Stacey. "But then again, did you even really make it to the top? As far as I can tell, James is still with Nikki, and once again, you have nobody."

That shot hits its mark. She flinches slightly and then shrugs. "Maybe I've turned my sights on something different. Vienna's other brothers are smoking hot, and I've heard they like to share. What do you think, Tori? Do I have a chance?" Her eyes light up at something behind me. "Or there's always that delicious man that seems to be your shadow. Why is that, Tori? You're obviously not keeping him happy sexually, so what is it?"

A hand slides around my waist, making me smile slyly at her, but before I can answer, he does. "Oh, I can assure you Tori keeps me completely satisfied." Sage nuzzles into my neck as his hand snakes farther around my waist, drawing me backward into him. The erection he's still rocking from before pushes against my ass, and I almost wince. That can't be comfortable. "But you would know all about that, wouldn't you?"

Sage's shot at her has more of an impact than mine did, and she winces.

Vienna has been quiet since her first quip at me, and I've been so consumed with my narrow-minded anger at Stacey that I kind of forgot she was standing there.

"Hmm, Stacey, it would seem to me that you are out of your league. Maybe you should stick to stealing Nikki's boyfriend. Neither Colton, X, or Tris will fall for your ways, especially when I tell them that it was you who raped Tori." She looks at Stacey in horror. "How could you do something so horrible like that?"

I struggle to contain my surprise. I thought Stacey would have caved and bragged to everyone about it by now. I'm also surprised that the new girl is standing up for me. I mean, I guess her adopted brothers are friends with Gio, but I don't know this girl from the next. I can't help but eye her warily. Is she trying for some angle?

Stacey rolls her eyes and sneers. "Please, Vienna, like you're so vanilla. Don't think that we don't know that you spread your legs for all three of your 'brothers.' You're not as innocent as you pretend to be."

"No, but everything I do is consensual. Taking away someone's choice is despicable, and only a lowlife does that."

"You keep telling yourself that, Vienna, but in our world, it's dog eat dog. Unless you're a woman who commands respect, you're going to become a doormat. That's all I did. I claimed my respect."

"Wow! Who wants the respect of misogynistic assholes who condone rape? No thanks." Sage and I watch quietly as the two women throw insults back and forth. It's getting more and more heated, and it's drawing the attention of everyone around us. Soon enough, a little circle of former school friends have gathered around as the argument devolves.

"We all know you are happy to get down on your knees for anyone who will help you climb up the social ladder. Last I heard, you fucked most of the football team. Plus, you're not happy to find your own boyfriend, and you continuously try to poach." Vienna's gaze drifts to where Nikki and James stand side by side. James's look of panic is there and gone so quickly that I'm not sure if I imagined it or not.

Nikki's eyes narrow, and she whirls on him. "Is this true? Does Stacey try to get in your pants?"

"Babe, no. I swear, I've done nothing with her," James denies, but I'm not paying attention to the two of them. I'm watching Stacey, and I see the exact moment she decides to go all in.

"Pfft, *nothing*? That's not what I'd call the blow job at the restaurant we went to for dinner," she scoffs at James before turning to Nikki. "Do you really think he was just going to the bathroom at the same time as me? We also fucked in his car after your last party when he offered to drive me home. See, if you were happy to actually spread your legs for him, then he wouldn't have to look for it elsewhere," Stacey sneers, and I watch as James blanches and Nikki looks like she's been slapped.

"I thought we were saving ourselves for marriage." Nikki sounds so hurt, I kind of feel sorry for her, but then I remember what a huge bitch she was to me and quickly get over it.

Stacey laughs maliciously. "That ship sailed a long time ago, even before you got together. He's been fucking side chicks the entire time you've been together."

Nikki glares at Stacey before turning to look at the twins, but Stacey waves a hand.

"Oh no, the Bobbsie twins are completely loyal, so they wouldn't touch him, but just about every other girl at school has, and they all laugh about it behind your back." Stacey really deserves what is coming to her, and I can't wait to dish it out. I might even invite Nikki. "Oh, except Vienna, because she is too busy with whatever she's got going on with her brothers to even look his way."

"Babe, please!" James pleads, but Nikki just turns her back, holds her head high, and walks away, followed by the twins.

I wave a waitress over. "Those girls' drinks are on the house for the rest of the night." I point them out to her. "And make sure they have a car to take them home."

She hurries away to do what I've ordered.

"Well, as entertaining as that was, I'm almost certain you're fucked now, Stacey," I remark as James hurls a hateful glare at her and storms away, followed by the rest of their friends, leaving Stacey and Vienna behind.

Stacey shrugs. "What do I care? High school is done, and I'm moving onto greener pastures. College is a whole new game with new meat and a chance for better friendships." She turns her body to study Gio and the boys who stayed in the corner, lost in conversation. He hadn't even noticed us throwing down earlier. Asshole! "Hey, who knows, I'm going to Suncity U, and I heard that Gio is attending this year too. Maybe I'll finally get a shot at him when you're not around to gate keep." She flicks her blonde hair over her shoulder before stalking off in the same direction of the football players.

"Is she really that stupid?" Vienna asks, unable to hide the disbelief in her voice as her eyes follow Stacey's path.

"Apparently. I'm Tori Russo, by the way. This is Sage." I introduce us to the girl I had never had a chance to be friends with. "Why did you do that?" I ask, unable to hide my own curiosity.

"Do what?" Vienna blinks owlishly at me, but I have a feeling it's an act.

"Tank your friendship with Stacey like that," Sage replies, sounding as suspicious as I feel.

She snorts. "Friendship? Are you serious? That girl is a piranha. After what she did to you on the first day of school last year, I was never going to be friends with her. If her supposed best friend isn't safe, no one is, but

I'm also not stupid. Haven't you heard the phrase keep your friends close and your enemies closer? There was no way I was going to let her get near Colton without me being around. I wouldn't put it past her to spike his drink either. I'm going to warn the others of that as well."

I reassess the redhead in front of me. There's a whole level of cunning there that I hadn't expected, and I begrudgingly have to respect that.

"Well, thanks anyway. It was kind of nice hearing you defend me even though I don't need it. Stacey is barely a blip on my radar at the moment." The three of us watch as Stacey changes direction, no longer following the football players as she beelines directly toward Gio and Vienna's "brothers."

"So what is the deal there?" Sage asks as we watch Stacey worm her way between Tristan and Xavier, fluttering her eyes at Gio and Colton with a bright smile.

"What deal?" Vienna asks Sage, not looking away from the scene in front of us.

"You're fucking your brothers?" Sage asks bluntly, and I can't stop my own snort from escaping.

"That sounds like a conversation that requires more alcohol than I've partaken in today," I tell him, and Vienna lights up, giggling. It's this musical tinkle that makes my heart go pitty-pat, and when I look at Sage, he practically has cartoon love hearts pulsing in his eyes. I mean, that could be the X too, but he doesn't seem unaffected by the redhead regardless.

"I guess. We were all adopted by the same person,

but before that, we lived in a group home. They were always my protectors. We would come and go, fostered out to different families, but we would always end up back at the same home. Eventually, as we got older, that protection turned into something more and, well, look at them. Did you really expect me to choose?"

Huh, that was not what I was expecting. I mean, I knew it wasn't some weird *Flowers in the Attic* shit, but for her to admit she is with all of them kind of throws me.

"But I thought Xavier and Tristan were a couple? They propositioned me," I explain, feeling guilty, though I have no idea why.

She groans. "Now why doesn't that surprise me?"

"That doesn't upset you?" Sage sounds as curious as I feel.

"Why should it? Tori's a gorgeous woman. I don't blame them. We're young, we're not tied down, and although we *are* committed, if they wanted to invite another into their bed, that's their prerogative. Same goes with Colton and me. Sometimes we all share." She looks at the two of us like she's considering how well both of us would fit in their bed.

Sage bites his knuckle, and it's his turn to groan. "Please introduce me to all of them. God, I'm still rolling, and my cock won't go down. At least this way I have excellent spank bank material for when I have to go home and take care of it with my own hand."

I smack him up the back of his head. "Sorry, Sage

has no filter. I really should have left him at home." I scowl at him, but she just laughs.

"Come on, there's been way too much drama tonight. Buy me a drink, and I'll even give you their phone numbers."

"Sold," Sage exclaims and hooks his arm through hers, and the two of them wander to the bar where he places an order before continuing on to join the rest of the boys.

I stay where I am to observe. Vienna and Stacey must exchange more barbs, because shortly after, Stacey places a kiss on both Tristan's and Xavier's cheeks before waving a breezy goodbye and disappearing into the crowd without a backward glance. I've got to admit, the girl has balls.

Gio glares at her the entire time. She has no chance with him, but Xavier and Tristan didn't seem opposed. I wonder if she even realizes how dangerous Gio and I really are, or if her dad has convinced her that she's protected because of our tentative truce with the Maricuso family. I bet he doesn't think we'd risk that to get even. I squeeze my hands into fists, the urge to follow after her and use my knife on her riding me hard. I may have to set up another rendezvous at the sex club with one of my subs soon if I don't get someone to torture in my chair in the near future.

My gaze returns to the group, zeroing in on the only woman. She smiles broadly as she introduces Sage. I'm not sure what he's saying, but from the way Gio rolls his eyes and the other three men's eyebrows jump in surprise, I'm sure it was something dirty. Tristan is the quickest to recover, and he must say something dirty in return, because he winks, and it's Sage's turn to look surprised. His mouth drops open, and everyone laughs, even Gio.

I can't help pondering what Vienna's angle is. She came to my defense rather quickly, and I'm sure it's because she's a decent person, but I still can't help but be suspicious. This is what Stacey has done to me. I can't even accept a supportive gesture at face value.

I'm not going to worry about it for now though. Instead, I'm just going to plaster a smile on my face and say hello to my brother's future roommates, because of course he's rooming with them again.

Chapter Three

"Tori, there you are. You remember Tristan and Xavier from my aborted attempt at college last year?" Gio greets me as I join the group, gesturing to his friends.

"Of course, how could I forget? It's nice to see you again." I'm super polite, but not overly warm. Close friendships aren't a possibility in our line of work, so I'm a little surprised that Gio is making such an effort. Sure, he's going to live with them for at least the next year, but he could maintain *some* distance. Becoming too friendly with them is a surefire way for them to be killed or used against us. I think that's one of the reasons Dad made Sage a Russo, to give him more protection.

"Hey, Tori, you're looking smoking hot. Still playing for the same team? Or are you ready to take a ride on the wild side?" Tristan smirks at me, and I roll my eyes.

"Tris? What the fuck?" Vienna scolds him,

smacking him on the back of the head. He winces but grins unrepentantly at her.

"Ow, knock it off. Tori's cool. She and I bonded last year over our mutual love of pussy licking."

I shake my head, amused at his antics. Nothing has changed, he's still a flirty fool. I remember our brief kiss in our kitchen when he tasted the pineapple juice from my lips and feel a twinge of regret. Maybe I *should* experiment a little. Between this and how I feel for Sage, not to mention how much I enjoyed playing with my new little sub, I almost have to face the fact that I'm not gay, but bi. However, it's like starting all over again. Sure, I'm definitely not a virgin, but having a relationship with a man hasn't been on my radar. One thing I do know for sure is that I need to avoid these particular men. Vienna has staked her claim, and no matter what she says, I will not poach another person's partner.

"Good to see you again." Xavier's nod is brief, and his words are gruff, but I can see by the look in his eyes that he's also admiring how I look.

"Hey, guys. I hear you didn't run while you had the chance and you're both stupid enough to want to room with this guy again this year." I point at my brother.

"Hey!" he complains, looking butt hurt.

"What? I've lived with you for eighteen years, so I know what I'm talking about. Just be grateful you aren't sharing an actual room, because he snores like a grizzly bear."

They all laugh, and Vienna puts a hand on my arm, drawing my attention. Her palm is soft on my skin, and goosebumps rise on my flesh. I hope she doesn't notice.

Vienna introduces me to the only stranger in the group. "Tori, this is Colton. I don't think either of you have met before." Colton has longish blond hair with matching stubble on his face, as well as black-rimmed glasses. He's wearing a pair of black jeans and a long-sleeved royal blue shirt that hugs his muscular physique. Like all of the others, he's unnaturally pretty. It's really not fair how pretty they all are.

"It's nice to meet you," I say politely, but all he does is nod his head. Okay, not a big talker, that's fine. "Listen, I hate to interrupt you, but I need to speak to Gio and Sage for a moment. Work stuff, I hope you don't mind."

"Now, Tori?" Gio whines, and I kind of want to shoot him in the knee. He's becoming more and more difficult. It's almost like he doesn't want to be the head of the family. I guess it can't be easy. He probably thought he had years before he had to take over, but he's not the only one who was robbed. At least he gets to go to college and pretend. Sage and I don't get that luxury. That would just leave the business open for a hostile takeover.

"Yes, Gio, now," I say through gritted teeth, and he heaves out a sigh.

"Fine. Why don't you grab drinks, and I'll be back as soon as we are done?" Gio gestures to a waitress who hurries over. "Can you clear out a booth for my friends? Their drinks are on the house," he tells her, and she nods, smiling at him.

"Sure thing, Mr. Russo. If you would all follow me, there's an empty one over here." She leads the way, and Gio's friends follow her.

"Are you going to join us later, Tori?" Vienna asks before she leaves.

"I'm not sure. I was just going to head home because I have an early meeting tomorrow."

"But aren't you going to help me move into the dorms again?" Gio sounds surprised, and I clench my fists to stop myself from reaching for the gun in my thigh holster.

Sage seems to understand how I feel, because he skillfully interrupts. "Come on, man. You know business comes before pleasure. Why don't you cut her some slack?"

"Well, you can at least have another drink before you go home." He pouts, and I cave.

"Okay, fine, one drink, and then I'm done," I tell him, and Vienna smiles prettily.

"Great, is there anything you want? I'll order it so it's here when you get back."

"Actually, I don't like anyone else ordering my drinks. I hope you understand," I tell her apologetically, and she blanches. Vienna knows what I'm referring to.

"Of course. I'm such an idiot. I'm sorry," she apologizes, but I wave it off.

"No big deal. We'll see you shortly." I lead Gio and Sage toward my office, stopping the conversation in its tracks mostly because I'm embarrassed that so many people have seen me vulnerable like that. Once it was taken down, it never actually resurfaced, but by then the damage was already done. I hate knowing she knows about it, let alone has seen it. I stomp down the corridor, my heels muffled by the rugs. I can hear Gio and Sage muttering behind me, but I don't stop. My buzz has worn off, and I want to grab another joint while I'm in my office. If I need to stay longer, I'll need fortification, and it doesn't look like I'll be escaping anytime soon.

I slap my hand against the biometric scanner, and when the green light flashes, I push the door open. The noise disappears as the door closes behind us, and I can't stop my sigh of relief. Going over to my desk, I flop down in the seat and pull my drawer open while Gio and Sage take the chairs across from me.

"What is so important that I had to leave my friends, Tori?" Gio asks, and I just stare at him in disbelief.

"Are you fucking kidding me right now?" I growl, unable to hide how pissed off I am now that we're alone. "When did you become such a clingy, whiny bitch?" I demand, not pulling my punches. "You're the head of the fucking Russo family, not a fucking sulking teenage boy who couldn't hang out with his friends. Get your shit together."

This has him sitting up straight in his chair. "Watch your mouth, Tori," he snaps.

"Why the fuck should I? When you act like a fucking child, I'm going to call you out on it. Right now, it seems like you don't even want the job. How about you step aside and let me take the role of head of the family, since all you seem to be concerned about is kissing those people's asses?" I stab a finger in the direction we just came from. I have a full head of steam now that I finally have a chance to get this all off my chest. "Not to mention you're shady as fuck, disappearing all the time. Where are you going? Who are you meeting? What are you not telling me? I thought we were a team." The last sentence comes out a little plaintively, and I want to kick my own ass at showing my vulnerability.

The anger seems to rush away from him, and he slumps again. "Nowhere. I just drive. It's a lot, you know. I didn't expect to have to do this for years. I thought once we had established our rule, things would be easier, but even though we've dealt with all the challenges here, more keep popping up." He slowly reaches up and tugs at his ear, and my stomach falls. The bastard is lying to me. I just don't know what to do anymore. I know he doesn't really want to be in this life. What is my next course of action? I can't kill my own brother. Can I?

"Dude, it's not cool. You get to go to college and have a semi-normal life, while Tori keeps control of the empire so it's still there for you when you decide to man up." Whoa, Sage isn't pulling any punches, and Gio scowls at him. "You need to be careful who you become friends with. We still know nothing about those people. They are not stupid, and I'm sure they know who you are now. How do you know they aren't using you for their own gain?" Sage points out, voicing exactly what I'd been thinking.

"And you know friends in our line of work are not possible. They will become targets. That's why Dad made you give up Casey last year." Gio won't look me in the eye, and I sigh. "I was actually surprised that she wasn't here tonight with them." He was adamant last year that she was *the one*, and I thought for sure that he would do what Dad suggested and send her letters, but I guess he wasn't as into her as he first thought.

"She doesn't like the clubbing atmosphere. She's more of a homebody," he replies, and my eyebrows shoot up. I guess he has stayed in touch with her. He shrugs, trying to seem nonchalant, but I can tell he's still interested. That will only end badly if anyone gets wind of his interest in her. He's going to fuck up her life, but I can't tell him that. I just hope she doesn't end up dead.

"Well, we need to at least run a background check on them. I'll have the tech team start on one tomorrow. I want to know everything about them, including what they ate for breakfast. I don't want any nasty surprises popping up when we least expect it."

Gio sighs and nods, knowing I won't take no for an

answer. "Fine, I will get them working on it tomorrow."

I sigh, knowing this conversation is going nowhere. I pull the slip of paper out of my dress and toss it across the table in front of them. "This is what I wanted to tell you about."

They both reach for it at the same time, but Gio is slightly faster than Sage, and he snatches it up. I open my drawer and pull out a couple of joints. Leaving one on the table, I light the other one and take a big drag as Gio quickly reads it. Scowling, he passes it to Sage who does the same thing.

"Well, that's not completely vague and obvious at the same time," Gio grumbles.

I hold the smoke in my lungs, enjoying the way they burn for fresh air before blowing it out again in a cloud. "That was my exact thought," I say, waving my joint around. I pull my laptop in front of me, but before I can open it, Sage comes around to my side and plucks the joint out of my hand. I scowl at him, but it will make using the laptop easier. He winks and takes a drag.

I huff and open the computer, accessing the security camera feed. I then find the camera covering the bar it had been left at and go back to the time when the waitress came and got me. Going back a little farther, I watch the security footage in real time, trying to work out who left the note for me. That's when I see it.

I watch as a figure wearing a black hoodie with the hood up and black jeans approaches the bar. They lean in and say something to the bartender before handing over the note. I can't make out anything, except I'm almost certain it's male. I use the zoom function to try and discern any other defining features, and apart from the hand when it passes over the note, I see no skin. The hand doesn't have any identifying tattoos, so I zoom out and see if I can make out anything else. As the figure turns away from the bar, I see a flash of blond hair poke out of the hood, but it quickly gets pushed back before the hood is pulled down.

"They know where the cameras are," Sage observes helpfully. "They know that's the only one pointing at the bar and manage to avoid it the whole time."

"Why is it the only one pointing at the bar? Surely they should be pointing at both sides," I grumble as I slap the computer closed in frustration. "That was no fucking help at all. We learned that he was male and might be blond, but for all I know, that was a wig to fool the bartender. I didn't think about asking him. Maybe I'll go back and see if I can get a description from him."

Gio rubs a hand across his chin and stands up. "Well, I don't know about you two, but I'm ready to get my drink on." He grabs the other joint from my desk and tucks it into a pocket. "No point in worrying about that. They weren't telling us anything we didn't know."

"No, you're right, but I'd really like to know who they were referring to. Are they the same people who killed Dad? Which, by the way, your tech team still hasn't been able to figure out. To be honest, I think they kind of suck and we need to find someone else. They are less than useless. A good hacker should have been able to tell us who posted the contract on that hit site."

It's an argument we've been having for a while, but I think Gio was so overwhelmed with everything and everyone else we had to take care of that the tech team hit the back burner. They swear they are loyal, but they are the ones responsible for digging into everyone we bring to them, so who's to say they have been truthful? I think it's time we hired a neutral third party.

"Fuck, fine, Tori. If I find you a new tech guru, will you give it a rest?" Gio snaps, and I exchange a surprised glance with Sage.

"Yes, that would be awesome, thank you," I say calmly despite the anger that rolls through me. I'm so fucking sick and tired of his attitude. Screw him. I thought we were a team, but I guess I was mistaken. I'm not sure why I'm surprised though. I should have expected to be let down, since it's becoming a pattern in my life. I've been betrayed and left by everyone who meant something to me. First there was Stacey, then Dad and Carla, and now Gio. This is why I won't let Sage get too close, because I know if I allow myself to care, to love again, he'll either let me down or leave me.

Standing up, I lean over and snatch my joint out of my brother's pocket. "Run along now. Don't let me keep you from your friends."

He blinks, and I'm not sure what he sees in my

face, but he blanches slightly before clearing his throat. "Yeah, okay, I'll see you back out there."

"Actually, I think I'm done for the night."

Sage watches the battle of wills and wisely stays quiet.

"But you promised them."

"I'm sure they won't miss me." I take another big drag of my joint, needing the floaty feeling to ease my anger so I don't shoot my brother.

A hand on my shoulder has me turning and glaring at Sage, but he gently shakes his head. "Come on, Tori. One drink won't matter, and you can always use a few friends."

I shake his hand off. "I don't need friends. All they do is let me down." Pushing past him, I stalk through my office, joint in hand, without looking back at either of them.

Hopefully there's someone who needs to be killed tomorrow, because I'm so angry that if I go to the sex club, I'll kill one of my subs, and that's frowned upon. No, tomorrow, I'm going to need to spill some real blood.

Chapter Four

Leaving Sage and Gio to make their way over to Gio's friends, I head straight to the bar. I order myself a drink and smoke the rest of my joint while I stand there waiting for it to be made. I must be putting off don't fuck with me vibes, because people avoid the space I'm in.

"Here you go, Ms. Russo," Jai, our VIP bartender, says as he places my drink in front of me. "Sorry that took so long," he apologizes, even though it took no time at all. He wipes the bar on either side of it, although it's clean as well. I think I make the guy nervous. Our staff isn't stupid, and they know we're not normal club owners.

"Thanks, Jai." I take it and make my way around the outside of the room. It's gotten crowded up here, and it is wall-to-wall bodies. A couple stumbles into me, and I end up being pushed into a small alcove. "Watch where you're going," I snarl at the two of them, but they are not paying attention, their mouths fused together as they stagger past the alcove, not even noticing me at all. Grumbling about horny, intoxicated idiots, I swap which hand my drink is in and run my tongue over the one that is now covered in alcohol.

"You know I've got something better for you to do with that tongue if you're interested." The voice is low and behind me, farther into the alcove. I spin around and peer into the darkness. I'm not worried it's someone who's going to kill me or anything, because I recognize the voice. I'm just a little surprised she's approaching me in public—well, sort of, since we are well hidden.

Felicity has cut her hair since I saw her last. It's no longer long and sleek like her sister's. Instead, it's in a blunt bob and frames her face, giving her an edgy look. Unlike her sister's body hugging dress, she's wearing a pair of black, cutoff denim shorts and a halter top that pushes her breasts up to perfection.

Striding across the alcove, I place my drink down on a small corner table and push her back against the wall, grabbing her hair and yanking her head to the side before running my tongue up her throat. She groans and tries to grab me, but I keep her at arm's length.

"Flic, as much as I enjoy our little rendezvous, after that little interaction with Stacey, I'm afraid I'm feeling too mean for you."

"But I like it when you're rough," she purrs, her pupils wide with lust.

"Oh no, honey, you might like it a little rough, but

you're no pain slut, and I'm afraid I would do too much damage to your pretty golden skin. You don't like to bleed, and I have a ferocious need to spill blood. Do you understand?"

She gulps, finally understanding what I mean, and shivers, but this time it's not from lust. This time she sees and hears the barely disguised violence that I'm trying desperately to keep at bay. Her throat moves as she swallows nervously, and she nods. I lean in and give her a kiss before shoving her and sending her on her way. She stumbles slightly, running her hands through her hair to straighten the mess I made of it, but doesn't look back. She's not stupid. She knows when to cut and run, and I admire that about her. Felicity was fun to corrupt, and she does beg ever so prettily, but I'm not interested in being her dirty little secret, and she really isn't that into me. She likes the thrill and the illicit meetings. No, it's time she got the guts to come out of the closet and find another partner. I'm done with that shit, although maybe I should introduce her to Candy. They could be good together.

By the time I leave the alcove, Felicity is nowhere to be seen, and I continue to make my way through the crowd, bracing myself for joining Gio and his friends. One quick drink and then I'm done. I have a meeting in the morning I can't miss, and to be honest, I'm at the no fucks left to give stage. Apathy, thy name is Tori. I just want my comfy bed and maybe some time to read or watch a movie.

Plastering on a smile, I join the others in their

booth. The booth is big enough that everyone is able to fit in it. Gio is on the end, talking to Xavier, then there are Tristan and Sage who look to be flirting outrageously with each other. Next to them are Colton and Vienna. Colton has his arm around her, and she is tucked in next to him while he quietly observes everything that is going on around him. I bet that boy doesn't miss anything. I'm going to have to keep an eye on him. I go to pull up a chair from a neighboring table, but Vienna pats the seat next to her.

"Come sit with me, Tori. It sucks being the only female at the sausage fest, so I need your moral support."

I look helplessly at Sage in the hopes he will jump in and save me, but he just grins and nods encouragingly. Asshole. I guess that's payback for fucking up his sure thing earlier.

"Ha, that's not what you normally say, V. Usually, you're giving instructions on where all the sausages need to go." Tristan winks at her, and she flips him off.

I feel my own cheeks heat at their casual sexual conversation. I still don't have the confidence to talk like that, and who would I talk to anyway? Gio would just gag, and Sage would take me up on any innuendo I threw his way.

"So tell me a little about yourself. Are you going to college with Gio this year?" Vienna asks, moving away from Colton and closer to me. Her thigh presses against mine, and her boob presses against my arm as she leans in so we can converse over the loud music.

Her breast is soft and round against my arm, and I wonder briefly what it would feel like in my mouth.

Fuck, Tori, get your shit together.

"Ah, no, I won't be. Our family businesses won't survive if we both ignore them to play college student," I tell her, and I guess maybe that sounded a little bitter, because one of her eyebrows rises in surprise. "And Gio was enrolled last year, so I told him to go and learn shit that will help benefit us. Maybe I'll take a turn when he's done," I lie to her. College is never going to be in the cards for me, and I'm actually okay with that. It all seems incredibly insignificant in the grand scheme of things. There are bigger things in life to worry about.

"What about you?" I ask her, putting the conversation back on her. I'm not sure what Gio has told his friends about what the family business is, and I don't want to be asked anything awkward that I can't answer, though clubs and casinos are a great public front.

"Oh yes, Colton and I will both be attending Suncity U as well. Actually, we will be sharing a dorm on the same floor that Gio and the guys are on with our cousin Casey. I think you met her last year." Vienna grabs Colton's hand and gives it a squeeze. "We're really very excited. It will be nice not to live at home anymore." There's an undercurrent of tension that I pick up from their exchanged glance. I'm not sure if it has to do with going to college or not living at home any longer. I was under the impression that their lives were good since they were adopted together, but maybe I was mistaken.

"Well, that sounds fun. What are you studying?" I keep the conversation flowing but pull out my other joint and spark it up.

"Oh, neither of us has declared a major. We're just going to see where our interests take us."

She watches my joint with interest, so I take another drag before offering it to her. I relax back into the soft booth behind me, the weed finally dampening the need to spill blood enough that I can function. I watch as Vienna wraps her pretty lips around the joint and takes a deep drag. Her eyes drift closed, and her long, black eyelashes sit on her beautiful porcelain cheeks like butterflies. She breathes out and opens them again, her hazel eyes sparkling with mischief. She takes another deep drag before handing it back to me and turning her head to Colton. She grabs hold of his cheeks and slants her lips over his. She breathes out the smoke, and he grabs her wrists, breathing it in. I feel my heart rate speed up at the exchange between the two gorgeous people, feeling a small wave of jealousy at their obvious intimacy.

"Oh yeah, I want a piece of that too." Tristan stands up and leans over, plucking the joint out of my hand. I growl at him, but he just shushes me. "Don't be greedy, Tori. Sharing is caring, and we love to share." He takes a big drag, keeping his eyes locked on mine, before he turns and does the same thing to Sage that Vienna had done to Colton. Sage startles, obviously not expecting it, but quickly gets into it. The kiss continues long after the smoke has been shared, and the joint gets passed to Xavier. Another irrational wave of jealousy washes over me at seeing my... Sage kissing Tristan. Yes, it's hot, but I also want to stab them both. What's with that?

"Okay, well, I think that's my cue to leave," I say, standing up now that my joint has become public property.

"Oh no, Tori, stay. We were just getting to know one another," Vienna pleads, but I've reached my limit.

"Come on, Tori," my brother calls, but I just turn to look at him, my stare turning dead, and he blanches and waves at Vienna. "Let her go. She won't be fun anyway, since she has an early meeting."

"Well, it's been fun. We'll have to do it again sometime," I lie and wave goodbye, not waiting for anyone to respond. Sage is so lost in Tristan that he doesn't even notice. I make it down the stairs and across the lower part of the club before I feel two people join me.

"Where are we headed?" Sam asks, clearing the path toward the exit for me.

"Anywhere but here. Do we have anyone at the warehouse at the moment?" I ask my minion as the crowd thins the closer we get to the exit.

Sam and Dean exchange a look before Dean clears his throat. "Ah, yeah, they picked up a couple of Mexicans sneaking around down by the docks. They brought them to the warehouse so we could ask them some questions."

I feel my smile spread across my face. "Perfect. Let's head there."

"Don't you want to let Gio or Sage know?" Sam looks back nervously in their direction.

"Fuck no. They are as useful as tits on a bull at the moment, and I certainly don't need their fucking permission to do anything. I practically run this family right now," I growl at him, and he holds his hands up.

"I know, but if you told them you were going home, they might worry."

I shrug as the double doors to the club open and we step out into the damp night air. There's a slight breeze, and some hardcore people are still waiting in line despite how the night has cooled.

"It wouldn't hurt for them to have to give a shit about something for a change. I'm sick of being the only one who is pulling their weight." I turn to the bouncer manning the door. "Are we at capacity?" I ask, and he quickly shakes his head.

"No, ma'am."

"Well, don't be an ass. Let these poor people in," I snap and gesture to the twenty or so people waiting. "Nobody wants to catch a fucking cold." I stalk down the stairs and into my car that the valet just pulled to the curb. One of the minions must have sent him a text when he saw me leaving. I take the keys from him as a couple of the waiting people call out a thank you to me, then I force a smile and wave before turning my back on them once more.

"But Sage pulls his weight," Dean argues as I get

into the car. He takes the passenger seat next to me, and Sam slides into the back.

"Yes, but he's on my shit list for a completely different reason tonight. Let it go, you won't win, and I might feel the urge to put the bullet I want to put in them in you if you keep it up." Both Sam and Dean fall silent as I pull the car out onto the road and put my foot down on the gas. The tires spin, and the back wheels try to slide out, but I keep firm control of the vehicle. We make it out of town and back to the city in no time. Luckily, there were no cops on the road, because I probably would have been arrested and the car would have been impounded at the speed I was going. I could hear Sam muttering a little prayer not long into the trip.

I pull to a stop, kicking up gravel in the deserted parking lot of the warehouse. I climb out and reach the door before Dean and Sam can even get out of the car. I hear their hurried footsteps behind me, but I'm already in the zone. I don't have my favorite knife, which is sitting on my bedside table at home. I didn't have anywhere to put it when I got dressed today, and I thought one thigh holster was enough—two would have been tacky.

I cross the deserted warehouse to the door that will take me downstairs. Putting my hand against the biometric scanner, I wait for it to beep, allowing me entrance. By the time I'm down in the outer room, I've stripped off my dress and removed my gun from my thigh holster. I pull overalls on over my panties and slip my feet into rubber boots.

"In a hurry today?" Sam asks, taking a seat at the table and throwing up his feet as Dean heads to the coffee pot. I look through the window at the three men seated inside the torture room and almost feel pity for them. What a crappy day for them to pick to get nosy. Instead of just getting roughed up, questioned, and sent on their way, none of them are going to leave that room alive, all because I happened to run into Stacey. What a shame.

Chapter Five

I have Sam and Dean separate them, and then I interrogate them one at a time. The first two men I use my tools on know nothing—less than nothing, to be honest. They die quickly and without satisfying my need for blood. I mean, sure, I spill heaps of it, but both of them died way too quickly for my liking. My bloodlust got out of hand, and I made a mess out of both of them, but as Dean brings in the last guy, he looks at me with worry in his eyes.

"Take it easy with this one. We kind of need any information he has in that brain. How about you start with the truth shit and then play with your tools once we have what we need." His tone is laced with disappointment, and I feel a pang of guilt.

"Yeah, okay, I'm sorry. I was just so angry. I'm better now. I'll get what we need from this one."

I hosed down the room between each victim. As much as I like to make them panic when they see all the blood, it really was a bloodbath, and this dude is not going to give me anything if he thinks his death is inevitable.

Dean places him in the chair and pulls off the black hood covering his face. His head lolls to the side in his unconscious state, and while I'm waiting for him to regain consciousness, I inject him with Trilimide, then I bang around on my tool desk in the hopes that he will wake up scared and confused. I do love seeing the terror in their eyes.

It takes about ten minutes, and I'm bored out of my brain by the time he does come around. Dean brought me a coffee and told me to chill the fuck out. Truthfully, caffeine isn't really going to help me do that. Only an orgasm or some weed ever settles my mind for a short while, but I am not interested in an orgasm from either of my minions, and I don't have any weed here. My mind is not a pretty place at the moment, and the less time I have to be lost in it, the better.

"Where am I? Who are you?" The words are slurred as the man looks around.

"Finally!" I get to my feet, put my coffee mug on the tool bench, and step in front of the guy.

His head flops back as he tries to get a good look at me. "Oh, I know you. You're the Angel of Death." A thrilled buzz of triumph runs down my spine at him knowing who I am, but he quickly ruins it. "Such a pretty, pretty angel. I'm sure the rumors are all made up. There is no way a pretty girl like you could do such horrible things."

"I wouldn't be too sure about that, buddy," I tell him, and he shakes his head, slurring his words.

"No way. I was telling my buddies at Quantico that there was no way a girl could be responsible for so much carnage."

My mind screeches to a halt. Quantico! Oh fuck. It's one thing to kill criminal scum, but this guy must be an undercover agent. My eyes swivel to the observation mirror. Sam and Dean are standing there with the same look of resignation on their faces.

I have to kill this guy. I have no choice now despite him not being one of the Mexican cartel. Fuck, I haven't had to kill law enforcement before. We mostly stay clear of one another. I think we have some high-level police in our back pockets, but Gio manages that side—or at least I hope he still is. He's been dropping the ball a lot. I wouldn't put it past him to fuck that up too.

"So you're an FBI agent, are you?" I ask, and he shrugs.

"What does it matter now? You're just going to kill me anyway." He sighs loudly. "All I wanted to do was rescue my sister from the sex trafficking that you Russos take part in."

"Hold up. Say what? We don't deal in skin, haven't for years," I argue, my mind running at full tilt now. I wonder if I can turn this to favor us.

"Bullshit," he slurs, scowling at me. "You started

back up six months ago, handing them off to the Mexican cartel where they disappear."

"Like hell we do. Gio and I have nothing to do with that." I cross my arms, stubbornly staring down at the man.

"Well, someone does. I have good intel that someone in the Russo family is in tight with the Nuevo Dios Cartel, and they made a deal that has them managing the West Coast skin distribution for a hefty cut of the sales."

I pace back and forth, frustrated that I killed those other two a little too quickly. How did we not know about this? Have we been so preoccupied with trying to figure out who killed Dad and maintain our hold that this happened right under our noses? My mind instantly goes to Lorenzo. This smells like something he would do. This FBI agent could be just what I need to get rid of him altogether. I wave to Sam and Dean through the window, and both of them respond quickly.

"What's up, boss?" Sam looks between me and the agent.

"Take this guy to the cells and feed him. I'll come back tomorrow once the drugs have worn off. I want to have an open and honest conversation with him. He may be the solution to my Lorenzo problem."

"Are you sure?" Dean looks doubtful as I head for the exit.

"Yup, and if he's not willing to play the game, we

can always kill him, but he has a vested interest in helping us out."

"His sister," Sam agrees, nodding and gently helping the agent to his feet. I appreciate his quick mind.

"Yes, and maybe we can kill two birds with one stone, or cut two heads off the Hydra, so to speak. Get rid of Lorenzo and the Nuevo Dios Cartel. That would certainly make our lives easier. If only I could deal with Penelope the same way."

I grimace at the thought of the meeting I have in the morning. I've been brushing her off for a month now, but she got screechy and threatened to make a scene in public if I didn't hear her out.

"Yeah, better you than me." Dean grabs the other side of the agent, and together, he and Sam walk him back to one of the cells.

I part ways with them, telling them I'll send a car back for them and quickly change into my dress and heels from before, making sure that I don't have any blood on me. I briefly consider going to the sex club, but it's a little short notice for any of my subs, and my bloodlust is still a little too high to be sure of their safety. Nope, home it is, and hopefully I won't run into Gio or Sage or anyone they may bring home with them.

The house is quiet when I return, and a feeling of melancholy washes over me as I wander through it. There's no noise coming from Gio's or Sage's rooms, and I realize I'm all alone in this giant house. I'm certain that when my great-great-whatever-grandparents built it, they never intended for it to be inhabited by just three people. It's large enough to have whole extended families living together without being on top of each other. It seems like such a waste, but neither Gio nor I trust anyone enough to invite them to live with us. I want to be comfortable and relaxed in my house. I don't want to worry about going to sleep and not waking up because someone stabbed a knife through my heart while I was sleeping. I pass my room and take the elevator to the indoor pool upstairs. I'm not quite ready to call it a night, since I have a whole heap of restless energy and my mind is racing. Ideally, an orgasm would settle my mind, but I have no great urge to call one of the girls I use regularly to take care of my needs, so a swim will have to be a poor substitute.

With the house surrounded by motion detectors and a couple of guards roaming the grounds, I'm not concerned about my safety. The house is only accessible via biometric locks, and once night falls, shutters come down over the windows, making them unbreachable. The only way in or out at night is through a few reinforced steel doors, so when I get to the pool, I feel comfortable enough to strip, dropping my dress and underwear on one of the lounge chairs, before removing my thigh holster and gun and placing them on top of it.

Taking a breath, I dive into the warm water, swimming beneath the surface for quite a distance as I enjoy the silence being underwater brings. My mind instantly clears of all its worries, and I just focus on holding my breath and going as far as I can. I surface and swim freestyle all the way to the end before turning and heading back the way I came. Yes, this is exactly what I needed—the repetitive, mind-numbing motion of swimming back and forth. I swim up and back, over and over, until my heartbeat is racing and my breaths are ragged.

I'm not sure how long I swim for, but when I finally surface, I'm breathless and weary. I'm also in the shallow end, so I slump against the side of the pool while I try to catch my breath.

"You were swimming like the shark from *Jaws* was on your tail. I'm exhausted from just watching it." The voice has me whirling and reaching for my gun, but I'm naked and in a swimming pool, and my gun is nowhere in sight.

My body slowly relaxes, however, as my mind focuses on the voice. I didn't turn the lights on in here when I came in, only the ones inside the pool, but I can see the red glow of a blunt and the stream of smoke as Sage takes a drag of whatever he's smoking.

"Tori?" he calls when I don't answer him, and I shrug, even though he can't see it.

"You know how it is. I've got a lot on my mind," I

tell him, sighing and walking up the steps at this end of the pool. I know I'm naked, but I have no fucks left to give. It's not like the lighting is all that good for Sage to get a good look anyway.

I grab a towel off the shelves along one wall and rub it against my hair. The water destroyed all the effort I put into straightening it before I went to the club, and it's now a tangled, curly mess. Once I'm sure it's not going to continue to drip, I wrap the towel around my body and drop down onto the lounger next to Sage. He hands over his blunt, and I take it. Inhaling deeply, I hold the harsh smoke before blowing it back out. I hand it back to him with a sigh.

"Thank you. How was the rest of your evening?" I ask and brace myself for his usual, golden retriever style response, but all he says is, "It was nice."

Silence falls between us, and it's heavy. Is he expecting me to ask him for details? Did he end up hooking up with someone to take care of his problem? What am I saying, of course he did, it's Sage, but was it one of Gio's friends or did he find someone random in the club?

Frustrated with myself, I growl and jump to my feet. "I'm going to bed," I tell him sharply. "I need to speak to you and Gio about something in the morning. It's important. I have that meeting with Penelope at ten in Suncity at the Lucky Diamond, so how about after that?"

I can't see his face very well, but I see him move his head in a nod. "Sure, we'll be there moving Gio's stuff back into his dorm. How about we have lunch in the casino together?" he suggests, and I think about it.

"We can have lunch, but this conversation requires no ears. We will need to meet in Gio's office before. It's soundproofed and swept for bugs daily."

"Okay, sounds good."

"Sage, I think it goes without saying, but don't bring the new friends," I warn him, and he scoffs.

"We're not stupid, Tori." He sounds insulted, but I don't care.

"That remains to be seen. Good night." I don't wait for him to reply, just sweep my clothes and weapon into my arms and quickly depart. That might seem like a chicken move, but I can only take so much drama in my life. My personal one is supposed to be drama free. Gio and Sage are supposed to be my rocks, and it's not turning out that way.

Chapter Six

My heels click loudly on the floor of the hotel foyer as I stride across it, heading toward the elevator. The receptionist behind the front desk looks up, and her eyes widen as she spies me. "Ms. Russo. Lovely to see you. Do you have a moment? Bryce was hoping he could have a word."

Bryce is the manager of the hotel who has been entrusted with running it since before Dad's death.

"Sure, where is he?" I ask, and she stands up.

"Just a moment, I think I saw him out back." He has an office on the same level as mine, but he's very hands on and can often be found elsewhere in the hotel.

She's not gone for five minutes before she returns with Bryce. Bryce is in his late thirties and is a tall, slender man who wears skinny leg dress pants with bright, colored shirts and ties. His hair is artfully done, and he has a gold earring in one ear.

"Tori, darling, good to see you." He comes over, and we exchange air kisses.

"Hey, Bryce, listen, I have a meeting scheduled in the conference room at ten, do you mind walking and talking?" I gesture toward the elevator, and he nods.

"Not at all. Now you know I love you and Gio, and the staff here does as well, but we're having a few issues with your mother."

My mother? I stop at the elevator and press the button before turning to him with confusion.

"What on earth are you talking about? My mother died years ago."

"Sorry, I mean Mrs. Penelope Russo. She's incredibly rude to our staff, and she threatens them with their jobs when she doesn't like being told no. That's really not acceptable, and I won't stand for my staff being terrorized by her anymore. She can't stay here any longer."

I could have been knocked over with a feather as the doors open and the two of us step in. "Penelope has been staying here?" I ask him, still slightly shocked.

"Yes, she spends most nights here, only occasionally staying away. She also has a man who has started joining her in her suite who is also incredibly rude and intimidating. He has bodyguards that stand outside the suite and frisk anyone coming and going."

I'm so shocked, we've been standing in a nonmoving elevator. Bryce leans forward and pushes the right button for the floor I need.

"There is no way that woman should be staying here. I'm assuming she's not paying?"

Bryce pales slightly at my tone. "No, of course not. Did we do something wrong?"

I sigh and pat his arm. "No. I guess Gio and I didn't realize she would still take advantage of her name like that, which was stupid of us, really. Penelope Russo has nothing to do with our business or family anymore. She was given the house she lived in and that was the extent of her inheritance. The businesses are all mine and Gio's."

"Well, that's what we thought, but then Lorenzo said that Penelope was still entitled to use your dad's suite. He is quite friendly with Penelope's new beau."

Warning sirens blare inside my head. "Have you told Penelope that she isn't welcome to stay here anymore?" I ask him, and he nods.

"Yes, she was informed yesterday that she had to vacate the suite by the weekend."

"I guess that explains her meeting request," I grumble, and his eyes widen.

"Is that who you're meeting now?" he asks.

"Yes. She demanded my presence here this morning, and I was curious enough to indulge her. At least I'm not walking in blind. Bryce, do me a favor. Can you tally a bill of her expenses for the last—how long has it been, six months?"

"Yes, since your father passed," he confirms.

"Okay, have someone in finance tally that up and bring me a paper copy to the conference room. Do you know if the man who has been visiting her is here?"

"No, he left late last night and took his goons with him."

"Excellent, so it will just be dear old Penny. Such fun." I must have reverted to my psycho smile, because Bryce takes a little step back. "I will make sure she is out of your hair by this afternoon."

The elevator stops at the right floor, and I step out while Bryce remains inside. "I'll bring you what you asked for ASAP," he assures me.

"Excellent, and could you book a table for three at Aces High for half past twelve for me please?"

"Of course I can, Tori. What about a massage after that? You're looking a little tense," he suggests, holding his hand up to stop the elevator door from closing, and I laugh out loud.

"I'm afraid a massage isn't going to fix that, and I don't have time today. My schedule is jam packed, and I have somewhere I need to be after lunch."

"Tori, I know you're a busy woman, but you're young, and I'm worried you're not making the most of it. You should be off having fun with your friends, not running a multimillion-dollar business." Russo Incorporated is the front for all of our legit businesses.

I'm quiet while I think about what he said. My life has changed so much in the last twelve months that I don't even recognize the person I used to be. It's like I was a caterpillar just wriggling through life, and when Stacey betrayed me, I entered the chrysalis phase, finally emerging as what I was always supposed to be—a badass avenging angel, or something along those lines. I'm okay with that, but I guess it occasionally gets lonely. Stacey cured me from the need for friends though. They only stab you in the back, betray you, and break your heart.

"I'm not sure if I would know how to have fun anymore, Bryce, and I certainly don't have any friends to do it with." Sympathy fills his eyes, but he knows better than to say anything else. He pulls his hand away, and the doors slide closed. Turning my back on the elevators, I make my way to the conference room. I have to pass the reception desk up here.

"Good morning, Ms. Russo," the girl behind the desk says politely. Sally is Bryce's secretary and right-hand woman. Gio and I use her as well when we are at the hotel, which isn't all that often.

"Morning, Sally. Could you show Mrs. Russo to the conference room when she arrives, please?"

Sally wrinkles her nose and rolls her eyes. "Sure. Are you going to deal with her?" she asks, not hiding her curiosity.

"Let's just say no one is going to have to worry about her upsetting any of the staff once I'm done."

Sally blanches slightly, and I laugh.

"No, not like that. I'm going to evict her, and I'm going to stick her with the bill. It should be fun."

I'm not sure if Sally looks relieved or disappointed. I know I'm feeling the latter, but killing her in our legitimate place of business is probably not a good start to the day, no matter how much my finger itches to pull the trigger.

Gio and I have had her monitored ever since the funeral, but she's boring, socializing on other people's dime. She did try to sue us for a share of the inheritance, but Dad's will was ironclad. Gio and I did give her a small sum of money, though, in a cash settlement just to get her off our backs. I had no idea she was living the high life here as well. I wonder how many other of our hotels around the country she's visited.

I push open the door to the conference room. The coffee machine on the sideboard is full, and the room smells delicious. I head straight there and make myself a cup before taking a seat and looking out the window across the back of the hotel. It's resort style, with a pool and lush green gardens. The pool has a few families with small children playing in the splash park we have there. The children look happy, and the parents look like they are relaxed and enjoying their vacation, which is exactly how we want them to be. Hopefully later in the evening, they will take advantage of the babysitting service and head down to the casinos and lose some of their hard-earned cash in there.

It's weird seeing happy families. I mean, sure, we were happy once, but we never really did the family thing. Not in public anyway. We would head to the cabin in the mountains and ski and fish and do outdoorsy stuff every winter, or we'd go to Hawaii and stay in a house we owned there. We didn't do hotels and resorts, which when I think back was kind of weird, considering how many we actually own, but I have to guess it was a safety thing.

I watch on as a father waves at two of his kids when they squeal with delight as a large bucket dumps a crap load of water over their heads. He then leans in and gives his wife a kiss. It looks intimate and loving, and she smiles at him like she knows that he'll be fucking her brains out later on. I wonder what it's like to love or be loved like that. I guess if it was horrible, people wouldn't get married and have kids, but how does one make the decision to trust one person for the rest of their lives? Especially when in today's society, it's all so temporary. I have no idea if what I'm seeing is real, or if when they are at home, he hits her and the children, or that when he goes to work, she's not bent over the couch by the man who cleans the pool. How does one decide to take a leap of faith and put all your trust in one person? It's unrealistic.

I think back to what Vienna told me last night. Although she made it seem casual, I kind of got the feeling that the four of them are ride or die. And how does it all work? Is there a schedule? Is it organic? When they do invite people into their beds, especially her and Colton, is it male or female? Are they both bisexual, or is it only one of them, and which one? I have so many questions, but asking them would have shown too much interest. I know Sage will have all the details by now, so I need to find a way to ask him without seeming interested.

I shake off my musings and concentrate on the

information I learned last night. I didn't really take the time to process it once I got home. I just needed to not think, but now I need to turn my full attention to it. Who could be in tight with the Nuevo Dios Cartel? My money is on Lorenzo. He wasn't happy when Dad stopped dealing in skin, but now I need to prove it. How has this been going on behind our backs? The Mexican cartels are nasty pieces of work with no honor whatsoever, and if they are trading in skin again, where is Lorenzo getting them? Obviously he's not being discreet if he's on the FBI's radar. Who would be stupid enough to kidnap an agent's sister? Hopefully I can get more information out of the agent when I speak to him this afternoon.

A knock on the door has me spinning my chair and pasting a blank look on my face. "Come in," I call and wait.

The door opens, and Sally enters, followed by a dolled-up Penelope. She's wearing a stylish dress in lemon yellow, and her blonde hair is swept back in a chic updo. She's carrying a little black clutch and has matched her sky-high heels with it. She brushes past Sally without a word and takes a seat on the other side of the desk.

"Thank you, Sally." I nod my appreciation, and she smiles before sticking her tongue out at Penelope's back. I smother a smile, and she leaves, pulling the door closed and leaving me with this woman I loathe.

"Penelope, you look well," I say benignly since she doesn't seem inclined to start the conversation.

She sighs loudly, opens her clutch, and pulls out a tissue. "I'm really not. I've been so depressed since Stefano's death," she sobs, and I resist the urge to roll my eyes. "I just miss him so much, and to know he didn't trust me enough to leave the business in my capable hands is such a stab in the heart."

I give her a moment to really sell her act, but then I can't stand the sound of her fake sobbing any longer. "Cut the crap, Penelope. You're not stupid. You knew you were never going to get your hands on the businesses, since they were always Gio's birthright. You knew that coming into the family. You didn't even provide him with a child who could be included in the will."

She gasps and clasps her tissue tightly. "That's because your fucking father got a vasectomy right after your precious mother died. He didn't want any more children. He was happy with his perfect boy and girl," she spits at me, forgetting to keep up her act. I ignore her attempt to get a reaction out of me. It will take a lot more than that to get me to crack these days.

"And we were more than generous after you tried to sue us. You get to keep the house for as long as you want, and we gave you a cash settlement, which is more than you deserve. But now I hear you've been living in our hotels, and on our dime as well. Not only that, but you have been inviting people to stay with you and charging everything to Dad's old account. Then, to add insult to injury, you throw your weight around, weight you no longer hold, even if you ever did, and treat our employees abysmally. How did you ever think that would be acceptable? You know how Dad felt about our employees. We have never and will never treat them like dirt."

"Your father was soft and weak. He was an embarrassment." She's done pretending now. "He wasn't a real mafia leader and definitely undeserving of being the head of the Russo clan. Gio isn't much better, going to college when he should be concentrating on expanding the business."

I take a moment to think about what she just said, not letting her get to me despite having had the same thoughts about Gio last night. I won't show her there is a rift between us though, that would just give her ammunition, but I need to play to her stupidity and give her enough rope to hang herself.

I pull my gun out from the holster under my jacket and put it on the desk between us before leaning back in my chair. "Well, why don't you tell me how you think that could happen. You were the right-hand person of the leader for so long, you must have some ideas on how things could be changed." She preens at my comments. I hooked her, so now I need to reel her in. "Do you know anything about the Russos being involved in skin again? Who was the forward thinker who decided to expand our business in that way?" She doesn't hear the underlying threat in my question, and I'm very careful to word it in a way that sounds like I am impressed with their initiative.

She leans forward, wearing an excited look on her

face, eager to share the information with me. "I facilitated a meeting between Lorenzo and Mario Maricuso. It was time we put aside our differences. Mario introduced him to a high-level Nuevo Dios Cartel leader here in LA. Mario has also been responsible for providing the supply chain for the women we ship to Mexico. It's been a very fruitful partnership so far."

Mario Maricuso, head of the Maricuso family and one of our remaining rival families here on the West Coast. So that's why they didn't make a play for Gio and me. I thought it was because of our very tentative alliance, but they have figured out another way to get their hooks into the Russo family. Fucking Lorenzo.

I had every intention of kicking Penelope out of the Lucky Diamond, but now I've reconsidered. If she's here, we can keep an eye on her comings and goings, or more specifically, Mario's comings and goings. I'm assuming that's who has been staying with her, but I will have to see some footage to confirm it.

"And Mario? What's he getting from this little arrangement?" I ask her, and she quickly shakes her head.

"Nothing. He's happy to act as the middleman for a small slice of the profit. Lorenzo and Mario worked it out between themselves. And of course, he enjoys my company." She smiles smugly, and I want to gag.

Damn, this woman is no better than any of my working girls. At least they get paid for being on their backs.

A knock on the door reminds me that Bryce is

returning with her bill. I need to change my tactics slightly, and he's going to be pissed.

"Come in," I call, and he walks in with a stack of papers. Holy hell, that's a lot of expenses, and now I'm going to have to give in to them all.

"Here's what you asked for, Ms. Russo," Bryce says politely, handing over the papers.

"Take a seat, Bryce. I think you need to be here for this." I make a show of looking over the accounts and grimace at the total at the bottom. Holy fuck, this woman has charged everything from room service to expensive items in the boutiques. "Do you know what this is, Penny?" I ask her, tossing the pages on the desk, and she shakes her head. "This is an itemized account of your expenses over the last six months."

Her eyes widen slightly before she adopts a stubborn set to her shoulders. "Your father always let me charge everything to his room," she argues.

"Yes, he did, but this is a huge total, and way more than I'm sure you've ever spent here before. From what I understand, you've been living here, not back at the house."

She picks up her tissue and dabs at her eyes once more. "I just can't stay there. Everywhere I look reminds me of him," she says quietly.

I sigh and adopt a look of sympathy. "I can imagine that would be hard for you."

Bryce stares at me like I've suddenly grown a second head, and I grimace internally, but I need to keep this woman content for a little while longer.

"Originally, I was going to make you pay at least half of this bill, but I can probably see myself waving it if you agree to a few terms." She raises a questioning eyebrow but stays silent, so I forge ahead. "You need to agree to be more polite to the staff. They will refuse to serve you if you are rude to them." She huffs but nods. "And stop spending in the boutiques. I don't mind comping your meals or your stay, but I will not be outfitting your wardrobe any longer. Go do your shopping somewhere else. Do you understand?" I ask her, and she nods quickly, agreeing to my demands. "Fine, and I will make sure to tell the staff that you will be polite, and if you aren't, then they are allowed to refuse service. You still go by the Russo name, Penelope, so do not give it a bad reputation."

She stands up, clearly hearing the dismissal. "I hope that one day soon we will be able to have dinner together. I would like to introduce you to Mario. He's been so kind since your father passed." And there it is, the real reason for this meeting. I was wondering when she would actually get around to mentioning it. "I don't see any reason why the Russo and Maricuso families can't form a firmer alliance. He is keen to speak to the family head and see if a tighter alliance can be formed."

"I will discuss it with Gio and let you know," I hedge, but I am definitely curious now that I know Lorenzo has been working with them. I'm sure it's a matter of time before they take a run at us, so it won't hurt to get all the intel we can.

"Please do. Mario really is a kind man. I'm sure you and his children would get along marvelously." With that, she breezes out of the conference room without even acknowledging Bryce.

"What the fuck, Tori?" he demands, huffing, and I slump in my chair.

"She has information I need. I'm sorry, but you're going to have to put up with her a little longer. Have anyone who deals with her given a bonus each week with their wages. I'm hoping it won't be for too long."

"Fine." He sounds anything but as he stands up. "It's your money, after all."

"Please send up whichever pit boss is on today, and the casino and cage managers. I want to have a quick meeting with them before Gio and Sage arrive."

"Will do." I can tell he's still pissed at me.

"Bryce, don't be like that. Book yourself a spa treatment and charge it to my account, and buy yourself a little something from the jewelry boutique," I cajole him, and the frown drops and he flutters his eyelashes at me.

"If you insist, boss." He's all smiles again, and I heave a sigh of relief. As high maintenance as he is, he's superb at his job, and I wouldn't want to have to replace him because Penelope is causing trouble.

He breezes out, and I groan and stretch before getting up to grab another coffee before my casino staff members arrive. Maybe I need a massage too.

Chapter Seven

My meeting with the casino management went well. I warned them to be on the lookout for Lorenzo. I wanted to know if he's running big amounts of cash across the tables or buying up chips. If he's laundering money for the cartel or the Maricusos, I want to know about it. I know this casino is loyal to Gio and me. I'll probably have to do a trip around the state and wider to find out if he's using our other establishments for the same thing.

The alarm on my phone sounds, alerting me to the time. It's now twelve, and Gio and Sage still haven't shown up. My teeth grind together in frustration as I think about the lack of fucking loyalty the two of them are showing at the moment. Fuck, is there anyone I can trust?

Standing up, I leave the conference room and stalk toward Gio's office, but just as I pass the elevator, it opens, and the two of them walk out.

"Tori, there you are. We missed you this morning," Gio calls out as the two of them walk toward me, smiling. No one was around when I left the house, so I'm assuming they had gotten underway early, moving Gio's crap to the dorm, though I have no idea why it took them all morning to do it.

"Yes, well, unlike you I don't have time to lounge around and blow off work. Things need to be dealt with, and one of us had to take responsibility for it." There's no missing my pissed off tone, and the two men exchange a glance.

"I thought you were okay with me attending college," Gio says, putting his hands on his hips.

My gaze slides to Sally who doesn't appear to be paying attention to our conversation, but I refuse to air our grievances in public, so I gesture to his office. "Shall we take this in there?" I suggest, not waiting for an answer. I push my palm against the biometric scanner that only the three of us are programmed into, and the door clicks open. I wave the two guys through before allowing it to close behind me. Gio starts to say something, but I hold up my hand and grab the scanning device out of his top drawer. I do a lap around the room just to make sure there is nothing, and when it comes back clean, I shove it back in the drawer and drop my ass down in the chair behind the desk. Gio can sit on the other side for a change. He frowns at me but takes a seat.

"What's making you so pissy?" he demands, crossing his arms and legs as he stares me down, but the days when he used to scare me are gone. I've lost respect for him, and that negates any fear I might have had.

"Seriously? You have to ask?" I scoff.

Sage stays silent, his eyes darting between the two of us.

"You didn't say shit when I announced I wanted to return to college, so why choose now to get your panties in a bunch?"

"When you said you wanted to return to college, I assumed it would be part time and you would live at home and continue to be the head of the Russo family. But no, now you're moving into the dorms and blowing off things to hang with friends. I learned important information last night, information we should have already had, but somehow, it slipped through the cracks. There are obviously more people on our payroll who are loyal to Lorenzo."

"What the fuck are you talking about?" Gio asks, uncrossing his legs and leaning forward. He's all ears now.

"Turns out the Russo family has started exporting skin again. A joint project with the Maricusos and the Nuevo Dios Cartel."

"What the fuck?" Gio jumps to his feet and starts pacing back and forth across the room, while Sage starts swearing up a storm. "Where did you hear that?"

"Three members of the cartel were picked up by guys who are loyal to us. They were found snooping around the wharfs and were brought to the warehouse.

When I left the club last night, I went and had a little one-on-one chat with them."

Sage blanches, and Gio stops pacing. "Are any of them still alive?" he asks carefully, and I shrug.

"One," I tell them, and they exchange a glance. "Mostly because by the time I got to him, I used sodium pentothal before my knives, and he may have admitted to being an FBI agent. I can't believe he passed the interrogation part of his training. He sang like a canary. Thank fuck the cartel hasn't done the same thing to him, because he would have lost his head instantly."

"Fuck, Tori," Gio hisses. "And you left him alive?"

"Yes, Gio. He had some interesting information to tell me, and I want to question him when he's coherent. I'm hoping we may be able to cut a deal."

"Who's to say he wasn't lying to get you to stop?" Sage asks, and Gio nods his agreement.

"Well, I did consider that, but I had a lovely little chat with Penelope this morning. She's too stupid not to brag about shit, and she confirmed that what the agent said was true, even copped to facilitating the meeting between Lorenzo and Mario Maricuso. Turns out she's spreading her legs for the enemy."

"And you didn't put a bullet in her brain?" Gio demands, and I sigh.

"See, this is why you need female minds in the higher levels of mafia families. We think more rationally than you males. No, I didn't. Penelope is going to be my eyes and ears. Remember the saying, Gio—keep your friends close, and your enemies closer. We're going to bug Dad's old suite here at the hotel and see what we can learn from her 'entertaining.' Apparently Mario has been a frequent visitor to her suite. She even implied she would like to have a family dinner with him and his children."

"She confirmed he has children?" Sage asks, leaning forward, his eyes brightening with excitement. "We've been trying to ascertain that for a long time now. It's one of the best kept secrets within the mafia families."

"Yes, I know. It sounded like the two of them have grown particularly close. I'm sure she would know one way or another, and she's too stupid to keep it a secret, or maybe she just liked showing she knew more than I did."

"Lorenzo will need to be dealt with." Gio is finally showing an interest in the family business. It feels like it's been months.

"Yes, but I thought I would give him enough rope to hang himself. I want to chat with our FBI agent and see if we can come to an arrangement. If we give him Lorenzo and the Nuevo Dios Cartel, hopefully they will leave us alone for the foreseeable future. I plan on going over there after we have lunch."

"I'll come with you," Gio says, and Sage holds up his hands.

"What are we going to do about the others? We said we'd play the tables for a little while with them after we ate."

Others?

"What are you talking about?" I ask, and Gio shrugs sheepishly.

"My roommates and their family wanted to check out the hotel and casino with us when they heard where we were going."

"Seriously?" I screech, and Sage waves a hand at me.

"See? I told you she'd be pissed."

"Well, what did you expect me to do? Blow them off?" Gio sounds frustrated, and I growl.

"Fuck you, Gio. Yes, I expected you to blow them off. This is our family business. Get your priorities right, or I may decide that you need to be replaced as the head of the family."

He steps up and places his hand on the desk, leaning over me. "What are you going to do, put a bullet in my skull?"

I stand up, not wanting him towering over me like that in a power play. "Maybe, or maybe you will have a small accident. The brake lines could be cut on your vehicle or, I don't know, maybe a gas leak in your dorm room."

He gapes at me in shock. Yes, that's right, bitch, I'm pissed off.

"I've suddenly lost my appetite. Why don't the two of you go to lunch with your friends? I'll just head over to the warehouse early and speak to the agent."

Gio is still speechless, but Sage quickly recovers. "Tori, no. They came here to see you too. They want to get to know you," he pleads, and I roll my eyes.

"What the fuck for? They seemed to have tamed the two of you, so why do they need another friend? Also, Sage, make sure you're not neglecting your own duties for the sake of your *friends*." I watch him, and I see the shutters come down in his eyes. He locks away his emotions, but not before I see the hurt in his gaze.

"Sure thing, *boss*," he says sarcastically before slapping Gio on the shoulder. "Come on, our *friends* are waiting." He emphasizes the word "friends" just like he did the word "boss" previously. Well, I guess a line has been drawn in the sand, and he didn't like it. I shouldn't be surprised. Why do I keep expecting people to pick me over anything else in their lives?

The two of them leave without another word, and the room falls silent. I turn my chair around and look out at the pool once more. More happy families are out there enjoying the beautiful California sunshine. It's a complete surprise when I feel a drop of water drip onto the hand I'm leaning on.

I reach up and discover I'm crying. Thank God neither Gio nor Sage saw my moment of weakness. I'll just allow myself five self-indulgent minutes before I get my shit together and get on with my day.

◆

After washing my face and plastering on my resting bitch face, I make my way through the hotel. Hotel employees smile at me but don't engage. I'm almost at the exit when I hear my name being called.

"Tori!"

For a moment, I almost pretend I don't hear it and keep walking, but then I remember how she jumped to my defense last night and that would be rude. Turning, I watch as Vienna hurries after me. Today, she's wearing a pair of black skinny jeans with a pair of red sneakers and a cute black and white polka dot top. Her red hair is tied back in a ponytail, and she's fresh faced. She looks just as gorgeous as she did last night despite not having any makeup on. "Hey, Gio and Sage said you were here, but you were too busy to eat with us. Are you done now? Do you have time to join us?"

I hesitate. I don't really have the time to be social. If it had just been Sage and Gio, I could have eaten and left, but now I'm going to be forced into conversation with everyone, and who knows how long it will be until I get a chance to interview the FBI agent.

I look back toward the valet, but she puts her hand on my arm. "Please. I kind of feel like we got off to a bad start last night, us being there with Stacey and all, but I want to reassure you she never was and never will be our friend, despite us all going to the same college and living in the same dorm."

"She's in the same dorm as you all?" Gio and Sage never said a word.

"Yes, we had a run-in this morning. Seems she was moving in at the same time we were. She's two floors below us, though, so hopefully we won't see her all that much."

I almost snort out loud. If I know Stacey, and I'm fairly sure I have a handle on her, she will do everything possible to throw herself in Gio's, Xavier's, and Tristan's paths, maybe even Colton's.

"Come on, we just ordered. If we hurry, we can add yours, and it will come out at the same time." She doesn't wait for me to respond, and I find myself being towed through the reception area back toward the elevators.

"What were you doing down here if you're having lunch upstairs?" I ask absently as Bryce raises an eyebrow as we pass the reception desk.

"Get it, girl," he mouths, and I flip him off behind Vienna's back.

"Honestly?" she asks as she presses the button. When she turns to face me, there's a slight blush to her cheeks. "I pressed Gio and Sage for information on your whereabouts. Sage was a rock, but Gio finally caved when Casey got involved. He said if I waited in the foyer, I'd see you since you had to pass through it to get your car from the valet."

My annoyance at Sage fades away. He knew I was pissed and wouldn't want to be interrupted, but my annoyance at Gio is just about at a boiling point. Of course he caved to the pretty little pixie. If he manages to pass college this year, I'll be surprised. I'm almost certain he's only going because she will be there.

"But why?" I ask, suspicion clouding my words.

She reaches out and squeezes my arm reassuringly. The elevator doors open, and we step into the empty space before they close behind us.

"Why not? You're a pretty girl, and I want to get to know you a little better. I've heard so much about Tori Russo through gossip and rumors. I want to know the real her. That's if you don't object."

I'm so bad at the friend thing, but I'm almost certain that her interest isn't purely platonic. The casual touches and the flirty tone all point to one thing, but I want to be clear on something.

"Look, if you're shopping for a threesome partner for you and Colton, I'm going to have to pass. I'm strictly into girls. I've never been with a man before, and I don't have any inclination now." Her eyebrows jump in surprise, and then she pouts prettily.

"Are you sure? I think between the two of us, we could probably blow your mind."

"Yeah, I'm good. I don't do relationships. Stacey killed any trust I had to give to a long-term partner, and I would probably just be a disappointment to you. I have control issues. I don't like to give it up, and I like things that scare other people."

Vienna sighs and drops her hand. "We never had a chance, did we?"

"No, not really. My life is pretty complicated, and starting anything with anyone would be a mistake. I like my sex uncomplicated and rough, and I use a service to give myself what I need. Not many people understand that." I try to hint at my proclivities, and from the widening of her eyes, I think she understands what I'm alluding to.

She leans in and places a kiss on the corner of my mouth. I breathe in, and her perfume fills my senses. It's something sweet with a hint of apple. It reminds me of Eve and the serpent, and I can't figure out which of us is tempting the other more. "Well, if you ever change your mind, we'll be here," she tells me as the elevator comes to a stop on the level the restaurant is on. "But don't think we're giving up." The doors open to the sound of clinking glasses and silverware on China, the sound of people talking almost violently loud after the silence of the elevator.

She steps back and grabs my hand. "Come on then. We may as well have a meal now that I have you here."

Chapter Eight

She drags me in the direction of the back of the restaurant and our family table. They must have seated them all there when they saw Gio and Sage with the group.

When we arrive, Colton, Xavier, and Tristan all get to their feet in a show of politeness that surprises me. Sage and Gio don't move. In fact, Gio doesn't even stop his conversation he's having with Casey, their heads bowed close to one another, and Sage seems to want to look anywhere but at me.

"Tori, you look lovely today." I startle at the words and turn to Xavier, who was the surprising person behind them.

I look down at my stylish pantsuit that reminds me so much of Carla and then back at the attractive man. "Thank you. How has your morning been? Did Gio get moved in okay?" I ask as Vienna takes the seat Colton pulled out for her.

"It was great." Tristan hurries around and, in a surprising move, pulls out a seat for me. I have the spare one between Vienna and Sage. Colton is on the other side of her and Tristan, and then Xavier is on the other side of Sage. That leaves Casey and Gio directly across from me. "He's right, you are gorgeous," he whispers in my ear before helping me sit. My eyebrows jump in surprise as he hurries back to his seat on the other side of the table next to Xavier.

"Gio and Sage said you were busy and weren't able to join us," Xavier says, waving over a waitress. "What would you like to drink?" he asks me.

"Just a sparkling water for me. I have another appointment after this," I reply. The waitress takes my order.

"Will you be having your usual for lunch, Ms. Russo?" the girl asks me, and I smile at her.

"Just a Cobb salad for me today. I don't want anything heavy, since I have a big afternoon planned," I tell her, and she hurries away to give the chef my order.

"So what are your plans for this afternoon? Anything you can blow off?" Vienna leans in slightly, her leg brushing against mine. "We thought we might play a few rounds in the casino and then maybe head out and go bowling after. It would be fun if you could join us."

Gio finally realizes that I'm at the table and does a double take. "Tori, you're here?"

"Yes, Vienna caught me leaving," I reply pointedly,

and he doesn't even have the grace to look embarrassed. He just shrugs.

"I'm worried about you. You work too much. That thing you have to do this afternoon can wait. It's not going anywhere. You need some downtime as well. All work and no play makes Tori homicidal," he jokes, and everyone around the table laughs—everyone except Sage. Sage is quiet as he watches me reach for the butter knife at my place setting. He puts his hand down over mine, stopping me from grabbing it.

"Leave her be, Gio," Sage snaps at him, and the laughter stops. "Tori is picking up your slack and allowing you to go to college. You should be kinder to her."

Gio frowns, properly put in his place by Sage, and I nudge his leg in gratitude. I'd been feeling particularly ganged up on, so it was nice to hear he still has my back. I thought he'd been dicktamatized by Xavier and Tristan last night, but maybe he's not as hooked as I thought.

"Tori, it's such a wonderful thing you're doing for Gio. You are really the best sister in the world," Casey gushes, her voice all tinkling and sweet, and again, I can see why Gio is so smitten. She really is the epitome of goodness and light, so different from everything in our world.

"Casey, it's lovely to see you again. It's been a while," I say to her. "Your hair looks nice." When I had seen her last year, she had a cute pixie bob, but now her blonde hair is sitting just below her shoulders in lovely ringlets.

She pats it and blushes prettily. "Thank you, I've been growing it out."

"So do you want to join us? We can play teams. Sage needs a partner to make it even," Tristan pleads, and I grind my teeth together. How am I going to get out of this? Fucking Gio set me up. A hand on my leg has me looking down. It's Sage's, and he squeezes my thigh.

"Come on, Tori. Just give yourself this afternoon. I promise I'll help you with that job tomorrow if you play hooky today and come hang out with us."

His hand is heavy on my thigh, but it's also comforting, and surprisingly, I feel myself relax under his touch.

I sigh. "Okay, fine, but it hardly seems fair to all of you for Sage and me to be on the same team. We're pretty much bowling experts." I wave a finger between us.

"Really? I don't see you as the type of person to bowl." Vienna laughs as she says it.

"Oh really? What kind of person do you see me as?" I ask her, and she shrugs.

"I don't know, but nothing as pedestrian as a bowler."

Gio snorts. "It's because we have a bowling alley at home, and they spend all their time challenging each other and trying to outdo one another. I've never known two people who are so damn competitive with one another."

"I don't know, that kind of thing sounds like foreplay to me." Tristan grins, looking between the two of us, and I roll my eyes.

"Sure, if your idea of foreplay is smack talking and being taunted when you lose." The table bursts into laughter, and Tristan shrugs.

"You'd be surprised what I consider foreplay, Tori." He winks at me, and I stick my tongue out at him. He's such a damn flirt. I'm not sure how Xavier puts up with him, but he just laughs with everyone else.

"If you have a lane at home, we should play there." Casey claps her hands together. "Then we won't have to worry about getting in anywhere."

Everyone else chimes in about what a good idea it is, but I study the girl closely. I try to see if there is any ulterior motive to her words, but she doesn't seem suspicious at all. She either doesn't know about our family, or she just doesn't care. If it had been Stacey, I guarantee it would have been about getting a look inside our house, but Casey just seems innocent. I will still watch her closely. I've been proven to be a terrible judge of character.

Gio bites his lip and looks at me hesitantly. The asshole is leaving it to me to shoot her down. Well, fuck you, Gio. "Sure, that sounds good. We actually have four lanes, so each of us can have one."

Her eyes widen. "Four lanes, wow. Where do you live?"

"I didn't see a four-lane bowling alley when we came to visit last year. Is it in the basement?" Xavier asks, looking between Gio and me, and Gio shakes his head.

"No, we've moved into a new place since then."

The serving staff arrives, and the conversation halts while we all dig into the delicious food the Aces High restaurant is renowned for.

"Oh, Tori, I may have a solution to our tech problem," Gio says out of the blue, and I frown at him. He shouldn't be talking about family business at a table full of strangers.

"Maybe we can talk about that later," I reply pointedly, but he shakes his head and points his fork at Colton, who has been silent the whole time.

"Colton here may be a man of few words, but it turns out he's a tech genius. Casey says he runs his own internet security business, and he's only going to college so he can stay close to the others."

"Oh yes, Colt is brilliant," Vienna gushes, beaming at her boyfriend. "You should really make use of his talents. He'll even sign an NDA if you need him to."

Fuck, how do I respond to this without insulting anyone?

"I'm not sure if the kind of work I need is something Colton will feel comfortable with," I hedge, not sure if Gio's friends know what the Russo family is famous for other than our legit business dealings.

Colton puts down his knife and fork and takes a sip of his water in front of him before wiping his mouth. He reaches up and adjusts his glasses before turning to me. "Let's be real for a moment, shall we? We know who you are. Gio is the head of the Russo crime family, and you are his right-hand woman."

I look around the table, and they all nod. I glare accusingly at Gio, who holds his hand up. "I swear I didn't say anything."

"No, he didn't. He's been trying very hard to appear normal around us, but I also don't let my family walk into situations without checking everything out first. We knew who you were when it first came out that Gio was going to room with Tris and X. I did my homework back then," Colton confesses unapologetically.

"And none of you care?" I ask, unable to hide my suspicion. I drop my voice. "You don't care that we deal in guns and drugs and prostitution?"

I'm taking a risk by exposing us like this to these people, but I can always put a bullet between their eyes if one of them turns out to be a snitch. It would be a shame to mar their pretty faces, but I will do anything to protect my family.

"None of us are from homes that were particularly savory, so we aren't strangers to that kind of world. Who are we to judge you for taking over the family business when your dad was assassinated? Any of us would have done the same for each other. Family is everything, even if it's the family you've made and weren't born into," Xavier states seriously, and I feel a shiver run down my spine. His words are close to what my dad would tell us all the time.

"Come on, Tori. You wanted someone independent, and Colton gives you that," Gio cajoles, and Sage's hand tightens on my leg with encouragement.

"I can give you references if you're still not sure, but I'd be happy to have a discussion with you about your needs." Again, Sage's hand tightens at Colton's words, and I know the dirty fucker is thinking about more than just my tech needs. I turn and raise an eyebrow at him, and he grins unapologetically. "And if I can't meet them, I may be able to point you to someone else in the industry who can."

I'm completely torn. I really do want a new tech person to do a deep dive into all of the people who pledged loyalty to us after Dad died. I also want to know who posted the hit on Dad, and none of our own tech guys have been successful in figuring that out. But can I trust Colton? I'm so messed up that it almost hurts to agree to allow him to help. If only my skills were in hacking, but I'm afraid the only hacking I'm good at is hacking up people.

"It's a big job. Would you work exclusively for me? Do you have time for both that and college classes?"

"Pfft. He doesn't need the classes. He's only doing them for fun and so he can stay in the dorms with us. He didn't even need to go to high school. He only did it so I wasn't on my own," Vienna assures me, and Colton shrugs his agreement.

"For the right kind of money, I'm happy to be exclusive," he tells me, and Vienna smacks his arm.

"Colt, no. We can't gouge our new friends," she scolds him, but I reach over and grab her hand as she goes to smack him again.

"No, don't, he's right. I'd much prefer to overpay him for his loyalty and silence than assume he's going to be quiet out of friendship with Gio. How about you and I meet tomorrow at my office in the club at Banebridge. I can go over everything I want from you."

"Or they could just stay the night at our place and then you could use my office at the house in the morning," Gio suggests, smiling at Casey and oblivious to the daggers I'm shooting at him.

Seriously? He's inviting them to stay at our house? It's the one place where I can relax and unwind and I don't have to worry about anyone stabbing me in the back. These people are complete strangers to me. I had thought they were to both of us, actually, but I guess Gio has been spending more time with them than I thought. I'm starting to get an inkling that every time he disappeared, he was with them... or one of them. My gaze moves to Casey, who seems to be just as smitten with my brother as he is with her. They are a little more familiar with each other than mere acquaintances should be.

"Only if that's alright with Tori. It's a lot to have your house invaded by five strangers. We take up a lot of space." Xavier has a small crease of concern between his brows, and I appreciate that he is at least being polite. My brother's brain has sunk into his pants.

It's then I make the decision that maybe I should get to know these people better. Gio obviously plans to have them in our lives, and nothing I say seems to be swaying him, so it's up to me to get to the bottom of things. Are they genuine, or are there ulterior motives? I'm the only one who seems to have a clear head. I didn't miss that Tristan and Sage were talking rather intimately during lunch, more intimately than just friends. Something definitely happened between them last night. I don't know whether to be angry, jealous, or turned on. I'm so confused, so instead, I will concentrate on all of this. I may have to get another independent tech contractor to give me background checks on all of them though. Colton isn't going to hand over their life stories, no matter how much I pay him.

"Tori?" I must have been quiet for too long, because Vienna sounds hesitant.

I wave a hand. "Sorry. That's fine, stay the night. I'll call Suzette and have her make up some rooms." I put my knife and fork together on my plate and wipe my mouth with a napkin. "I won't join you for the casino, but I'll see you back at the house later. I'll arrange for the car to pick you up so you can have a few drinks without worrying."

"Oh no, are you sure you can't stay?" Vienna pleads, but I shake my head.

"No, sorry, I have one meeting that I really can't

blow off. It's pretty damn important, but it shouldn't take too long. I'll probably be home before you. Don't forget your swimsuits. There's a pool we can all use after we finish bowling." I soften the refusal with a smile, and it seems to do the trick.

"A pool too? Wow, that must be some house," Casey gushes, and I feel a little sorry for her. The house is really going to be a shock to her.

"I'll see you all later." I stand up and push in my chair.

"Can't wait," Tristan calls as the others say good-bye. Gio is strangely silent, but I'm done with him now. Once again, I will pull all the weight while he plays college kid with his friends.

Sage stands up. "I'll come with you," he tells me, to the dismay of the others.

"Really? You have to go too?" Tristan pouts, and Xavier grabs his neck and gives it a squeeze. I see him shudder under his hand.

"Stay," I urge him. "I have Sam and Dean, that's all I need."

The direct dig hits, and he flinches, but Colton of all people chuckles.

"You have friends called Sam and Dean? Are they brothers whose last name is Winchester?"

Gio snorts. "Their names aren't actually Sam and Dean, that's just what Tori calls them, and they are not her friends, they are her bodyguards."

"Bodyguards?" Vienna gasps, and I roll my eyes.

"Actually, they are my henchmen." Her eyes widen

slightly. "Anyway, they will be enough for today, so you go have fun," I tell Sage, patting his hand. He tries to grab mine, but I yank it away before he can and whirl around. I can't look at him. I don't want him to see how jealous... annoyed... hurt I am about everything.

"See you soon. Prepare to have your butts kicked," I call back over my shoulder before breezing through the restaurant and down to the valet to claim my car.

I'm halfway to the warehouse before I realize my eyes are leaking again. My damn allergies must be acting up.

Chapter Nine

The FBI agent, Gabriel Garcia, and I had a nice little chat. I proved, unlike everyone's opinion of me, that I can listen and be a reasonable adult.

"So you're saying you and Gio Russo had no idea this was going on under your noses?" He sounds skeptical, and I don't blame him. I had the boys bring him into the interrogation room and sit him down. He is uncuffed as a show of goodwill. They both stand behind me just in case, but he's relaxed and appears open to making a deal with me.

"Our transition to head of the family has been a little rocky since Dad's passing. I guess we have been so focused on trying to track down who killed him and keeping hostile takeovers from other families at bay that we didn't think to look internally." I shrug. "But that stops now. The Russo family hasn't dealt in skin trafficking since before my grandfather was in charge, and we will not return to that disgusting habit.

Work with us to shut it down, and you can have Lorenzo on a plate. It will take care of both of our problems."

"You'd just hand him over to us? No questions asked?"

"You'd need a solid case that he couldn't wiggle out of. We will help you bug his residences, and I have it on good authority that Mario Maricuso is also involved. I will arrange to have the suite he stays in at the Lucky Diamond bugged as well. "

He starts to look a little excited. "If we could shut down their supply chain, the Nuevo Dios Cartel would be dead in the water. They have put all their eggs in one basket since you have a lock on all the drugs and guns coming in and out of the West Coast."

"Why, Agent Garcia, I have no idea what you are talking about. My family runs legitimate clubs and casinos, and to suggest otherwise would be slander." I flutter my eyelashes at him, and he grimaces. We have put up roadblocks for everything the cartel tries to bring into the West Coast. I will not have them flood it with their filthy meth, fentanyl, and dirty, disgusting D-grade crap.

"Sure, sure. Whatever. Look, if you can give us this, then we can probably be persuaded to find interest in something else for a little while."

"I will have my tech guy work on it. Now that we know, I'll have someone follow Lorenzo. We should meet again in a couple of weeks, that should give me enough time to get you some solid evidence. You keep working your angle in the cartel, but be careful. You're no good to us dead," I warn him, and he nods.

"You're going to have to work me over. I can't go back to them like this, they'll think I snitched."

"Which you did," I point out, standing up. "Your interrogation skills need work. Don't let the cartel question you under the influence of drugs. You'd sing like a canary and be headless before you could take your next breath."

"I'm too low on the totem pole for them to worry about. I'm just a grunt. It's why I am having trouble getting details on exchanges and meetings. The cartel tasked me and the other two you caught to find a hole in your security down at the wharfs so the next shipment can be transferred safely."

"We can provide you with a hole if that will help you with the bosses." I look at Sam and Dean, and Sam nods.

"Diego, who is in charge of security at the docks, likes women. It would be easy enough to distract him with a whore and keep him busy for a couple of hours. He wouldn't even blink at it."

I grind my teeth at the fact that one of my employees is so easily distracted, but it's the opening we need. I can deal with him later.

"We need to make sure that both Mario Maricuso and Lorenzo Russo are at the exchange. That way we can do a raid and sweep them all up together in one go. What happened to the two guys I was with?" Agent Garcia asks.

"There was an unfortunate accident on the way here, and neither of them survived." I'm lying through my teeth, and he knows it, but there is no way I'm admitting to anything.

"Fuck, so you're really going to have to work me over. We need to come up with a legitimate reason for you letting me go."

"Without making it sound like I've gone soft," I growl.

"You can take a message back to the cartel, it's the only reason you were left alive. If any more of their members are caught sneaking around, they will be coming back in body bags," Dean suggests, and Gabriel shrugs.

"I guess it's as good as anything I can think of. They respect violence, so make me look good."

"Jesus, that's going to fucking hurt. Just drug him unconscious before you kick the shit out of him. I can't watch this," I tell my minions, and Sam grins.

"Going soft on us, boss?" he teases, and I shudder.

"It's no fun if it's not real." Gabriel blanches at what he sees in my eyes, but for now, we have a truce, and that's good enough for me. To be honest, I have enough to worry about, so if he's handling the cartel, then that takes one thing off my plate. I'll worry about the traitor in my family and the circling sharks.

When I get back to the house, no one is around. Shit, I'd forgotten to call and let Suzy and Ben know we were having guests. As the elevator opens up on the first level, instead of going straight up to my room to get changed, I head in the direction of the kitchen and their living quarters which is attached to it. They have a lovely two-bedroom suite with a small living area. They also have permission to use any of the recreational facilities in the house, but I don't think either of them do apart from the pool. Ben swims laps early in the morning.

"Hello?" I call out as I enter the kitchen.

They are both sitting at the island with coffee mugs in front of them. They complain that they have nothing to do because Gio, Sage, and I are the only ones who live here, and we're fairly self-sufficient. None of us like our bedrooms to be cleaned, but all three of us are terrible cooks, so we happily allow them to do that. I think Ben has taken to the upkeep of the garden and outdoor areas. There isn't anyone to butler for, so he doesn't really have anything to do. The housekeeping staff are kept busy dusting and cleaning the huge house, and Suzy keeps track of them. Apart from that, it's not really a taxing job.

"There you are, pretty girl. I feel like I haven't seen you in days," Suzette exclaims, and I chuckle.

"You saw me at breakfast yesterday," I remind her, and she sighs.

"Yes, but it was just you, and this morning, it was just the boys. I never see you all together anymore, and soon it will just be you and Sage. Gio is leaving the coop."

"Yes, my beautiful cinnamon bun, but I bet the cooking at the college isn't anywhere near as good as yours." Ben cups her cheek affectionately before patting her face. "College life is not all it is cracked up to be. I'm sure he will return home before long. It's the thought that sounds wonderful, but he is a man who has been looking after himself for a while. I think he will find college rules will chafe at his nature."

He's not wrong. How is Gio, head of the Russo family, who is used to getting what he wants when he wants it and playing by his own set of rules and morals going to adjust to having to live the normal life of the average college student? It's not going to work, and I tried to tell him this, but he would not listen.

I will wait and let it play out, and when he does return, I will try not to rub it in his face... every day. "So Gio invited some friends of his to come over and go bowling and stay the night. Would it be possible to make up a few rooms for them?"

It's comical how their eyes widen in surprise, and I snort as I go to make myself a coffee with the automatic machine. You just press a button, and it does everything for you. I just need to add milk and sugar when it's done. The beans grind loudly, so Suzy waits until it's finished before she says anything.

"Friends, coming here?" she checks, and I nod, and they exchange a glance.

"Are these 'family' friends?" Ben asks, using finger quotes when he says "family."

I shake my head and sigh. "No, these are his college roommates and a few others."

"And he invited them here?"

"Yes, apparently they have known who we are since they found out he was going to be their roommate. Their adopted brother is a genius tech wiz, and he did a deep background dive into Gio, so I guess Gio figured we don't need to hide who we are. They may as well come and stay here. Of course we will stick to the top levels, since they don't need to know what's below ground."

Now that their confusion is cleared up, Suzy starts to look excited. She jumps to her feet and hurries over to the walk-in pantry and disappears inside. "I'm going to have to go get some groceries. How many extras will there be so I know how many rooms to make up?" she calls from within the depths of the pantry.

I grab the creamer out of the fridge and give myself a generous helping before adding two spoonfuls of sugar. Ben pulls a face, but I just poke my tongue out at him. "There will be five extras, but only make up three rooms. Four of them are couples. Actually, I think four of them are a quad, but I'm not sure if they like to admit it with how judgy people are." To be honest, I don't think there's any chance that Gio will let Casey stay anywhere but his room if he has his way, but who am I to assume she will cave to his demands? It's better that we are overprepared than under.

"A quad, that is fascinating." Ben sounds so posh with his English accent. "And do we like these friends?" Ben asks, raising an eyebrow while Suzy continues to mutter to herself within the pantry.

"We haven't come to a decision yet," I tell him.

"It would be good for you to have some friends. You work too hard and isolate yourself too much." Suzy comes bustling out of the walk-in with an armload of recipe books. She allows them to fall onto the counter. I guess she must be planning a feast for dinner tonight.

"You know you don't have to cook, right? We can just order in."

She gasps. "Order in? No. I finally get a chance to show off my skills, so do not take this from me," she pleads, and it doesn't take much for me to give in. Suzy is an amazing cook, and I will gladly eat anything she offers.

"Suzy is right, you know. You could do with some friends. All work and no play gets to a person after a while. You need a close inner circle. Your father had your mum, Carla, and Mickey, not to mention Suzy and me. There were two more in his inner circle as well, but both of them were killed when you were little."

I'm not surprised to hear him say that he and Suzy were in Dad's inner circle. When we first moved back into the mansion after the Stacey fiasco, I could see how close they all were. Penelope would pout because she was never included, and Ben and Suzy were down-right frosty to her.

I sigh and take a seat next to him. "But how do I know who to trust? Do I just take a leap of faith and cross my fingers that they won't betray me? I don't know if I can do that."

"You trust Sage, don't you?" Suzy leans across the counter and grabs my hand, giving it a squeeze. "What made you trust him?"

I think about my crazy friend and how we had become close. "Because Dad did, and he doesn't want anything from me," I reply, and Ben chuckles.

"I wouldn't be so sure of that. We see the way he looks at you."

I shake my head quickly in denial. "I could never go there with him. I wouldn't want to jeopardize our friendship. He would betray me eventually when he got bored and moved on, and I'm not sure I would recover if it happened a second time."

Suzy spits out a string of French swear words. "Don't let what that bitch did to you dictate how you go through life, because then she is truly winning. You and Sage would be good together. That boy loves you, and you just have to let him."

"I'm not even sure I'm interested in men. I've only ever been with women," I say quietly, unable to look at either of them.

"The fact that you say you're not sure means that you could be open to the idea. Don't close yourself off to it.

I'm not saying you have to have sex with him straight out the gate, but there are other things you can do to test the waters. Make out with him on the couch. Hold his hand and be affectionate. You'll soon know whether it's something you are interested in or not," Suzy suggests gently.

I think back to my last time at the sex club. I was certainly turned on by my sub, but was that because I was making him bleed, or was it because it was him? I closed myself off to the idea that I was bisexual for so long, mostly to spite Stacey, I think. Her stupid idea started with wanting to impress boys, so after what happened, there was no way I was going to show interest in boys. Stupid, I know, but it was one way of me regaining control over my sexuality after she smashed that to smithereens.

"I don't know if I can," I say, and their eyes fill with sympathy.

"Life is going to be very sad and lonely if you don't. Try, sweetheart. We want you to be happy. Use tonight as a practice run. Commit to making an effort to be friends with Gio's friends. If that doesn't work out well, then I'm sure you can figure out a way to find your own group of friends, and stop closing your heart off to Sage or anyone who piques your interest. Who says you can only have one love in your life? You deserve many." Suzy pats my hand.

"Hmm, maybe the quad could become a quint," Ben jokes, and I roll my eyes, but Suzy nods enthusiastically.

"Oh yes, that would be fun. Now go and get

changed. Ben, I need you to run me to the grocery store so I can get a few things." And just like that, I'm dismissed. Suzy mutters about different dishes as Ben stands up and presses a kiss to my forehead.

"Sorry, duty calls. Never get between a French woman and her recipe planning. I need to go and find my keys."

I wave goodbye, and since they are both leaving, I take my mug of coffee and head upstairs to my room. Although I didn't do any killing, or even any maiming this afternoon, I feel like I need to wash off the metaphorical dirt from dealing with the FBI agent. Do I feel bad about setting Lorenzo up? Hell no, but I just hope making a deal doesn't come back to bite me in the ass. Just in case, I think I need to burn the warehouse down. We have plenty of others we can use for interrogation, and no matter how well you clean up, you never know for sure if you leave evidence behind. Nope, better to cut our losses and move to a new location. So tonight, after everyone has gone to bed, I'm going to have to make a quick trip and take care of yet another problem.

Chapter Ten

My hair is still damp when Gio and the crew arrive home. They all look a little awestruck as they follow Sage and Gio through the front door. I heard them arrive, so I came down to greet them.

"Holy shit, you live here?" Vienna's hand is in Colton's, but her eyes are wide as she looks around the foyer.

"Yeah, we moved in last year when I deferred from college. It's been in our family for generations," Gio explains.

"I would have thought that was something you already knew," I ask Colton, and he shakes his head.

"No, we have your address as a different place, though I did try to uncover who owns this place just out of curiosity when the kids used to talk about it during our senior year. It's hidden under layers and layers of corporations and shell companies." He doesn't sound guilty at all. I like a man who owns his shit. He's a hacker and proud of it, and he doesn't care who knows. It shines a whole new light on the quiet, sexy man.

"Yes, there's no way this home could ever be seized no matter what happens." Gio shrugs and takes off through the house with Casey glued to his side, their heads together as they talk quietly.

"Hi, honey, I'm home." Sage throws out his arms and wraps them around me. I can smell the alcohol on his breath, and I know he's been indulging. I think about what Suzy and Ben said, and I allow myself to relax into his arms, hugging him in return and placing a kiss on his cheek. I almost laugh out loud when his body stiffens in surprise. He pulls back and holds me at arm's length. "Who are you, and what have you done with my Tori?"

"Stop it, Sage, you're being silly," I scold him, but he still won't let it go.

"Did you help yourself to my X stash?" he asks seriously, and I grind my teeth and lean in.

"No, I had a little talk with Suzy and Ben, and I am trying to do better, but if you don't let me go now and stop making such a big fuss, I will shoot you in the toe." His arms slide from my shoulders and down to my waistline, where he feels around before snorting with laughter. He reaches in and pulls out my gun before stepping back.

"Trust you to be carrying a piece in your yoga pants at home." He waves the gun, and Vienna gasps.

"You had that on you?" she asks with no judgment, just curiosity.

"It's rare that Tori doesn't have one on her, or a knife. I swear she sleeps with one under her pillow." Sage shoves it into a sideboard drawer and waves his hand. "Would you like the grand tour, or shall we get to the ass kicking?" He throws down the challenge, but all four of them are still looking at me with various expressions.

"Uneasy lies the head that wears the crown," Xavier says quietly, and I give him a small nod. There is no disgust in their eyes, instead there's a lot of respect, and Tristan looks slightly turned on, but I've come to realize that he and Sage could be two peas in a pod. I think a light breeze would turn them on.

"Ah, there you are. I'm so sorry I wasn't here to greet you. Suzy has kept me busy playing sous chef for her." Ben comes out, wiping his hand on a dishtowel before shoving it into his back pocket.

"Benny, my man!" Sage shouts, and they exchange a manly hand greeting. "Does this mean your sexy French crumpet is making us a feast for dinner?" I have no idea how Sage does it, but he has Suzy and Ben wrapped around his little finger. If anyone else talked about his wife like that, Ben would knock them the fuck out before they'd even finished talking, but Sage gets away with it.

"Ah, Sage, you are in for a feast for your senses. She's worked herself into a tizzy wanting to prepare you a masterpiece."

"You guys are really in for something. Suzette is an amazing chef," Sage gushes. "This is Ben. If you need anything while you're here, he's the man to get it for you."

Ben bows slightly at our guests. "There is a phone in your room. Just press one, and it will connect to me no matter where and when."

"Ben, this is Vienna, Colton, Xavier, and Tristan." I point each person out one by one, and they exchange greetings. "Gio just dragged their cousin Casey off somewhere. Did Suzy get a chance to make up some rooms yet?" I ask him, and he shakes his head.

"No, our apologies. The grocery store was busier than expected, and then she wanted to get dinner started right away. I will see to it now. You said three, right?"

I turn to look at the four in front of me. "Do you each want rooms, one for each couple, or do you just want to share one room?" I ask, laying it all on the line, remembering Vienna told me that they are some kind of polycule.

They exchange a glance, and Sage holds up his hand. "Completely no judgment here, right, Benny?" He turns to our butler, who shakes his head.

He's keeping a straight face, but his eyes are alight with interest. "None at all. I have had many strange requests over the years, and that is the least of them. We have one room which has two Alaskan king-sized beds. You can push them together and zip the mattresses together to make one giant bed if you wish."

"We do?" I ask him in surprise.

"Young people don't have the monopoly on orgies, young Tori. Your mother and father threw some wild parties in their day." I grimace at the thought of my mom and dad being involved in anything like that. "Obviously the beds have been upgraded since then, but I'd be happy to do that for you."

"Benny, my man, you're the best," Sage says as the four guests have a silent conversation with their eyes.

"That would be great, thanks, Ben." Xavier takes the lead for the four of them, which doesn't surprise me in the least. He puts off major big dick energy, although it seems to simmer deep down.

"Very good. Why don't you give them a tour of the house while I do that? I'll have one of the staff help me."

"Staff?" I ask, sounding slightly confused. We don't have any others apart from the housekeeping staff, and I don't think today is their day.

"Yes, I'll get one of the young men to help me."

Ah fuck, of course there will be someone underground doing something. We got a shipment of guns the other day that needed to be cataloged, so there's bound to be someone doing that. Not to mention we have guards patrolling the grounds. I'm an idiot.

"Sweet, so let's get this tour on the road, come on." Sage heads to the elevator behind us. "Down here are the boring rooms. Dining, lounge, kitchen, ballroom, meeting rooms, and offices. The good stuff is upstairs." He presses the button, and the elevator opens immediately. Everyone steps in except Xavier, who looks back in the direction Gio and Casey went.

"I will find the master and let him and your cousin know where you have gone," Ben assures him, and Xavier fights with himself until Vienna puts her hand on his arm.

"Don't stress, baby. She will be fine." I guess she's decided to give up any pretense of pretending to be with just Colton. We are a judgment free zone here, and them all being in a relationship together is the least of our worries.

"Gio is a lot of things, but he would never do anything to hurt your cousin. He's completely infatuated with her," I admit to him, and we watch as the tension bleeds away from his shoulders, and he sighs.

"Yes, I think it's mutual."

"You don't like that?" I ask, feeling slightly defensive as he steps in and the elevator doors close. Sage pushes the button for the top floor. That's where all the fun stuff is. The middle floor has bedrooms, bathrooms, and a couple of living areas, including my favorite library.

Before he can say anything, Tristan jumps in. "It's not that we don't like Gio—he's awesome—but we also know what life with him would be like. Casey won't be safe, and she's really not cut out for this kind of life."

"She's soft," Vienna says bluntly. "She's been protected all her life, first by her parents, now by her uncle."

"Unlike the four of you?" Sage asks, not hiding the curiosity in his question.

Once again, the four exchange a loaded look that seems to speak volumes.

"Come on, you know everything about us thanks to Colton," I accuse, feeling rather annoyed. "We can't know anything about you?"

"It would go a long way to building some trust between us," Sage suggests gently, putting his hand on me to get me to ease up.

"We all had rough lives growing up. All of our parents were junkies, and some were worse than others. They were friends and shared the same dealer, so we have known each other since we were in diapers. Mostly for us" —Vienna gestures between her, Tristan, and Xavier— "they were neglectful at best and mean at worst, but Colton's mother and father were psychotic, and he didn't come out of it without a few scars. Some you can see, but most you can't."

I eye the quiet man with a new perspective, and now that I look closely, I can see the haunted look in his gaze that tells me he's seen trauma. "My parents were smart and very careful never to hurt me where people could see or where it would leave a mark. They knew how to ride that fine line and took sick pleasure out of staying just on this side of it."

"How did you get out of there?" I ask him, my eyes not leaving his.

"By the time I was thirteen, they were making me cook their heroin before they injected it. Everyone's parents were over for a party, and I was charged with having to make eight syringes so they could all shoot up together. I made them all hot shots. Idiots trusted me not to betray them, but if I thought I could get away with killing them, I would have done it sooner to stop all the pain." He shudders, and both Tristan and Vienna embrace him.

"The cops didn't suspect a thing?" Sage asks, looking at Xavier who shakes his head.

"Nope, we waited until the next morning to call them. We claimed we'd all been asleep at the other end of the house while they partied, and we woke up to that. The cops believed us. They didn't care, because as far as they were concerned, it was a mass overdose, bad heroin. They called Child Protective Services because none of us had family, or if we did, they had cut off our parents years ago. We've been together in a group home ever since. We were fostered out a few times, but it never took, mostly because we didn't want to be without the others, especially once our relationships grew into something more."

I'd love to ask more questions about how that happened, but the elevator doors open, and we step out.

"Fuck, okay, I don't know about you, but I need a drink." Sage blows out a deep breath, trying to lighten the heavy atmosphere. Tristan and Vienna are still standing close to Colton, offering emotional support.

"If you're offering up some of that weed from last night as well, I wouldn't say no." Colton kisses both

Vienna and Tristan on the cheek, and it's all I can do to stop my eyebrows from jumping. "Stop fussing, I'm okay, I promise," he assures them and follows Sage.

Tristan hurries after them with Xavier, their heads together as they whisper, leaving Vienna behind with me.

"That's the most he's talked about it since it happened," she offers. "If that doesn't tell you that he is open to trusting you, I'm not sure what will."

"So you weren't kidding when you said the four of you were a thing?" I ask, changing the subject in a quiet acknowledgment of her truth.

She turns to face me, arching an eyebrow as we let the heavy subject drop away for now. "No, I wasn't. Those three men are my life, and the four of us would do anything to protect each other."

"And Tristan's little interlude with Sage? Is he going to break his heart?"

Vienna shrugs. "No more than you have been."

Ouch, that was a direct hit. She may not have a weapon in her hand, but she certainly knows how to hit a target. I decide to give her a little of my own truth since they were so open with me.

"My life is not easy. It never will be, and after what Stacey did, trust is hard." She nods, and I carry on. "You know it wasn't even the rape. Yes, that was bad enough, but to use it as her springboard to popularity..." I trail off, unable to finish as a lump of emotions develops in my throat.

"You can't get much lower than that." Vienna steps

forward, and I startle when I find myself caged between her body and the wall. "But it really didn't work. Sure, she was included in the popular crowd, but despite how Nikki seems, she's not stupid. She didn't learn anything new last night. She's known about James's cheating ways, but she got a sick sense of pleasure out of denying Stacey what she wanted. If she was still dating him, then Stacey couldn't. You don't think Nikki was being faithful to James, do you? She was just better at hiding it. That 'let's wait for marriage' thing is an act. She just didn't want to catch anything from James. And now, Stacey better watch her back, because Nikki has some friends at the college, and Stacey's climb to the top might be a little bumpier than she thought it would be."

I feel a smile creep across my face at this information. Although I've kept tabs on her whereabouts, that's about all we've had time for, what with running the family business, so having some of this inside information actually makes me feel better.

"Ah, there it is." Vienna cups my face and brushes her thumb across my lips. "You know, you're gorgeous with a resting bitch face, but you're downright mind blowing when you smile."

I can feel her body pressed against mine—her round breasts, her flat stomach, and the swell of her hips—and I itch to reach out and run my hands over it, but I fist them so I can't. She looks down at them and chuckles, but I shake my head.

"I don't poach other people's partners. It seems

like you have a good thing going with your guys, and I don't want to fuck up that dynamic."

She leans in, her lips a breath from mine. "Ah, but then you wouldn't learn how I could rock your world."

She brushes her lips against mine, in just the briefest of lingering touches, before pulling away.

"And then we could let them rock both our worlds." With that, she turns and walks in the direction they all went, leaving me reeling.

Chapter Eleven

I compose myself after my interaction with Vienna. I guess that answers my question about who is bisexual in her and Colton's relationship—both of them. I wonder how that came to be. They said they have always been friends before the relationship developed into more, and I am dying to know all the nitty-gritty details, but I'm going to have to wait. I slowly follow after them, thinking about her offer to let the guys rock both our worlds.

Is she inviting me to be a participant in their relationship? A new toy for them to have some fun with until they discard me to the side. And is that what they want from Sage too? I don't know how I feel about that. I just came around to considering Sage as a sexual partner, so I'm not sure I'm willing to just throw aside everything I thought I knew about myself because a pretty, intriguing woman asks me to.

I stop and smack my hand against the wall. Fuck, my life is complicated. Sometimes I wish it was just easy, and that I was a normal kid preparing to go to college just like they are, but it's not, and I can't, so I have to make the most of what I've been dealt. Maybe I can do as Ben and Suzy suggested, though, and put a little trust in my best friend once more. I'm going to be really sad if I have to shoot him if he betrays me however.

"Tori, come on." Sage sticks his head out of the gym where he must be showing the others the facilities.

I hurry after them as Sage shows them the indoor pool, the theater, and the game room before hitting the bowling alley with the attached bar. He slides behind the polished wooden counter and waves his hands like a game show host. "What will your poison be?" he asks the others while I reach into a cigar box on top of the counter and pull out a couple of joints, rolling one toward Colton before lighting up my own.

Oh yeah, that's what I needed. I feel the tension I was carrying bleed out as the weed takes effect, while Sage pours our new friends drinks. Colton smiles gratefully at me and takes the other one. I pass him my lighter, his fingers brushing against mine as he takes it, and I feel goosebumps break out across my thighs. Luckily, they are covered by my yoga pants, so no one notices. What was that? The mere brush of someone's fingers has never affected me like that before. Maybe it was because I was surprised by the roughness of them.

He has calluses, but I thought they'd be smooth from using a computer. I guess there's more to him than what meets the eye.

"And a Jack and Coke for you, my lovely lady." Sage places a drink in front of me with a flourish, and I quickly take a sip.

"Thanks, Sage, you're the best." I blow him a kiss and move toward the lanes, but not before I register the stunned look on Sage's face at my flirting.

Vienna chuckles and follows closely behind me with a glass of wine in her hand. "Girl, what are you doing to him? Poor Sage looks like he's been hit by a two by four."

"I'm just taking some advice someone I trust gave me not too long ago and opening myself up to some opportunities. Stacey has ruled my mind for too long, and I'm trying not to let her win." I overshared, but despite all the conflict I'm experiencing, I'm feeling lighter than I have in ages.

"Hmm, I like the sound of that," she whispers in my ear, brushing her body against mine as she stakes her claim on the lane on one side of mine and Sage's. Tristan and Xavier take the one on the other side, leaving the one on the far end for Gio and Casey.

Sage flicks a few of the buttons on the control panel behind the bar, and all the lights turn on and pins drop down into place. I wave at the rack of balls on the wall.

"Take your pick, but know that the black one with

the gold flecks is mine, and the rust-colored one with the weed leaf is Sage's." The four of them put down their drinks at the console on their lanes and head over to pick their balls. The door to the alley opens, and Gio and Casey walk in, giggling. They both look flushed, and their hair is in disarray. It's not hard to guess what the two of them have been doing.

"About fucking time," Sage grumbles, leaving the bar and going over to grab his ball and mine at the same time. He comes back and hands it to me, and I put it on our ball return.

"Hey, what about our drinks?" Gio asks, looking between Sage and the bar.

"Get your own. If you have time to make out, you have time to make your girl a drink." Sage turns his back on Gio. Hmm, what is going on there? It's unusual for Sage to be frosty toward Gio. Gio just huffs out an annoyed sigh and slides behind the bar, gesturing to Casey.

I turn back to look at my best friend.

"You okay?" I ask him quietly, and he shakes his head.

"I'll tell you later when there aren't so many ears around."

I let it go, but I'm going to interrogate him later.

The other four find their balls and join us at the lanes, and it's not long before Casey and Gio do as well, drinks in hand.

"Hey, that's my lane." Gio points to the one Vienna and Colton are at, and I shake my head.

"Sorry, bud. You snooze, you lose. You get that one." I point to the remaining one, and Gio looks like he's going to argue, but Casey puts her hand on his arm, and he melts like a pat of butter in a frying pan.

"Can you help me, Gio? I've never been very good at bowling." She blushes, and he leads her to the lane before hurrying over to the rack of balls and grabbing one for both of them.

"What the actual fuck?" I mutter under my breath, watching my hard-ass brother become someone completely different. He's soft, gentle, and kind. I should be thrilled for him, but I'm just suspicious. What are the odds that Sage is going to confirm my suspicions, and that's where Gio has been sneaking off to?

I'm not actually sure how I feel about this. Sure, I'm relieved he's not a traitor, but I'm pissed as fuck that he's blowing off family business for something personal and leaving me to deal with all the crap. Gio and I used to be a solid team. Together, we could take on the world, but now it seems like team Russo is no more. Just another blow to my fragile psyche. And Ben and Suzy wonder why I don't trust easily. Why couldn't he just be honest with me? Sure, we might have argued about it, but in the end, I just want him to be happy.

He turns back to face me, and our eyes meet. I'm not sure what he sees in them, but he flinches slightly and puts himself between me and Casey. Ouch, that kind of hurts. He's protecting his girlfriend from me, his sister, the one who has had his back for all of our lives.

I turn away from him, no longer able to look at him in case I break and show some emotion. I take a long drag of my joint and blow out the smoke, but I'm tense once more with the realization that Gio and I are growing apart. I'm not sure what that means for us, but we need to sit down and have a long, overdue chat about everything.

"Okay, should we draw straws to see who bowls first?" I ask, and Sage goes over to the bar and grabs four, trimming them at different lengths, then he comes back, holding them level.

"Shortest straw bowls first." He holds out his hand. Colton, Xavier, and Gio all reach for a straw and hold up what they have picked, leaving Sage with the remaining one. "Whoop, look at that. I guess Tori and I are up first," he crows as the others grumble good-naturedly.

"You totally rigged it," Gio complains, but Xavier just shoves him in Casey's direction.

"Alright, why don't the two of you show us what you've got?" He drags Tristan back, and they take a seat on their lane and wait their turn, his arm casually thrown over Tristan's shoulder.

Tristan smiles widely and winks. "I saw some of Sage's moves last night, and I can't wait to see yours, Tori."

Fuck me, my partner in crime and bowling blushes before picking up his ball and lining up to throw.

"What the fuck did you do to him?" I ask and point my finger at Tristan. "I don't think I've ever seen him blush before."

"Well, if you come over here, I could give you a hands-on demonstration."

Vienna, Colton, and Xavier burst into laughter as I scowl at him.

"I'm almost certain you would be happy to give anyone a demonstration, so I'm going to take a pass on that," I deflect, even if I am interested deep down.

He clutches at his chest. "Ouch, Tori, that kind of hurts. I would have you know that I am faithful to my lovers, and we only pursue anyone with each other's permission."

Tristan is telling me something, and it takes me a moment to realize it. All four of them must have discussed both me and Sage, because Tristan and Vienna both made moves on us. When did they discuss us? Last night was the first time I'd seen them in a year, and I'm not sure they'd ever met Sage before. I must ask him. Maybe Gio had introduced them in the past.

Colton sits down on their couch and pulls Vienna into his lap. She leans back into his chest, and he presses a kiss to her temple. I feel a pang of envy over how comfortable they are with one another. Maybe I do want something like that. All the one-night stands in the past were just me protecting my fragile heart, but what good did it do? I just succeeded in isolating myself further.

The sound of the ball hitting pins has me spinning and checking out what Sage's first roll was.

"Strike!" He fist pumps the air and turns around, heading back to me and holding his hand up for a high five. We slap hands as the others jeer behind us, then I input the strike into the computer console in front of our couch.

"Bah, that was just luck, you won't be able to keep that up," Gio calls, but Sage ignores him and pats me on the ass.

"Your turn, love." Usually I would slap his hand away, but this time I pat his butt.

"Good job." I might give it a little squeeze and wink at him.

His mouth drops open before he shakes his head and smiles. "Good luck."

"I don't need it. We've got this in the bag." I stab out the end of my joint, pick up my ball, and make my approach. Blocking out the surrounding sound, I draw my arm back before letting it fly. It hits true and knocks all ten pins down on the first go.

"Woo-hoo, that's another strike. We're on fire." Sage pushes the buttons to put up my score as I return to our couch.

Tristan and Xavier are grumbling about home court advantage as Vienna gets up to take her turn. I grab my drink and down the rest of it before heading back to the bar to pour another.

When I get there, I flick the button on the

surround sound, and music comes through the speakers.

Vienna was just starting her approach, and at the music's loud intrusion, she turns around and scowls at me. "Are you trying to distract me?" she accuses, and I shrug.

"Hey, whatever works." I smile to soften my words, and she uses her fingers and points to her eyes then me.

"I'm watching you."

"They are dirty cheaters, I'm telling you," Gio joins in, and I flip him off.

"Watch out, Casey, your partner can be a bit of a sore loser. I hope you've got something up your sleeve to distract him when he goes down in flames." My smack talk is on par this evening, and Sage whoops and claps.

Vienna restarts her approach, and if my eyes drift to the curve of her ass in her tight jeans, well, I'm not going to apologize. She has good form, and her ball knocks down six of the ten pins.

She waits for her ball to return, and I see Colton giving her tips on where to place the next one to knock over the remaining pins. I throw some more ice into my glass before picking up the bottle of Jack and pouring myself another generous shot. I grab the soda gun and top up the last inch with coke as three of the remaining pins fall, leaving her with only one.

"Hey, that's not bad," I say, returning to my and Sage's sofa and sitting down. Vienna takes a bow as the pins reset.

"We might have some competition," Sage agrees as Colton lines up and takes a shot, getting a strike. "Well, at least more than Gio ever gives us." He leans back and puts an arm on the back of the sofa, his hand grabbing a piece of my hair and twirling it. I don't pull away like I normally do. I'm really going to try, just like Suzy suggested.

"This is fun." Vienna picks up her wine and drains the rest of it. "It beats going out to a club and having to put on a fake facade."

"But then I don't get a chance to get my hands on you on the dance floor." Tristan jumps to his feet, while Gio takes a turn. They drew the longest straw, so they'll go last. He grabs Vienna by the hand and twirls her around before bringing her close, and they dance to the music that's pumping through the speakers.

"Nothing is stopping you from dancing here," Sage points out.

"Too true," he agrees, and I get my first look at their polycule in motion. He dips Vienna deeply before following her down and kissing her. Their tongues tangle, and I feel Sage's hand tighten in my hair. I turn slightly to look at him, careful not to rip my hair out. I was expecting to see jealousy, but it's not there. There is only heat and lust.

I turn back to the couple who have now broken apart and watch as Gio helps Casey. I examine how I feel about what I just saw. I was most certainly turned on by Tristan and Vienna, and I could see Sage was too, but how do I feel about that? I think about how I would feel seeing him with either Vienna or Tristan and quickly discover that's not something I'm opposed to. Surprised but happy with my thoughts, I lean back into him as Casey's ball drifts into the gutter, and she stomps her foot in frustration. Gio assures her it's fine and that it doesn't matter, but she seems so disappointed, and no matter how I feel about my brother at the moment, I won't let her pay for it.

I stand up and head over to their console and erect the gutter barriers. The things slide into place so her ball can no longer roll into them. Gio blinks owlishly at me before smiling and nodding his thanks.

"Just until you get used to the weight and flow of everything," I tell her, and she smiles brightly. I'm momentarily blinded by her golden light. Shit, this girl is just too bright for my brother. He's going to end up muddying her.

"Thank you, Tori. I was so worried I was going to let Gio down, it was making me more nervous," Casey confesses, but Gio throws his arm around her shoulders and kisses her on her temple.

"I'm just happy we can be together," he tells her.

"Please, Gio needs all the help he can get," Sage teases, "so you're helping him."

Gio flips Sage off while I think about his last comment. I guess it would be a relief for him to be able to hang out in private and not worry about who can see him being affectionate to her. Someone's always looking for leverage against him, so maybe I can understand the secretiveness a little better, but I'm still hurt he wouldn't confide in me.

"Alright, let's get this party started. It's on like Donkey Kong." Sage whoops and heads back to the bar for more drinks. I'll have one more and then stop. I've got another errand to run tonight, but it won't hurt for them to all be out due to intoxication.

Chapter Twelve

We got in two rounds of bowling before Ben announced that dinner was ready. We were all pretty intoxicated by then, so getting some food in our stomachs was an excellent idea. We headed down to the formal dining room, which is where Suzy decided we needed to eat. It was the first time since Dad has been gone that we used it, and it was slightly bittersweet seeing Gio sit in his spot.

The table is ridiculously long, made for large family dinner parties, so instead of sitting down at the other end, I found myself sandwiched between Colton and Xavier with Tristan, Sage, and Vienna on the other side of us. Casey took Gio's right-hand spot, which traditionally would have been mine. I didn't care though. I smoked two joints and had four Jack and Cokes, and I was feeling no pain. Usually I don't indulge in alcohol and weed at the same time, since I like to keep my wits about me, but I know Sage will have my back no matter how besotted he seems to be with our guests. I also still have enough time to sober up before I need to take a little trip later this evening.

Our guests are certainly not what I had expected. To be honest, I hadn't really thought all that much about them after Gio deferred college and we did our thing with Dad. It wasn't until last night—shit, was it only last night?—that they'd crossed my mind again. Turns out they weren't there with Stacey and Nikki, and it was a coincidence. They'd been invited by Gio when he had originally invited Casey to join him. She had declined, claiming she didn't like clubs, but the others had taken him up on the offer.

We talked and got to know one another. Like Gio, they are all doing business related courses. Their adoptive father pushed them into it, and they caved to his whims. I tried to ask more about their situation and how they came to be adopted by the same person, but they weren't very forthcoming. Seems like it might be a hard subject for them, so I let it go. I know what it's like not to be able to share every detail of my life.

They were happy to share other things with me though. Tristan loves to draw and would like to be a tattoo artist, so he's using the business classes as a gateway to have his own parlor. He has a part-time apprenticeship at one not far from the college. He says they get a lot of drunk college kids making bad decisions, but he lights up when he talks about it, and the other three look at him with such pride.

He designed the rose tattoo I'd been so fascinated

about on his chest at our first meeting. They all wear it. He did it on the others, but of course someone else had to ink it on him. The three guys wear theirs in the same place above their hearts, but Vienna's is in the middle of her chest just below her breasts. How do I know this? They all lifted their tops and showed me when I expressed my appreciation of Tristan's. I'm pretty sure Sage and I both nearly swallowed our tongues at all that pretty exposed flesh. It took me a moment or two to get my brain back into the conversation.

Colton has his tech business, which I know works in shades of gray, straddling the line of legal and illegal depending on what is needed to get the job done. He and I still have a meeting set up for tomorrow to go over my requirements. He wasn't very forthcoming with what he was interested in, but the others talked about his love of gaming, and Sage has challenged him to a Mario Kart showdown, which he claims he's the king of. From the way Colton rolled his eyes but agreed good-naturedly, I'm almost certain Mario Kart is not the kind of gaming he's into. Xavier whispered in my ear that he's also programming his own game, but that he doesn't like to tell anyone about it.

Xavier is into fitness and trains at one of the local MMA clubs. He claims it keeps him fit, but Tristan brags that when he gets in the ring, he's lethal. Apparently, he is also musically inclined. He plays both the piano and the guitar. I found that strange since they all grew up in a group home and music lessons weren't something I thought they would have the opportunity to partake in, but Vienna bragged that he plays by ear.

They are so into one another, you can tell it's for keeps. Each one took the time to talk up the others if given a chance.

"Last year, you and Tristan were on the football team. Is that something you're doing this year?" I ask Xavier, but he shakes his head.

"No, that was just for a bit of fun, but our guardian wants us to concentrate on our education this year. I am teaching a self-defense course on campus, so that should be interesting." Oh yeah, I can imagine how packed it's going to be with females once they figure out the instructor is smoking hot.

"What about you, Vienna?" Sage asks, shoveling some of Suzy's delicious food into his mouth and chewing quickly before swallowing. I'm not even sure he tasted it. "We've heard all about the guys, but nobody's mentioned what you want to do. We know you're taking business classes, but once you finish up, where do you see yourself going?"

Vienna blushes, the color of her cheeks almost the same color as her flaming locks, and her guys chuckle while Sage and I exchange a glance.

"Are we missing something?" I ask cautiously, and she shakes her head.

"No, but I don't have any real ambitions or hobbies," she says quietly, and Colton grabs her hand and squeezes it.

"Yes, you do, you just don't think it's one a girl

your age should have, so you won't share them with people. We keep telling you that's silly. You know we're just waiting to finish college, and then the three of us will give you exactly what you want."

"What do you want?" Sage asks, sounding as confused as I am.

"I want to be a mom. I love baking and cooking and keeping house, and nothing would make me happier than having a family to raise and look after." She doesn't look at either of us as she admits it, staring down at her hands that are wringing together.

Huh, that was not what I thought she was going to say. I thought she'd admit to wanting to be anything but a mother.

"Like Vienna said, our parents were neglectful at best. She wants the chance to do better. Even though she's the youngest, when we were all together, she was the one who made sure we were eating and going to school and had clean clothes," Xavier explains, looking at the redheaded beauty with such love and affection in his eyes I'm almost breathless.

"And when we didn't, she made sure we got those things in whichever way she could. She's a warrior," Tristan says fiercely, and Vienna finally looks up and smiles at him.

"I became proficient at shoplifting at a young age, but we ate and we were clothed, and that's what matters."

Tristan grabs her neck and pulls her to him, kissing her hard on the mouth before pulling away.

"Vienna is a nurturer, and nothing makes her happier than caring for the ones she loves. It's why it was so hard for us last year when the guys lived in the dorms, and we were home in Banebridge. This year will be better for all of us," Colton explains.

"Yes, I only have to walk across the hall to make sure you're both eating right." She smiles brightly at Tristan and Xavier.

"Which, hopefully, will mean you'll sleep better now that all your chicks are close by again," Colton deadpans, but she shrugs unapologetically.

"I know I will."

"So a baby, huh?" Sage asks the question that had been rolling around in my brain too. "How do you decide who gets to be the father?"

She quickly shakes her head. "It doesn't matter because that child will be all of ours and the most loved child in the universe."

"With four parents, it certainly won't be lacking for attention," I say kindly, though I'm slightly horrified because I'm the least maternal person in the world. I freak out at the thought of having to hold a baby, and forget about babysitting. What would I even teach a child? How to remove a toenail or fingernail effectively? Or a thousand ways to cut someone so that they enjoy it? No, fuck that, I would completely suck as a parent.

Now Sage would be a good parent. He'd be the fun, irresponsible dad who revved the kids up until they were hyper and then hand them to the mother to try and get them to bed on time, but he'd love them with all his heart. That's another reason why I probably shouldn't be contemplating a relationship with anyone. I'm just not the right person to be planning a family with.

"Are you okay?" A whisper in my ear startles me out of my thoughts, and I turn to face the controlled man next to me.

"Ah, yeah, I'm fine, I was just thinking about parenthood."

"Not a fan?" Xavier asks, and I cock my head to the side, thinking about the question.

"My dad was amazing. He always made time for us, and I never felt like I missed out on anything, but we lived in a different house our whole childhood. He was away a lot on business, and I know now that was for our protection. The only mother figure I've known was disinterested in me completely unless she was telling me how I was less than useless. I would be a terrible mother." I realize the whole table has fallen silent and is listening to me, so I turn my attention away from Xavier and look at Vienna. "But I can see how it could appeal to someone. Why were you embarrassed?"

"Come on. I saw the way you and Sage reacted. It's not exactly something an almost nineteen-year-old should be thinking about, is it?"

"Why not? Shit, eighteen months ago I never would have imagined myself as an enforcer for the mafia, yet here I am, and I'm very good at it. Sometimes life just takes you where you need to be, and sometimes you know exactly where you need to be."

"Tori busts heads and takes names, and you better watch out if you end up on her radar." Sage does his own bit of bragging, and the ones who weren't in the know look at me differently.

"You're the head enforcer? That's not actually something we knew." Tristan sounds incredulous, and he looks at Colton accusingly as a smile spreads across my face.

"Would you like a demonstration?" I ask the flirty man, but he quickly shakes his head, shuddering.

"No, thank you. I've seen some of the enforcer's handywork, and it's gruesome. Are you sure that's you?" He still sounds like he doesn't believe me.

"Oh yes, Tori is known as Azrael in our circles," Gio says proudly, and Colton gasps.

"The Angel of Death."

"How have you seen my work?" I ask Tristan carefully, fully realizing what he just said.

"Oh, ah, I pulled up some police pictures that were speculated to be the result of the Russo family. When we heard that Gio was returning to college, I did another round of checking into you," Colton quickly butts in before Tristan can answer me.

The atmosphere has gone from relaxed to tense, and I'm not sure if I believe him or not, but I will give him the benefit of the doubt. He has been fairly transparent with us so far, and Gio seems to trust them, though I'm pretty sure he's ruled by his dick and not his brain.

There's an awkward silence now that is only filled by the sound of cutlery scraping across China.

"I like to knit," Vienna blurts out. I guess the silence was too much for her to take.

"Hey, so does Tori." Gio points his fork at me, grasping the new conversation like a lifeline. "She always has a set of needles in her hands when we're in the theater room."

"There's a set in the limo too," Sage adds, smiling.

"Well, the drives to some of our assets are long and I get bored."

That was enough to move the conversation onto more benign things, but it's not long before we've finished up the delicious meal.

"Would you like dessert?" Suzy asks as she comes in to clear the table. Tristan, Xavier, and Colton all stand and start helping her. Sage joins them as soon as he realizes what they are doing. She tries to shoo them away, but Sage just puts a finger to her lips.

"Hush, woman. If we help, it's done quickly, and you can get back to whatever it is you and Ben do in the evening." He winks, and she shakes a finger at him.

"Never you mind what we do, you naughty perv."

"I think we might leave dessert for now. Is that okay with everyone?" I look at our guests who all quickly agree.

"That was delicious, Suzy. Would you mind

sharing the recipe with me?" Vienna asks, and Suzy beams.

"Oh, you wonderful child. Of course I will. I have been waiting for the day when Tori might show an interest, but I quickly learned it was not meant to be. I would love to share anything you want." Suzy's French accent thickens in her excitement.

"That's it, you've done it now, Vienna. You've replaced me in Suzy's heart." I press my hand to my forehead dramatically. "Whatever will I do?"

It's my turn to get a finger shaken at me. "Stop it now. Take your new friends up to the pool for a soak in the hot tub. It's great to relieve any tension."

Suzy leads everyone back to the kitchen so we can put all the dirty dishes on the counter for her, but of course Tristan slides past me and leans in, whispering, "I have another idea on how we can relieve our tension. Care to find out?"

Before I can answer, Vienna gives him a shove. "Leave her be, you horn dog."

"Hey." He acts wounded. "That's not what you say when I'm balls deep in you."

I feel my eyebrows jump on my face at how blatant they are being, but they both disappear through the double doors before I can respond.

"Ignore them. Vienna and Tristan are like a dog with a bone once they have an idea." Xavier stops next to me with a couple of dirty plates in his hand.

"And that bone would be me or Sage?" I ask, not

shying away from the conversation. It's time to pull up my mafia pants and meet this head-on.

"Not you *or* Sage, you *and* Sage," he confirms, holding my gaze.

"But why? You guys seem to have a good thing going. Why mess with that dynamic?"

"Because Vienna likes girls. Oh, we know she would happily settle down with us and pop out a few babies, but why deny her when we can give her everything she wants? She wants you, and Sage is part of that equation, because we can see how in love with you he is, even if you are still trying to deny it."

I cross my arms defensively, but before I can say anything, he keeps going.

"Look, just keep an open mind and see what happens. It may go nowhere. We may have a hot fling and then go our separate ways, or it may become one of the most important things in your life. Just don't let your past dictate your future, because you could miss out on so much." With that, the quiet man who puts off an aura of silent, coiled violence follows everyone into the kitchen, leaving me behind with Casey and Gio who are still seated at the table.

"What was that about?" Gio calls across the room, nodding in the direction Xavier just went.

"That was nothing you need to worry your pretty little head about. Now what did you do with everyone's gear when you first arrived? I'm assuming you stopped back at the dorms to pick up swimsuits and things."

Gio pushes his chair back before helping Casey out of hers. "We left it in the trunk of the limo."

"Well, how about we go grab it, and then we can show them to their rooms? By then, the food would have settled enough so we can swim without worrying about puking it back up."

"That sounds like a great idea," Casey replies. "I can't wait to see the pool. A swim to cool off is just what we need after all that bowling."

"Well, the indoor pool is heated, so I'm not sure how much cooling we will do, but I guess we can swim in the outdoor one." Gio looks at me, and I shake my head.

"Nah, I swam last night, and it's the perfect temperature. Let's stay inside so we can use the hot tub too. I have a few muscles that need soaking."

"Yay, I love a good soak in a hot tub," Casey cheers, jumping up and down. Gio's eyes lock onto her breasts. Scoffing, I turn and head in the direction of the elevator, not needing to see the two of them being so lovey-dovey with one another, but there is definitely a hard conversation in my and Gio's future, and heaven help him if he tugs his fucking ear.

Chapter Thirteen

Casey, Gio, and I grabbed everyone's bags from the limo, and by the time we returned, the others had finished helping Suzy clean up.

"Okay, how about I show you to your rooms?" I announce as I walk into the kitchen. Casey and Gio stayed on the elevator while I went to gather the others.

"The room next to Sage's is where we put these four, Tori, and Casey is in a room next to Gio's," Ben tells me.

I raise an eyebrow at him, and he smirks. The man is infuriating, but his heart is in the right spot, I guess. Out of all the rooms in the damn place, the meddling man put them as close to me as possible.

"Thanks for dinner, Suzy," Colton tells her politely, and the others chime in with their thanks again, and she beams at them.

"We're going to retire for the night, but there are snacks in the library on the floor you guys will be on.

Help yourselves to anything. Breakfast will be served at eight, Tori, if that's okay with you?" she tells us, and I go over and give her a kiss on the cheek.

"Sounds perfect, thank you."

We wave goodbye, and the others trail me back to the elevator.

"Thanks for grabbing our gear." Xavier picks up a backpack and throws it over his shoulder, as does Colton and Tristan. When Vienna goes to grab the last one, Xavier beats her to it.

I press the button for the next floor, and the elevator takes us straight there. We step out and turn to the left, passing the grand staircase on our way toward our rooms. We pass Gio's and stop at the one on the other side.

"This will be yours, Casey." I open the door to the pretty yellow room. I'm just going to pretend she will actually stay there and not spend the night in Gio's. Thinking about her and my brother having sex is just wrong.

"Come on, let's get you settled." My brother drags her into her room and closes the door behind them. I hear a growl behind me, and I can't figure out which guy it came from, but Vienna slaps Colton.

"Stop it. She's a big girl and can make her own decisions. Jesus, it's not like you guys haven't been defiling me for years, yet you expect Casey to be different."

"I'll show you defiling," Colton growls and grabs for her. She dodges quite impressively and takes off down the corridor, laughing. Colton is right on her heels, and the rest of us follow, laughing at them. It feels strange to just be hanging out and messing around with people my own age, instead of trying to hold onto my position in the family with every bit of strength that I have. If I'm not home, I'm at the casino, the nightclub, or the strip club. There, I have plenty of acquaintances, but not friends.

They go past my and Sage's rooms, so I have to call them back. I open the door to the room next to Sage's and peer in. I explored this house when we first moved in, but I haven't really bothered since. I know the housekeeping girls clean all the rooms once a week whether they have been used or not, but my mouth drops open at what I find inside this room.

"Holy shit, that bed is big enough for a fucking giant," I exclaim, pausing in the doorway. It's seriously the size of two Alaskan king-sized beds pushed together and is covered with four separate comforters. This room is done in blues and grays and has a little sitting area similar to the one in my and Sage's rooms.

A pair of hands grip my waist, helping move me forward into the room, before letting go and they step up next to me.

"Wow, if that's not an orgy bed, I don't know what is." Sage whistles as the other four join us in the room.

"Wow, this room is gorgeous." Vienna goes over and runs her hand across one of the comforters as the guys drop their backpacks on the sofas in the little sitting area.

"Whoa, this is huge." Tristan throws himself backward onto the bed, taking Vienna down with him, and her musical giggles fill the room.

"That's what you usually say," Xavier jokes, running and jumping like he's going to land on them. They both screech and hold up their hands, but at the last minute, he changes trajectory and lands on the other side of Tristan.

Colton joins them, and Sage and I are left staring at the four of them as they wrestle on the bed like kids. I have a strange urge to join them, and I guess Sage does too, because he takes a step toward them, but I grab hold of his arm and drag him backward.

"Please make yourselves at home. We'll leave you to get changed and meet you back in the corridor. Is ten minutes enough?" I ask them, and they stop roughhousing and look at the two of us sheepishly.

"Ah, yeah, sorry." Colton sits up, pushing his long blond hair back, but a boyish smile crosses his face. "We got a bit carried away."

"Don't stress yourself. I did the same thing when Gio showed me my room here. I'm across the hall, and Sage is next door if you need anything tonight, but we'll leave you be for now."

I drag Sage out of the room, but not before he calls, "Don't do anything I wouldn't do."

I pull the door closed behind us, rolling my eyes. "I'm not sure there isn't anything you wouldn't do, so that's not really great advice."

He puts his hands on his hips, looking affronted at

my remark. "I will have you know that I am not into any kind of bestiality." He tips his head to the side in thought. "Unless it's you and you're dressed in a furry costume, and then I'm down for anything."

I consider my reaction, and I decide to give him one he's probably not expecting just to test the waters a little more. I step up to him and run a hand over his shirt. "Be careful what you wish for, it just might come true." I smack his ass at the same time I kiss him quickly on the lips. He's so confused, he has no time to react to either before I pull away and open the door to my own room. He starts to follow me, but I quickly close it, leaving only a gap to call through. "Ten minutes, Sage." Then I close it fully.

It's not long before there's a thud on the other side, and I laugh, knowing that's his head.

"You're not being fair, Tori. You better not be playing with me and getting my hopes up. Know this, if you're not being real, please stop. It hurts, and I die a little more every time you reject me." The words are said just loud enough for me to hear them, and I know it cost him a lot to say them.

"I promise I'm not. Just be patient with me," I tell him through the door, and I hear him open his own before going in and closing it behind him.

My own head bangs back on the door I lean against as I heave out a sigh. I'm not a fan of change. Sure, I adapted like a duck to water when I thought I was joining a mafia family ran by my father, and I was just going to be a loyal soldier. Then we had to adapt again with Dad's death and the subsequent attempts at hostile takeovers. I don't know if I have it in me to adapt for a third time. I like my life. Mostly. Sure, it gets lonely, and tonight has been the most fun I've had in months, apart from when I go to the club and play with my subs. Maybe I do need something different. Change is as good as a holiday, and I could sure use a week-long stay by the beach with sun, sand, and a cocktail in hand, but I will settle for being open-minded to this change in my relationship with Sage and be open to accepting Gio's new friends as mine too. At least there are no preconceived notions on anyone's behalf, and they didn't seem too terrified when we talked about my role within the business.

"Okay, Tori, get your shit together. Take a swim, and then you'll have to put your business face back on and commit some arson. Just another fun packed evening in my life."

My pep talk does the trick, and I push off the door and go search through my closet for my swimsuit. I grab a plain black one piece before turning to go and get changed in the bathroom, but I stop and look at the sedate piece of material in my hand. "Come on, Tori, that's not sexy, and you promised yourself you were going to try harder with Sage."

I throw the one piece back into the drawer and dig deeper into the pile of fabric. I have lots of suits in here, but I've barely worn any of them, since I have no time to do any of the aforementioned sitting by a beach. I pull out a deep, blood-red triangle bikini top and matching bottom set. The bottoms are basically held together with a couple of pieces of string too.

I feel a smile stretch across my lips as I think about how Sage is going to react when he sees me in this. He'll probably swallow his tongue. If it gets a little attention from four of our guests as well, then I won't be upset.

I hurry through getting ready and take a good look at myself in the mirror, grimacing when I see how pale my skin is. "You look like a slutty Snow White. Damn, Tori, you need some sun," I tell myself and make a note to use the outdoor pool and the sun loungers on the next hot day.

Tying back my unruly locks, I grab a coverup from the closet and a towel and head back into the corridor to wait for everyone. Sage took my Glock and put it in a drawer downstairs, and I feel a little naked without it, but there are some guns in the indoor pool area if I need one, and really, where would I stick it? It's not like my swimsuit bottoms would cope with having it shoved into the back of them. I giggle at the thought, and I'm still giggling as Sage comes out of his room.

"Hey, that's not a sight I see very often," he says as he pulls his bedroom door closed, but I barely hear what he says. He's only wearing his swim shorts, so the rest of his body is on full display. I mean, sure, I've seen it before, but today, I'm looking at it with new eyes, and I quickly run a hand across my mouth to make sure I haven't started drooling. Fuck me, Sage is ripped. He has been from the start, but he's bulked up slightly since we first met, and there isn't an ounce of fat on him, just lovely sculpted muscles. Not roid muscles like a lot of the guys that work for us—no, his are just from dedication and hard work in the gym. All three of us make use of the one here at the house on an almost daily basis. You never know when you're going to have to run or fight your way out of a situation.

"What's that?" I ask when I finally get my head back in the game.

"You giggling like a little schoolgirl. It's nice to see you happy for a change."

"I'm happy, I smile." I scowl at him, and he chuckles.

"No, babe, that there is your default look most days. It's okay, I get it, being you is hard and, well, no one would respect you if you went around smiling like a beauty queen, but your eyes are always so sad. It's nice to see a little bit of joy in them." He reaches over, pulls me to him, and gives me a quick hug. I don't struggle, I just go with it and allow my body to sink into his. It feels really nice to be held against all that naked flesh, and I think about one time, when I was high, when I stuck my tongue out and licked him. I'm tempted to try it again, completely sober this time, but the other door opens before I can, and Sage and I break apart as the other four join us.

"Oh great, you're all here, shall we go?" Sage grabs my hand and drags me in the direction of the elevator with the others following behind. When I glance back,

Vienna is looking at our joined hands with a small smile on her lips.

We stop at Casey's door, and I knock, silently hoping that he didn't convince her to have a quick fuck while the rest of us were getting ready. I need to speak to him about being a little bit more respectful when her cousins are around. She's not a skank he can treat poorly.

Thankfully, the door opens, and Casey comes out on her own. "Where's Gio?" I ask, peering behind her, and she giggles, flushing slightly.

"I sent him to his room to get changed, otherwise, we might never have been ready."

"Good for you standing your ground. I know how persuasive my brother can be. Getting him used to hearing no now will go a long way in your relationship." I give her that little piece of advice quietly, and she nods, her eyes serious.

"I can imagine, thank you."

I nod as Sage pounds on Gio's door. I thought it would take a minute or so, but he appears within seconds, like he was just waiting on the other side of the door for us. His eyes go straight to Casey, and it's like the rest of us don't even exist.

"Well, let's get moving, shall we?" I mutter and take the lead, but Sage quickly catches up. We bypass the stairs again for the elevator. There is another sweeping set that leads up to the next landing, but I'm feeling lazy.

The trip up to the next level is quick and quiet.

"How about some more drinks?" Vienna says, breaking the comfortable silence.

"I wouldn't say no," Xavier rumbles, and Colton and Tristan agree.

"No more for me. I'm still feeling lightheaded after dinner," Casey decides, and Gio wraps an arm around her in concern.

"Are you sure you're okay? We don't have to swim. We can go back to your room and you can go to bed."

She pushes his hand away from her forehead. "Yes, I'm fine, silly. I just think I'll stick to water for the rest of the evening. I don't like feeling out of control."

"I think I'll join you, I don't like to feel out of control either," Gio agrees, and she beams at him. He's not lying to her. He doesn't indulge very often, none of us do, and it's only when we're here in our house. When we're out, we keep tight control of everything.

"There is a fridge in the pool area that is fully stocked, and if it doesn't have what you want, we can head back to the bowling alley and make something in the bar there."

It doesn't take long until we're in the pool area and the others are oohing and aahing over the space. I must admit it really is a thing of amazement. Fake rock work forms a grotto with a waterfall flowing over it, leaving a space behind it with a jacuzzi in it. Actually, I don't remember the last time we turned that section on. Usually I just use the bit that is long enough for me to do laps in. Sage goes into the control room and flips all the switches, turning on the lights, and the smoke, waterfall, and grotto section lights up. Casey squeals with delight.

"That's awesome." She tosses off the dress she put on over her swimsuit, and before anyone else can stop her, there's a splash and she's diving into the water, swimming in the direction of the grotto. She takes a breath and stands up just as she gets to the waterfall. She turns around and gestures to us. "Come on, the water is lovely," she calls just before she ducks under the waterfall and disappears.

Gio looks at me, and I shrug. "Go, I'll get everyone drinks," I tell him, and he dives after her. Just as he surfaces before the waterfall, I call out, "No fucking in the grotto, Gio."

He flips me off without turning back to look at me and follows Casey under.

Chapter Fourteen

I grumble under my breath as I head in the direction of the fridge, while Sage turns on the hot tub and sauna.

"Help yourselves to whatever." I pull the fridge open and turn back to look at the others. "Same with the facilities. Use the sauna or the hot tub, whatever you'd like."

Xavier reaches into the fridge, his muscular, tattooed arm brushing against me as I continue to stand there holding the door open. He pulls out four beers and hands them to the guys, keeping one for himself. "What do you want, babe?" he calls to Vienna, who is looking longingly at the hot tub. "There's a vodka cooler thingy in here."

"I can get you another bottle of wine or champagne, too, if you want it," I offer, and she turns away from the tub to look at us.

"No, don't go, Tori. Come and sit in the tub with me. Let Xavier wait on us. I'll just have whatever is in the fridge." She strips off her coverup and tosses it onto one of the loungers next to the pool, and the five of us are mesmerized as she sashays to the hot tub and walks down the two steps before sinking below the water. Her curvy body has a smattering of freckles across her porcelain skin, but her bikini doesn't do much to cover anything. Her top is basically a swatch of material covering her breasts with no straps. They are a delicious full handful, so I'm not sure how the top even stays up, to be honest, and the bottoms are a thong, displaying her round, tight ass, and I just want to sink my teeth into it.

"Holy crap," I mutter under my breath, but I'm obviously not quiet enough, because Xavier chuckles.

"She's fucking hot, right?" When I turn my gaze away from the mouthwatering sight, I find him grinning, but no sign of jealousy.

"Yeah, she really is. Seems like you guys really hit the jackpot. Gorgeous inside and out."

"You could have that too," he says, his smile dropping as he grabs two of the girlie drinks, hands one to me, and pops the lid off the other before stepping back so I can close the fridge. "Just keep an open mind."

He leaves me and joins Vienna in the tub. He gives her a long, lingering kiss when he gets to her before handing her the drink. Colton and Xavier are quick to join them, leaving Sage and me as the only people not in the water. It's almost like they are giving us a preview of what we can have too.

"Come on, Tori. Don't overthink it, just go with

the flow," Sage urges quietly, and so I hand him my drink and use both hands to peel off my own coverup.

"Jesus have mercy," I hear him mutter as it joins Vienna's on the lounger, and I have to smother the smile that wants to cross my lips. This is fun, and it's nice to be admired. All of my previous relationships—no, hookups, were all about instant sexual gratification, so there wasn't much flirting or fun stuff. Now, I'm enjoying this dance that is courting.

"What's wrong, Sage? Cat got your tongue?" I ask him, and he shakes his head.

"Not yet, but I know a pussy that my tongue would lovingly appreciate."

"Hmm, tempting, but we have guests. Rain check?" I ask him, and his eyebrows jump in surprise before he's quickly nodding. "Good, I'll hold you to that. I think it's time for me to see if you can put your money where your mouth is."

His eyes flare with lust, and he reaches for me, but I skip out of his reach and hurry over to the hot tub, laughing.

"You minx, just you wait. I'll prove I'm not all talk. I'll prove it as many times as you need me to," he calls after me.

I step down into the tub, aware that there are four sets of eyes on me, these ones just as heated as Sage's, but before I can sit down, a pair of large hands circle my waist.

"Gotcha." Sage's heated breath brushes my ear, and I lean back into him as he nibbles on the shell of my ear. I feel my nipples pucker and my toes curl, but I'm cognizant of the fact that we're being watched, so I push him away and take a seat next to Vienna.

"Wow, that's a gorgeous swimsuit on a gorgeous body," she says as Sage looks around the tub for somewhere to sit. He starts to make his way to my other side, but Tristan grabs his hand and drags him over to sit next to him.

Sage looks back at me, and I give him an encouraging smile. I'm not going to stop him from exploring whatever he's building with Tristan. I think we're both fully aware that if we start anything with these four, it's an all-in kind of situation, so we may as well embrace it.

"Ugh, this feels awesome," Colton mutters, leaning his head back on the cushioned edge of the tub, stretching his body out to make the most of all the jets. "With the move and everything, I've been so tense. I really needed this. Thank you, Tori." I think, apart from during dinner, that's the most I've heard him say at once, and my mouth drops open just a little bit.

Vienna giggles. "It takes Colt a while to start to open up, but when he does, sometimes you can't shut him up. Wait until he starts telling you about the game he's designing or a particularly tricky something he's had to hack for a client. I swear my eyes just glaze over and I nod at the appropriate times while trying to work out what color I want to paint my toenails next." Her mouth is close to my ear, so he can't hear what she's saying about him, but she looks at him with so much love in her eyes, I feel a pang of envy.

I glance around the tub. Xavier, Sage, and Tristan are involved in an intimate conversation that I can't hear over the sound of the hot tub, and I'm okay with that, but is this a snapshot of our possible future? I never imagined myself in a relationship with multiple people, especially one with men, but I'm not hating the idea. In fact, the more I think about it, the more I kind of like it. With multiple people in a relationship, no one is going to care too much when the business keeps me so busy I have no time for them, or when I retreat into that world where the only thing that makes me happy is spilling blood. Those episodes are still quite frequent, but the club helps me keep my most homicidal tendencies at bay. That is another stumbling block though. How am I going to explain to this group that it's not something I'm willing to give up? I can't even claim it's not a sexual thing, because it really is. How are they going to feel about me going off to a sex club to splash blood around and score an orgasm? It's probably something I need to address soon before we get too far into whatever this is. I can imagine it would be a deal breaker for most people.

My eyes flick back to Sage. He knows about my proclivities but has been very tight-lipped on them, not wanting me to feel judged or shame, but it's a conversation I need to have with him too. I would never ask him to allow me to cut him. I'm aware of the abuse he suffered under the hands of his own foster parents, but knowing him, he would do it because I asked, not because he wanted to.

"So are we still on for that meeting in the morning, Tori?" Colton's voice jolts me out of my musings, and I turn to look at him. There's a long piece of damp hair hanging in front of his face, but his eyes look super blue in this light. Without his glasses in front of them, they are even more intense than normal, and that's really saying something.

"Yup. Does after breakfast suit you? I have to take a trip out of town, but I don't have to leave until the afternoon."

"Aww, you're going away?" Vienna asks, pouting prettily. "For how long?"

"Just a couple of nights. I have to go up to San Jose and check in on our Kitty Kat Club there and the casino we have in the Napa Valley. Then, next week, I have to fly to Vegas and then Seattle and do the same thing in both of those states. At some stage, I'm going to have to fly to Arizona and Texas as well and do the same thing."

"Well, that's a bummer. Today has been so much fun, I was hoping we could do it again soon."

"Leave Tori alone, sweetie. You're going to have to worry about classes starting next week anyway, and I'm not sure how much time you'll have for playing," Colton warns her, and her pout gets bigger.

"It's just that I've had so much fun, and I'm sad that Tori and Sage won't be joining us at school."

"Sorry, one of us has to keep showing their face at

our businesses, or people are going to start thinking we've lost interest."

"And then they start to take over, right?"

"Yup. No rest for the wicked, I'm afraid," I reply, confirming Colton's guess. We fall silent for a while, and I take a sip of my drink, downing half in one go. It will be my last for the evening.

I wonder if I just sealed the nail in our coffin. Vienna may only be interested in someone who is available twenty-four seven, and that is neither me nor Sage. He's coming with me to San Jose. In fact, he comes with me most of the time. Back when we moved into the house, Dad made the decision to move most of the drug operations to another underground basement below another warehouse of ours. He didn't want the illegal stuff happening in a house we were going to reside in. The only thing that remained was Sage's weed plants. There was no way he was going to hand over his little propagating and strain experimentation to someone else. If he's not with me, you can find him down in his lab playing with his plants. It makes him happy, so I'm happy. Sad Sage is a downer and annoying as fuck. He whines, and he has practically made it an art form.

We do have a new chemist, but he follows all of Sage's instructions and knows not to deviate from them. Sage threw an almighty fit the one time he suggested we try something different, but he seems to have the recipe down to an exact science. There are very few accidental overdoses from any of the drugs we put on the street.

"That's okay. Let's swap numbers so we can text while you're away, and then you can message me when you're back. I'm hoping maybe we can go out and do something together."

"Ah, yeah, sure, that sounds good." Pleasantly surprised at what she suggested, I close my eyes and lean my head back so she can't see the questions in my gaze. "So all of us again?"

"No, Tori, I was hoping maybe you and I could go out, just the two of us, on a date." I feel her hand slide into mine below the water. My eyes fly open as I feel her move closer to me.

"Oh, ah, yeah, okay, we can do that," I stammer and then blow out a huge sigh. "Look, please don't take this the wrong way, but, well, being gay…" I pause and look around the tub before returning to Vienna. "Or bisexual, I guess, is kind of frowned on in my line of work. One of the reasons the rumors about Sage being the enforcer is because he's always with me. People assume that he's actually the one who wears the pants in the relationship and that I'm just pretty eye candy, but my name legitimizes him despite Dad adopting and giving him the Russo name. If I were to appear in public with another woman, it would just add fuel to that already burning bush I try desperately to stamp out."

"The misogynism in the older generation is so rampant they can't see that sexuality plays no role in whether you are a competent person or not," Vienna grinds out from between clenched teeth.

"Ah, so you've experienced something similar."

"Hasn't everyone?" she asks, and I guess she's not wrong.

"Probably," I agree, "but most people don't have to worry about being stabbed in the back, literally, or having a bullet put between their eyes, so I have my quiet, private little flings with women in back rooms. Relationships are nothing I've ever wanted or considered trying before." She opens her mouth to start arguing, but I put down my drink on the side of the tub and lay my finger over her lips to stop her. "That's not to say that I'm not willing to see where this might go... between all of us. But for now, it's something that's going to have to be kept private here at the house, in hotels, or private dining rooms in restaurants, or even out of state. But there are a few things I'd like to discuss with you all before we get too far into this."

"That sounds pretty serious," Colton remarks, and I shrug, removing my finger, and Vienna smiles and nods.

"Look, it seems like if we want this to work, even if it's temporary, we need to lay all our cards on the table, and there are things that you guys need to know about me that might not work for you."

"Well, what?" Vienna demands, frowning, but I shake my head.

"Nah, let's enjoy today for what it is, some fun and relaxation, and when I return from San Jose, we'll have you over for dinner again without Gio and Casey, because they don't need to be involved in that conversation. We can talk about it then." I'm still not one hundred percent sure I'm all in with this. I want to have a conversation with Sage privately first, and that's something we can do on our trip. There's no point in telling them about my enjoyment in cutting if the two of us decide not to go ahead.

When I look across the hot tub, I find Tristan and Sage lip locked. Whoa, that is sexy. I watch, completely entranced, as Xavier reaches up and grabs Sage by his damp curls and pulls his mouth away from his boyfriend's. I tense for a moment, waiting for him to go ballistic, but all he does is turn Sage to face him and swoop in for a searing kiss as well.

"Fuck me," I mutter, and Vienna's hand slips out of mine and onto my thigh, her thumb stroking back and forth as Colton slides closer to me.

"It's sexy, isn't it? I love watching Xavier and Tristan seduce someone. They are so fucking good at it, and it reminds me of what they'll be doing to me later."

"And you? How does it make you feel?" I turn my head toward Colton and discover he's so close, his plump lips brush across mine. I startle backwards, and the previously quiet and shy man gives me a quick wink before crossing the tub. He straddles Sage's legs and leans in, joining their kiss. I watch as the four of them swap with one another, their tongues tangling, and I find myself panting with excitement.

"Hey, are you guys going to come for a swim or what?" Gio shouts from the pool, his voice easily heard over the sound of the hot tub.

The loud and unexpected intrusion breaks the building sexual tension, and I feel Vienna blow out a sigh before removing her hand from my thigh. "Fucking clam jam," she mutters as the boys all break apart as well. I can't help but snort with laughter at her reaction, and before long, all six of us are giggling like caught school kids.

"Come on. Gio will be annoying as fuck if we ignore him. Now that they are not doing whatever in the grotto, I can show you that." I stand up, and the five of them watch intently as the water runs over my body. I preen internally before grabbing my drink and climbing out of the hot tub. Vienna follows closely behind me, but the guys take a little longer. I guess raging boners are not that easy to hide in swim trunks.

I drain the rest of my drink and toss the bottle into a nearby bin before crossing over to the pool and diving in, swimming over to the grotto. Gio and Casey are sitting on one of the ledges on the side of the pool. I duck under the waterfall and come up in the grotto. The hot tub jets are on in here and it's not long before Vienna is following me in. There are fake plants scattered on all the rock walls, giving it a very tropical feel, and she squeals with delight.

"This is awesome." She pushes her mane of red hair back off her face and steps over to where I made myself comfortable. She doesn't sit down but stands in front of me, taking both of my hands in hers. "I'm okay with whatever you need. If we have to keep whatever this might become behind closed doors, then that's okay with me. It's not like we haven't had the same issues in general. That's why we appear as two couples, so that all those judgmental assholes can't give their unwanted opinions about our unconventional relationship. I'm just thrilled you're actually considering it. I thought for sure you'd shoot us down."

"Someone I trust recently told me my life would be pretty lonely if I didn't start to open up a little, and that I was letting Stacey win if I continued the way I was. There is no way I'm going to let that bitch win."

"Good girl," Vienna praises, and I feel an internal pulse and almost moan out loud.

Fuck me, please don't tell me I'm developing a praise kink as well. I'm already so messed up, I don't need that also.

The guys, Gio, and Casey join us, and the conversation moves on, but in the back of my mind, I can't stop picturing the four boys together and imagining what it would be like for me and Vienna to be involved as well.

Chapter Fifteen

The party breaks up late in the evening. Everyone stumbles off to bed around one in the morning, but I just jump in the shower and wash off the chlorine before drying my hair and throwing on some dark clothes—jeans and a hoodie so I can hide my face. I need to remember to grab my Glock from the sideboard on the way down to my car. It's probably half an hour later when I crack the door to my room, hoping everyone has gone straight to sleep.

The moans and groans coming from the door across the hall tells me that our guests are putting that big bed to good use. I groan quietly and bite my lip as I ease out of my room and pull the door shut behind me. It closes with a quiet click, but the soft creaking of the bed and the accompanying cries of pleasure don't even pause. Fuck me, that sounds like a good time. Vienna's pants and cries sound sweet, and I wouldn't mind being a part of wringing those sounds from her lips. I reluctantly push off the door, but before I can go anywhere, the door to Sage's room flings open.

"Where are you going? Can I come?" he demands, naked except for a pair of tight boxer briefs. Fucking hell, that's an even worse tease than the sounds from next door. A particularly loud grunt breaks the silence between us, and he looks ruefully in that direction. "They have been at it since we went to bed. I've already rubbed one out to the sound of it. Don't make me listen anymore," he begs me.

"Get dressed in all black," I tell him, "and meet me in my car."

He retreats back into his room without another word, and I continue on my way. I use the stairs this time instead of the elevator. I don't want Gio to hear me, but when I pass his room, the sounds of pleasure coming from it has me wrinkling my nose. Gross! It seems everyone but Sage and me are getting laid tonight. No rest for the wicked, I guess.

I retrieve my Glock from where he stashed it and use the elevator to ride down to the garage, then I grab my keys from the box hanging on the wall and start up my car. Next, I shoot a message to the guard at the gate to open it, so I don't have to stop and risk anyone hearing the loud rumbling of my car, despite them being preoccupied at the moment.

The passenger door opens and Sage climbs in, and we get moving. "Shit, I think I'm still drunk." He rests his head on the glass window and closes his eyes. "Where are we going?"

"Just need to take care of the warehouse," I tell him, not looking away from the road.

"Which one?" he asks, sounding surprised.

"The interrogation one. Although the agent was blindfolded while coming and going, I don't want to risk them searching it out later once our deal has concluded. He's not stupid, he knows what that room was for."

"Ah, yeah, good call."

"Sam and Dean supervised a crew to remove anything of importance this morning. They did another sweep with bleach and then steamed the room. That, combined with the fire, should make it nearly impossible for them to identify any blood residue if they find any. They have installed a boxing ring in the basement, so it will explain any remaining traces of blood."

"Oh snap, that was smart." Sage sounds impressed, though he still doesn't move from his place of rest.

"Not our first rodeo."

We fall into a comfortable silence, but I know he won't be capable of holding his tongue.

"So," he starts, and I smother the chuckle that I feel bubble up. Although I've decided to see where things between us might go, I'm not going to make this easy for him. "Tonight was fun, wasn't it?"

"You certainly looked like you were having fun in the

hot tub," I say lightly, but even I can hear the jealousy in my voice, and I kind of want to punch myself in the tit. A shared relationship is going to take some getting used to. I guess I kind of wanted to keep Sage to myself for a moment now that I've decided to pursue this. Hell, maybe I just wanted to be involved too, and not watching from the sidelines. Watching isn't really my kink.

"Ah, yeah, it was kind of awesome, but kind of intense too, you know?"

"No, I really don't. Why don't you tell me?" I turn my head to look at him. He's finally opened his eyes, and he is watching me carefully. He shrugs and pushes off the door, sitting up.

"I don't know. Three different sets of lips and three totally different styles of kissing was sort of sensory overload. And that topped with you and Vienna watching, I almost came in the hot tub," he confesses, and I squirm slightly in my seat, my foot pressing down harder on the accelerator.

We're quiet for a little while longer, and the street-lights of the city disappear as we hit the stretch of forested road between Banebridge and Suncity.

"How did you feel seeing it?" he asks, finally breaking the silence.

"Fuck! Confused, turned on, and a little jealous—" I break off, but Sage isn't willing to let it go.

"Tori?"

I huff out a sigh, my thumbs drumming against the steering wheel. "Look, Sage, Stacey fucked me up. Big time. I was so pissed off, not just at what she did, but the reasons behind it."

"Revenge on you?" he asks quietly, and I shake my head.

"No, not that. The whole thing started, or so she claimed, because she wanted to be popular with boys. Having sexual experience would help her sleep her way to the top, I guess. I thought it was ridiculous, but she was my best friend, and I would have done anything for her to keep her happy. It also didn't hurt that I enjoyed kissing her. Despite being high on X, I fucking loved everything we did at the start. It felt incredible to make her come like that and give her pleasure. I felt powerful when I was driving into her from behind with the strap-on."

It's Sage's turn to wriggle in his seat, and he adjusts himself beneath his tight black jeans.

"So even with her drugging me further and raping me, I came to the conclusion that I was gay. I didn't need or want to be popular, so there was no need for me to impress boys, and fuck, it was the reason I was in the position I ended up in. Fuck Stacey, and fuck all the guys who would benefit from my pain. So I closed myself off to the idea I was into anything but girls, despite enjoying flirting with Xavier and Tristan when I first met them, and even enjoying the little stolen kiss Tristan managed to scam."

A wry smile crosses Sage's lips. "He's a dirty perv, isn't he?" His voice is full of affection, and I can't help but smile as well.

"I also closed myself off to ever letting down my guard to trust anyone again, and then I met you, and Dad forced us together."

"It wasn't all horrible, was it?" he asks, and when I turn to peer at him through the darkness, I can see he's serious again. I take one hand off the wheel and reach for his.

"No, it wasn't—isn't. I value your friendship more than anything, especially with Gio being so sneaky, though I think I've worked that out now." I see him give a decisive nod. "But it's because of that friendship that I locked myself off to anything else I was feeling."

"Did I make your core tickle?" he asks in a teasing voice, trying to lighten the mood, and I snort, pulling my hand away from his and putting it back on the steering wheel.

I ignore it and keep going. "But someone I trust recently said that I shouldn't close myself off, that my life would be very sad if I went through it alone. Even Mom and Dad, and then just Dad once she was gone, had their inner circle, people they would die for, and they didn't keep them at arm's length. He loved them with all his heart."

Sage gasps. "Mickey and your dad were lovers?"

"What? No! Or I don't think so. I don't think it was that kind of relationship." I pause for a moment, contemplating it before shuddering and shaking my head. Nope, not going there. It doesn't matter anymore. "All I'm saying is that I'm trying to be open minded. There's no denying that I love you, but I was trying to keep that strictly in the friend zone."

"And now?

"All I can say is that if you betray me in any way, Sage Russo, I will shoot you in the dick."

He's quiet for a moment, and I feel myself stiffen. Fuck, have I said the wrong thing? Did I just destroy this friendship by thinking he wanted more than just that? Shit, Sage flirts with anything with a pulse, it's his way. Maybe he didn't actually mean any of the suggestive things he said to me in the past. Maybe everyone who's told me that he's clearly in love with me was reading it wrong.

"I knew it. You want to kiss me and hug me and touch me," he sings, doing a little victory dance in his seat, and I let go of the breath I was holding. "I am going to completely rock your world. I will love you so good the memory of Stacey and what she did to you will fade into the past."

He shifts his body so that he's facing me and starts playing with my ponytail. Normally I would smack his hand away, but the low-key affection feels good, and I need to embrace this new normal, not push it away. "And the others? How do you feel about them?"

"Is it a deal breaker? If I don't want to pursue anything with them, does that mean you and I are done?" I ask cautiously, wanting to see where I stand.

I expected him to think about it, but he replies instantly. "No, Tori. If all you want is you and me, then I will be happy with just that. I don't want you to think that I require that. I know you enjoy women sexually, just as I enjoy men, so I think this gives us the chance to have the best of both worlds. Why should we settle if we don't have to? Especially with our lives as fucked up as they are. Things are never going to be normal and easy. We're never going to have the white picket fence with the two point five children and the dog, so why not embrace what they are offering?" He's not telling me he won't, he's just suggesting that we can have our cake and eat it too.

"And you're okay seeing me with the guys as well as Vienna, or will it be you and the guys, me and Vienna, and you and me?"

He answers my question with two of his own. "Is that what you want? Do you want me to stay away from Vienna?"

"No, I like the idea of both of us loving her together," I tell him as we reach the outskirts of Suncity, and I drive the car in the direction of our warehouse.

"And I can't wait to see you writhing beneath Xavier's, Tristan's, and Colton's attentions."

I blow out a big breath. "So we're doing this?" I ask, looking at him, and he nods decisively.

"Yes, for as long as it suits us, but you and me, we're a team. Any decision we make, we make it together. Any problems we have, we discuss it before they blow out, just like we always do. Okay?"

"Yeah, that sounds good to me."

I pull the car into a deserted alley not far from the warehouse. I know there are no CCTV cameras in this area, so it's safe for us to leave it here. We both get out and pull our hoodies up over our heads. Before I can shove my keys and hands into my pockets, though, Sage is around my side of the car, caging me in with his body. He smiles down at me mischievously.

"What are you doing?" I ask him curiously.

"Why, I'm kissing my girlfriend of course." He leans in, giving me plenty of time to stop him, but instead, I reach up, grab his head, and pull him toward me. Our lips fuse, and his tongue thrusts into my mouth, tangling with mine. The kiss is full of heat and passion, and when we pull away moments later, we're both panting.

"Wow." I blink owlishly at him. Yeah, we kissed once previously, but it was nothing like this. This was indescribable and unlike any other kiss I'd had before, except maybe with Stacey, and it was more than just going through the motions. This one was laced with feelings, feelings I'd never allowed myself to feel before. Anything before this had just been the path I took to get to the main event, which was sex, but this was so much more. I kind of get the whole making out thing now, and I'm ready for more.

"Ah, yeah, wow." Sage is as shaken as I am, and we both stand there a moment as we try to collect ourselves before a cocky grin spreads across his mouth. "I completely rocked your world. Wait until we have more time. You are going to wonder why you didn't cave sooner." He brushes another quick kiss across my lips and pushes off the car, freeing me.

"Okay, fine, but get your head in the game. We have something to do first, and then maybe we can have a little post arson celebration." I push away all the messy feelings and emotions and turn on the part of me that compartmentalizes everything perfectly. "Come on."

Chapter Sixteen

We walk toward the warehouse, sticking to the deep shadows of the surrounding buildings in case there are any CCTV cameras around. In the darkness of the shadows and with our hoodies, there's no way anyone would be able to tell who we are if anyone ends up looking any closer into the fire.

When we get to the warehouse, Sage picks up a nearby brick and hurls it through a window. The sound of smashing glass is loud, but there are no residences close by, so the likelihood that anyone heard it is slim. He carefully knocks out the remaining glass, and then the two of us climb through the window frame, careful not to cut ourselves and leave behind any DNA evidence.

Once we're inside, the warehouse is lit from the outside streetlamp, and there are boxes stacked in one corner. Sage frowns. "I thought Sam and Dean had the warehouse cleaned out. What's all this?"

"They cleared the basement, but it would look a little suspicious if it went up with nothing in it. Open one of the boxes," I tell him, and he rips the tape from one of the edges and pulls back the flaps.

"What are these?" he asks as he uses the flashlight app on his phone to get a better look.

"I had some of the paper supplies from the hotels stored here so they wouldn't question why the ware-house was empty," I tell him, picking up napkins with the Lucky Diamond Casino logo on them. "A few of the boxes have our playing cards in them, and those ones over there are boxes of napkins and coasters from the Kitty Kat Club. All legitimate business expenses and proof that this warehouse is nothing more than storage. Not to mention fuel for a fire lit by a vagrant who broke into the place to keep warm."

From behind the boxes, I pull out a couple of old blankets that may or may not have gasoline splashed on them and place them in front of the boxes, then I grab some napkins and a couple of boxes of playing cards and set up a small fire. I then place a trail of napkins over to the staircase leading into the basement and down it. I make sure there are enough napkins down there for them to catch fire and return to the other level. I pat my pockets, looking for my lighter. "Fuck, I forgot my lighter. Do you have one?" I ask Sage, and he grins, pulling both a lighter and a joint out of the front pocket of his hoodie. He lights up the joint and takes a deep breath before holding it out to me. I frown and shake my head, but he just jiggles it.

"Jesus, Tori, you're so tense, just relax a little. I know the world is usually resting on your shoulders, but it's just you and me. I'm always going to have your back, and I'll never judge anything you do."

I shake out my shoulders and stretch my neck from side to side before reaching out for the joint. "God, Sage, I have to have my barriers up twenty-four seven, so it's going to take me a little while to get used to this." I gesture between the two of us while I take a drag of the weed. The familiar skunky taste crosses my taste buds, and I feel my body relax instantly. I blow out the smoke before saying, "Speaking of barriers and trust and getting everything out before we go any further, let's talk about my little trips to the Black Rose."

His eyebrows jump, and he cocks his head to the side. "The sex club?"

"Yes, you know why I use it."

He nods, his brow furrowing. "Yeah, I do, but cutting isn't my thing." There's a hint of fear in his voice, like he's worried I'm going to ask him to go under my knife.

"Oh, I know," I quickly assure him, and I see him sigh with relief. "It's not what I want from you, but how are you going to feel when I still go there and play with my subs? It's not something I'm willing to give up." I take another long drag before holding it back out for him, but he just avoids it and steps up, wrapping his arms around me.

"I know, and I would never ask you to. I know why

you need the club, and if you need to keep going, that's fine with me. Do you have sex with them?" There's no judgment in his tone, only curiosity. This is something we've avoided talking about in the past, something too intimate that I've never wanted to burden him with, but our relationship is changing, and we need to be open with one another.

"Occasionally with my female subs, but usually the act of cutting and rubbing myself in their blood was enough to bring me to orgasm." I feel him harden against me as I describe it.

"And do you have any male subs?" Again, no judgment.

"I have recently acquired one," I admit, and he nods before pulling away and looking me in the eye.

"And how do you feel about him? Have you had sex with him?"

I quickly shake my head. "No, but I can't deny that I wasn't turned on by more than his blood the last time I was with him. I let him come all over me, and I rubbed it into my body as well as tasted it."

Sage lifts his fist to his mouth and bites down, groaning. "Fucking hell, that's hot. Let's torch this place and get out of here. You can tell me more about it on the way home." He adjusts himself under his tight black jeans and grabs the joint from my hand. We pass it back and forth until we both have a good buzz before he flicks it at the pile of napkins.

The two of us stand there and watch as the fire catches, slowly burning the tissue paper, before spreading to the small boxes of cards and eventually the blankets. Sage tips one of the big boxes over, and stuff goes everywhere, catching fire. That's our cue to leave. We hurry back out the broken window and walk leisurely back to our car so as not to attract any undue attention.

As I unlock the doors and we climb in, the car fills with the smell of smoke, so Sage winds down a window to air it out a little.

"We need to put these clothes in the washer as soon as we get home," he says as I get us moving. "Are we worried it's going to be put out before it can burn the basement as well?"

"No, Sam and Dean assured me that the industrial-sized containers of hand sanitizer that are being stored in the basement will catch alight quickly, and everything down there will burn as well."

"Ah, so that's why you did that little napkin trail. I wondered." He leans his head against the glass as I turn the car in the direction of home.

"Yup, and if the fire alarm was tampered with and had a delay so it wouldn't alert the fire department for thirty minutes, then that is unfortunate. There are no residences in the area, so there's no one around to call it in. That fire should be good and blazing by the time anyone comes to put it out, and hopefully arson detectives won't find anything but the evidence of vagrants using the place overnight."

By the time we arrive back at the fortress, it's almost four in the morning. I grumble as the two of us make our way to our rooms. "Ugh, we have to be up in three hours. Lorn and Castiel will be here for training."

The elevator lets us off, and we quietly make our way to the laundry room. There, we remove our smoky clothes, leaving us both in just our underwear. Giggling like school kids, we streak through the house and up the stairs to our level, where we tiptoe, trying not to make any sound to wake our sleeping friends. Thankfully, the sounds of pleasure from before have stopped.

When we get to our rooms, I stop. "So, that was fun. Thanks for your help," I whisper to Sage, and he backs me up against the wall again.

"This is not how I thought I'd get you out of your clothes once we returned home, but I'm not complaining." He leans and takes my mouth with his again. I pull his body against mine and wrap a leg around his waist, grinding myself against his rapidly hardening length. Our bodies are warm against one another, but my skin prickles with desire from feeling our flesh pressed together for the first time. I moan loudly into his mouth and fist his hair in my hands. He grunts but pushes even harder against me, like he wants to mold our bodies together. I'm not sure how long we stay like that, but when we come up for air, we're both breathing heavily.

"Do you want to come in?" I ask him, reaching out and shoving the door to my room open.

He backs away, shaking his head, and my heart sinks. "You have to be up soon for training," he explains, obviously seeing my crestfallen expression, and I feel a wave of relief wash over me.

"Fuck sleep. Who needs it anyway?" I tell him and grab his hand, dragging him into my room, but not before noticing the door across from us is cracked open, and I can see Vienna standing there in the gap. I consider inviting her to join us, but I decide to be selfish with my first time with Sage. Plus, she just got a good dicking, so I'm not sure if she would want to anyway. She winks at me before closing the door, and I smile, dragging Sage farther into my room and closing the door. Before I can get any farther, he scoops me up bridal style and hurries to the bed. I'm giggling and breathless by the time he throws me onto it. I reach up to drag him down, but before I can, he moves away.

"Ever since I saw you sleeping on this bed the first time, I have had a fantasy play out in my mind." He tugs at the drapes tied to the bed posts, releasing the ties before spreading out the drapes so they completely surround the bed. They are thick, heavy velvet curtains that block off everything outside of the bed. Finally, he climbs through the gap in one side, tugging it closed behind him with a wicked grin on his face. "The thought of having you all to myself, wrapped up in this little slice of heaven, has lived rent free in my mind. It's one of my favorite fantasies to tug one out to, and I'm going to make it come true."

"Oh, and what happened in these fantasies of yours?" I ask him, and he brings his hand from behind his back, and in it are the ties for the curtains.

"How do you feel about letting me be in charge?" he asks gently, and I feel my heart rate increase as I consider letting him tie me up. It's never something I've contemplated in the past. I was always the one tying up others. Candy suggested she should tie me up once, and I freaked out. It was the idea of not being in control, a reminder of what Stacey did to me, that had me running in the opposite direction, but when I think about Sage tying me up, I realize I'm not actually scared, just turned on.

"Okay, but if I say stop, you have to," I agree, pushing my arms back over my head, and he grins wickedly.

"Your safe word is Skittles," he tells me, and I freeze and sit up, frowning at him. "What's wrong?" he asks.

"Why did you pick that word?" I ask him, remembering that Romeo, my sub, had used the same word, but there's no way Sage is Romeo. I would recognize him, and he doesn't want to be cut.

"Oh, Vienna and Colton grabbed a bag from the pile of snacks when they headed back to their room. Sorry, we can use something else. They got Twizzlers too." He seems confused, and I shake off my own concerns.

"No, Skittles is fine, you just surprised me, that's all," I tell him, not wanting to ruin the mood any more than I have by telling him that my sub uses that as his safe word. I lie back down, and he gently ties my hands together and to the headboard. I pull against them and realize if I really wanted to get out, I could. Sage is already looking after me, so I settle back as he lays his body next to mine.

He runs his hand in light circles on my stomach. "Tori, have you ever been with a man?" he asks as his caresses move up and over my breasts, across my shoulders, and down my arms. The light tickling sensation makes me squirm. I'm more of an instant gratification kind of girl, and foreplay is something I considered too intimate in the past. This is going to be a whole new experience for me.

"No," I reply quietly, not looking at him, and he grabs my chin and turns me to face him.

"I'm going to love you so good you're going to be questioning why you didn't let me do this sooner," he promises me. "But I need to know a few things in light of your past trauma. Are you okay with penetration?"

I think about what he just asked. Originally, when I first became sexually active after the rape, I avoided any kind of penetration with my female lovers. Sure, I would wear a strap-on and use it on them if they wanted it, but I wouldn't let them use it on me. Eventually, Candy convinced me that penetration wasn't a bad thing. We started slowly with her fingers, then small dildos before working up to allowing her to fuck me with a strap-on. It didn't happen very often, but I think that was more me getting off on being dominant over her. I did swap to a strap-on that had an internal piece for me when I fucked her though. I got over my aversion to it, and when it comes down to it, it wasn't about fear, it was about being in control. I became good at topping from the bottom. I'm just not sure if I can get out of my head enough to enjoy Sage.

I explain all this to him, and he smirks. "Oh, baby, if I can't get you out of your head enough to enjoy it, then I'm doing it all wrong."

Chapter Seventeen

Sage rolls his body onto mine and settles between my thighs, so most of his weight is still on the bed. He then pulls down the strap of the bra I'm still wearing, popping my breast out of the cup, before doing the same to the other side. His eyes light up as he gets his first close-up of my breasts.

"I always wondered what these would look like." He leans in and kisses each of them lightly. His mouth feels so different. He has a dusting of stubble across his jaw and top lip that rasps exquisitely against my skin. He has the perfect amount of suction, which causes a tingle deep inside my core.

My body becomes relaxed and pliant, and I'm putty in his hands before he decides to slide his body lower. He places kisses between my breasts before kissing a line to my navel, which he gives a quick lick to before looking up at me and grinning. I roll my eyes but smile at his playful ways. He keeps moving lower, his line of kisses trailing over my stomach and pubic bone until he gets to the top of my panties. Once there, he sits up and leans over me, reaching behind my back and deftly flicking the catch on my bra, before drawing the straps up my arms and out of the way, grinning wickedly as he wraps it around my hands as extra restraints. He then lifts a questioning eyebrow as he reaches for my panties and pauses. I give him a quick nod, and he grabs the band and strips them off me. Sage looks his fill at my now naked body.

"Tori, baby, you're even more beautiful than I had even imagined," he whispers reverently before pushing my thighs apart. My body starts to tremble with nerves and anticipation as I allow him to do that. He must see the hesitation in my eyes, because he settles his body between my thighs and places a kiss on them before nipping each sensitive limb. The sharp, painful bites help clear the nerves and get me out of my head. "Are you with me?" he asks as I look down at him, and I nod. "Good, because I want all your focus on us, nothing else. No painful memories are going to ruin this for us, okay?"

I nod quickly.

"You're a good girl, and good girls get rewarded." His voice is low and husky, and I feel my body tremble again, but this time it's really good. He leans in and runs his tongue through my folds. We both groan at the contact, and I strain desperately against my restraints, wanting to have use of my hands so I can run them through his hair. But I keep my lips closed and the word Skittles off them.

I feel him chuckle against my pussy before moving to my clit and flicking his tongue against it, then drawing the whole thing into his mouth and sucking. I moan, and my back arches. It's so intense I'm not sure if I want him to keep going or pull away. Before I can make up my mind, however, he pushes down on my raised hips and holds me in place as he completely goes to town on my pussy. He kisses and sucks and thrusts his tongue as far as he can get it.

I feel him run two fingers through the mess he made before he gently feels around and slides them deep. My head thrashes back and forth as he slowly and gently moves them in and out.

"God, you're so tight, baby. I'm going to have to stretch you a little before I can get in there." He goes back to licking my clit as he gently scissors his fingers in and out until I'm all but riding his digits. He drives me to the very edge of my orgasm without letting me fall over the edge, then he stops and waits for my pussy to stop fluttering before starting all over again.

"Sage, please," I beg, tugging harder on my restraints wanting him to move, but he just chuckles again.

"No, baby, you need some more stretching." He takes his fingers out, and this time when he returns them, he uses three.

He's a little more forceful, and I pant and moan like a porn star. My orgasm builds again, and it feels different this time. He's curling his fingers upward and brushing against my G-spot with every pass. My toes curl, and my legs tense up, but just as I'm going to fall off the cliff, he stops once more.

The sound that leaves my mouth could be compared to a harpy screech, and I clamp my legs shut.

"Shh, it's okay, I've got you," he tells me and pries my legs open, crawling up my body and taking my mouth with his. Our tongues tangle, and I can taste myself all over his lips and tongue. He kneels between my thighs and runs his thick cock through the mess between my legs, getting it good and wet. "You ready for this?" he asks, and I look down at it, and my eyes widen. I mean, I've gotten a handful of it before, but wow. "It will fit, I promise. It's going to feel so good when your pussy chokes it."

Sage's dirty talk flat out does it for me. Who'd have guessed?

"Okay, do it, Sage," I tell him and slam my eyes shut as he lines up. I wait for the pain, but it never comes, so I open my eyes and find him looking at me patiently.

"There you are. I want to see those pretty eyes when I make you mine for the first time." With our eyes locked, he slowly sinks into me, bit by bit. It's unhurried but perfect, and my greedy cunt sucks him down, practically opening and inviting him in. Finally, he's balls deep, and the two of us sigh with relief. I can see strain around his jawline and the muscles in his arms where he's braced above me.

"Fuck," he mutters. "I have been dreaming of this since I first met you, and now that it's finally happening, I'm going to lose it before I can make you feel good. Your pussy is so wet and hot and tight. It's like it was made for my cock," he praises and kisses me again. As we get lost in the kiss, he starts to roll his hips and move in and out of me. He angles so every thrust brushes my G-spot, and it's not long before I'm at my peak again.

He pulls away from my mouth and leans down, taking one of my nipples into his mouth while pinching the other with his fingers. His pace speeds up, and my pussy flutters and tightens, and I feel my whole body balancing precariously on the edge. Just then, he pulls back, and I wrap my legs around his waist, holding him to me so he can't escape.

"Don't you dare go anywhere," I growl at him. "If you deny me my orgasm again, I will shoot you."

"I just wanted to look at you when you came for me." He braces himself over me and really starts to move, fast and hard, and I go over. I throw my head back and dig my heels into his ass as I scream, my orgasm flooding through my body like a tidal wave. My pussy clamps down hard, and he continues to try and thrust through it, but it's too late, he can't hold out any longer, and he stutters, his eyes rolling backward.

"Oh, baby," he groans, deep and guttural, as we ride our orgasms together. I watch him as he enjoys the pleasure coursing through his body, and I feel another flutter, this one somewhere around the region of my heart, but I'm not ready to acknowledge that one, so I focus on the one between my legs.

"Best fucking orgasm ever," I mutter as he gives me another couple of small thrusts, milking this for all it's worth.

He smirks at my words and reaches up to untie me before rolling to the side, taking me with him. We're still joined, so I end up sprawled across his chest and he massages my wrists to ease the ache. "Told you so," he says smugly, before wrapping his arms around me and nuzzling my neck. "So fucking good."

We make out for a little while longer, and his dick finally softens and slips out of me, but we don't move. Instead, we stay wrapped together, enjoying each other's bodies until, eventually, we fall asleep, even if it's just for a moment.

My alarm goes off soon after we fall asleep, and I'm so warm and snuggly with Sage wrapped around me that the last thing I want to do is drag my ass out of bed. I hit snooze and wiggle my ass back against the hard body behind me.

"If you wiggle that ass any harder, I'm going to think you want me to stick something in it." Sage's sleepy voice comes from behind me as his hand grasps my hip. I freeze at his words, and he nuzzles into my neck, his warm breath washing over my skin and causing it to prickle. "Oh, is ass play something you haven't tried yet?" he whispers, and for the first time in a long time, I blush as I shake my head. "Oh, honey, we have some fun times ahead. Especially with three other boys who want to play. We need to make every hole available for use."

And that's my cue to bail. Not waiting for the snooze alarm, I try to roll off my bed, but I'm not quick enough, and before I can get halfway to the side, he rolls and pins me underneath him with his fat cock nestled between my thighs. Before he can say anything else, I tackle his mouth with mine. If I keep him busy kissing me, maybe he won't mention anything else about anal, because it's not really a conversation I want to have so early in the morning after very little sleep.

But of course Sage won't let me go, and after kissing me breathless, he pulls back and grinds down on me. "Don't worry, I'm an expert. I'll make it good for you." He grins, and I roll my eyes, shoving him off me.

"Whatever, but I don't have time for that now. It's bad enough my whole body aches from our extracurricular activities last night. Lorn and Castiel won't take it easy on me," I tell him, going to my bathroom to pee and splash water on my face. When I look at my hair, I grimace, but I don't have time to shower, since I needed to be in the gym ten minutes ago. Sage comes in and lifts the seat, his bare ass flexing as he pees too, while I try to tame my hair into some semblance of tidiness. Up and back is going to have to work. I don't want it in my face for training.

Sage groans and sounds like a racehorse peeing, but finally, he's done, and he puts the lid down and flushes before coming over and washing his hands in the sink. He leans against the bathroom counter, completely unconcerned that he's naked. His own hair looks like he's been well fucked, the cute curls sticking out all over the place. "So," he begins as I throw my brush back down.

"So?" I prompt, cocking my head to the side and getting a good look at his naked body in the bright light of the bathroom. Sage is taking his own look, and I watch on in fascination as his cock starts to thicken and rise.

"It wasn't as horrible as you thought it was going to be, right?" he asks, but I'm completely entranced by his body's reaction to seeing my own. It's kind of exhilarating knowing I can cause such a strong reaction in someone. "Tori?" he calls, and I run my hand across my mouth to make sure no drool dribbled out.

"No, Sage, it wasn't horrible. In fact, it was pretty damn awesome." I smile and reassure him, giving him a quick kiss before escaping to my room to get dressed. I pull out some yoga pants, a crop top, and some underwear, pulling them all on before spraying on deodorant and grabbing some socks and my shoes. Heading back out, I find Sage sprawled out on my bed on his back, his hands behind his head. I sit down next to him to pull my shoes on.

"Yeah, but on a scale of one to ten, how awesome was it?"

I pause and turn to look at my best friend, and I can see the insecurity in his gaze.

I put my shoe down and lean in to kiss him gently, brushing his hair back from his face.

"You were the best sex I've ever had with a male," I tell him cheekily, hoping to see him smile, but the same worry is still behind his eyes.

"Sage, if you want to know if I still want to have sex with you after last night, then the answer is yes. Not just yes, but hell yes. You are a master at the tongue, and your cock could make angels sing. Is that enough reassurance for you?"

The worry floats away and is replaced with a smug grin. "I knew it. I've never had any complaints before."

"Yeah, yeah, you're a regular sex machine, but mentioning previous lovers is a surefire way not to get a repeat of last night," I growl at him, and he grimaces.

"Right, ah, sorry."

"Are you coming to work out?" I ask him, and he shakes his head.

"No, not today. I need to do some work in my grow room."

"Do you think that could wait until after the guests leave? I don't really want them asking questions about where you disappeared to." I stand up and head across the room to my door.

"Yeah, sure, that sounds smart. So I'm just going to roll over and breathe you in then until breakfast." I watch as he rolls over and grabs my pillow, shoving his face in it and taking a deep breath before pulling the blankets back over him.

"Fine, but don't be late, or you may miss out on all the goodies Suzy makes us." He just waves a hand at me, so I leave him in my bed, feeling completely satisfied at the idea that he's there.

I practically skip down the hallway to the elevator and head up to the next level with the gym. Thankfully, Lorn and Castiel aren't there, so I turn the Bluetooth speaker on and pair my phone to it, putting on my favorite workout playlist. It's all angry, angsty rock music, but it's motivating. I step up onto the treadmill and start my warmup, replaying my night with Sage over in my mind.

<hr />

Lorn and Castiel must be in shitty moods, because they work me hard. Gio never shows up, but it's no surprise if he has Casey in his bed. I'm a panting, sweaty mess when I head back to my room just before eight to shower and change.

I wonder if Sage is still in my bed or if he managed to drag himself out of it. I'm excited to see. My trainers worked me too hard to think about anything other than not falling on my face, so I wasn't able to take a moment to consider how I feel about this change in our relationship, but as I examine my emotions, I realize there's nothing there to worry about. I wasn't lying, the sex was incredible, and snuggling afterwards was not awkward or uncomfortable like I thought it would be, it just felt right. Even this morning, waking up next to him and the banter between us was light-hearted and fun despite the underlying seriousness. I have a feeling Sage is insecure under his big personality, but I don't resent the need to reassure him. In the past, I would have run for the hills if someone was so needy, but all I want to do is make everything right for him.

I'm lost deep in thought, so when the elevator doors open, revealing Vienna and her guys, I startle slightly.

"Oh, hey, guys, how are you this morning?" I step out so they can get in, but instead, they let the doors shut.

"Hey, Tori. You look like you've been busy this morning. If I'd known, I would have come and worked out with you." Xavier looks low-key put out, and the others laugh at him.

"Ignore Xavier, he's a grump in the morning if he doesn't get his own workout," Tristan tells me, hip bumping his boyfriend who growls at him.

"Well, I will definitely let you know next time. I could use another sparring partner. Castiel and Lorn, our trainers, were assholes this morning. But feel free to use the gym after breakfast if you want. Colton and I have that meeting before I have to leave, so why don't you make use of it while we do that?"

Seriously, it's almost like watching a sunrise as the

frown disappears, and he beams at me. "Really? That would be great. There's nothing better than starting the morning with exercise."

"Actually, I can think of one or two things that are a better way to start the morning." Tristan winks suggestively, and none of us miss what he's implying.

"Did you go near a fire last night?" Vienna asks me, wrinkling her nose and leaning in to sniff my hair. "Your hair smells all smoky."

"Wow, Vienna, boundaries much?" Colton tugs her back from me with an apologetic grimace.

"Must be from the weed we smoked yesterday." I give them a lame excuse, and I can tell she doesn't really buy it, but I don't care. I don't need to explain myself to them. "I'm just going to grab a quick shower, but head downstairs. I'm sure Suzy probably served breakfast in the dining room again. I won't be long."

I press the button for the elevator, the doors opening instantly, before waving goodbye to them all. I don't wait to see if they get in. There's not much I can do if they decide they want to snoop. I was so preoccupied with Sage and the warehouse, I didn't think that they might. I'll check the security footage of the house from last night. There are cameras everywhere but the bedrooms and bathrooms. Even if they did snoop, though, there's nothing to find. The offices are locked with biometric measures, and the lower basement requires an access code for the elevator before it will go down there. Nope, all they would have found is a very big, very empty house.

I hope for our blossoming friendship that they stayed in their rooms, but I can't really fault them if they didn't, since I probably wouldn't have either. It's nothing to worry about now though. I just need a shower to wash off the funk, and then I'll head downstairs. I'm starving. Who would have thought that really good sex would work up such an appetite? There is no way I'm telling Sage. He's already smug enough.

Chapter Eighteen

The dining room is filled with the sound of laughter when I finally make it down there ten minutes late. Suzy scolds me as I pop my head into the kitchen to say good morning to her and Ben, but when they see how happy I am, they quickly shut up and share a secretive, knowing glance. I just flip them off and continue on my way.

The food smells delicious, and I hurry to my seat, but not before stopping and giving Sage a kiss on the mouth. The room falls silent, but I just ignore it as I take my seat in the same place as last night, between Colton and Xavier.

"Wow, Tori, you look radiant. You must have slept really well last night," Casey gushes enthusiastically.

"Something like that," I reply as I reach for the pot of coffee in the middle of the table and pour some into the cup at my place setting.

Sage is grinning like the cat that got the canary, but

I can see clouds brewing in my brother's eyes as he looks between the both of us.

"What the fuck was that?" he grinds out through gritted teeth.

I take a deep breath before taking a sip of my coffee. "What was what?" I ask him, taking the plate of bacon that Xavier passes me now that he and the others have recovered from the surprise of seeing me be affectionate with Sage. Everyone else continues on like nothing happened, but I can see that my brother is spoiling for a fight, and I am happy to give him one if he is going to make a big deal of this.

"That." He stabs a finger at Sage.

"What?" I ask innocently, and he growls again.

"You kissed him. You don't like boys, you're a lesbian."

"Seriously?" Tristan slams his fork down and stares at my brother.

"You stay out of this," Gio growls at him. Tristan goes to argue, but Sage puts his hand on his arm and nods in my direction.

"Tori has this."

"Oh, so it was alright when I was just fucking girls, but now that I show an interest in boys as well, you have a problem with this."

"You can't just change your mind, Tori. I don't want you fucking with Sage. He's too important to this organization."

Oh no he fucking didn't. He's making this about the family business that he hasn't shown any regard for in the last few weeks. He actually doesn't care about me or Sage.

I put down my cup of coffee so that I don't spill it in my annoyance. "I'm not sure what my sex life has to do with this organization, and to be honest, who I have sex with and what gender they are is none of your fucking business."

"Yes it fucking is," he shouts back, standing up and towering over me.

"Oh really? You want to do this now? Because I won't hold back, and out of respect for our new friendship with these people, I think maybe you should sit your ass down and shut up until later."

"No, we talk about it now," he demands, and I see red.

"I apologize for anything I'm about to say. I like you guys, I really do, but nobody disrespects me like this," I say to our new friends. "Casey, please don't take any of this personally, it's nothing against you, just family stuff."

The pretty young woman turns pale and sinks down in her chair slightly as I turn back to look at my brother.

"So now you want to throw your fucking weight around? Shall we get into where you've been disappearing to over the last twelve months? Who you've been sneaking off to see? You see, at first, I thought you were being a shady fuck and dealing with our enemies, because there is no way you would disobey a directive from Dad, but I now see I have this completely wrong.

Even though Dad warned you to stay away from Casey until things were more settled and established and you could protect her, you continued seeing her, isn't that right?"

I look around the table and see the answer in everyone's eyes and the clench in Gio's jaw.

"Everyone at this table knew except me, your sister, the one person who is supposed to have your back, while you have mine."

"In my defense, I didn't know until this week either," Sage says, raising his hand. "I would have told you."

"Which is why you didn't know," Gio sneers at him, and I slap my hands down on the table and stand up.

"But he shouldn't have had to tell me, you should have, so even now that I know what has been going on, I mind my own business. You both seem happy, and your relationship is none of my concern. You're a big boy and can make these decisions no matter how unsafe it is for your partner, so at least have the same respect for me and stay the fuck out of it."

"When you get tired of pretending not to be gay, you'll break his heart, and then that will fuck everything up," Gio argues, not hearing a word I said. I flinch at his words, they hurt more than I expected.

Before I can respond, Sage does. "That's enough," he states with deadly calm, leaning forward. "That is none of your business, and right now, I suggest you walk the fuck away, Gio, before you say something you can't come back from. I have no idea what your problem is all of a sudden. You had no problem with anyone else's sexual orientation at this table, or have you just been hiding your bigoted opinions?"

Gio looks around and blanches when he notices everyone's attention is on him.

"I think I'd like to know the answer to that," Xavier says, crossing his arms and staring my brother down. I have to admit, I'm impressed. Gio Russo is no slouch when he's angry, and he can appear terrifying, but Xavier just meets his anger head-on without a hint of fear.

"No, of course not. What you do in your personal life has no bearing on me whatsoever," he starts, but Sage interrupts him.

"So Tori's shouldn't bother you either. You know her past, you know she's suffered trauma, and she's slowly healing from that trauma. Instead of knocking her down for it, you should be her biggest cheerleader. I've got to say, man, I've respected you since I met you, but today, I'm disappointed. I would bet your dad would feel the same way. All he wanted was his kids' happiness."

"Then why did he say I had to stay away from Casey?" Gio shouts. "I love her."

"It wasn't permanent, it was temporary until we had everything in place to protect her, but you were too blind to see that. You are fucking lucky she's still alive and nobody has found out, Gio," I tell him, losing my head of steam. Gio has always been so reckless when he sets his mind on something, and this is no different.

"Mark my words, someone is going to get hurt, and don't come crying to me when it blows up in your face. Either of you." Gio slams his chair back from the table and hurries out of the room. Tears stream down Casey's face, and Vienna gets up to comfort her cousin.

"I am so sorry," I apologize to our guests, but Colton holds up his hand.

"You have nothing to apologize for, but Gio does. To both you and Sage."

"I have no idea what's wrong with him. I'm so sorry, Tori, and I didn't know you didn't know about us. I just thought we never hung out here because we had to be secretive," Casey sobs, and I shake my head.

"Don't be, Casey. Gio likes his world in a neat order, and when things he thought he knew change, it throws him for a loop. He's not very flexible."

"I've never seen him like that before," she argues, and Sage and I exchange a glance.

"Look, Casey, I like you, I really do, but our life is not easy, and it will never be. Things regularly get heated and blow up here, and you need to decide if that's the kind of life you can see yourself living," I tell the girl gently. "Now, how about we forget about Gio and eat some of this delicious food Suzy made for us? She'll be in here flapping over us like a mother hen if we don't."

Breakfast is quiet for the most part with subdued, stilted conversation. Gio never returns, and Casey keeps looking at the door he left through with worry. I stay long enough to put together a bacon and egg sandwich with one of the bread rolls before I take my leave.

"Sage will show you to the office once you finish eating," I tell Colton and leave before anyone else can say a word. Hopefully our meeting will be over quickly, and the five of them will leave. I could use some peace and quiet before we have to board the helicopter to San Jose.

About ten minutes later, there's a knock on my door, and Sage opens it, allowing Colton to enter.

"I'll let you discuss business. I'll see you around, Colton."

"Oh, are you off, man?" Colton turns back to look at him.

"Yeah, I've got some work to do, and I'm heading to San Jose with Tori this afternoon. We won't be around all that much for the next couple of weeks. With Gio starting college, it's up to us to make sure everything continues to run smoothly. Tori, shoot me a text when you're ready to head to the airport."

"Will do," I tell him, and he pulls the door closed. "Take a seat, Colton. I'll tell you what I want, and you can tell me whether it's in your scope of expertise."

He's dressed in dark blue jeans and a fitted, light blue shirt which makes the blue of his eyes really sparkle. He has his glasses back on, his blond hair is tied back, and he has a backpack slung over one shoulder.

He grabs a seat and puts his backpack down at his feet, before leaning forward and removing a laptop out of it and placing it on his side of my desk. He then pulls out his phone and holds it up for facial recognition to do its thing and open it for him.

"Do you mind if I take notes?" he asks, holding out his phone and showing me the notebook app.

"No, not at all, as long as there is no sensitive information."

"I won't even put your name. I just like to jot a few things down to keep them straight for me."

"Okay, but I will kill you if you betray me. You are aware of this, yes?" I ask him before I go on, and I see him swallow, but that's the only outward sign of nervousness.

"Yes, Tori, we are very aware of the seriousness of this situation, trust me." It almost feels like there's more to what he's saying, but I don't have time to think about it now.

"Right, these are all the Russo family associates' files." I gesture to a filing cabinet built into the book-lined walls.

His eyes widen. "You only have hard copies?"

I chuckle at his disbelief. "No." I pull open my top drawer, take out a thumb drive, and slide it across the desk to him. His sigh of relief almost has me laughing out loud. "That has all of the previous background checks Gio's tech crew has run. I don't trust them, and I would like an unbiased second opinion, a deep dive into their lives, especially in the past six months since Dad's passing. I want to see if anything sticks out as suspicious."

"Okay, seems easy enough."

"Also, I need you to see if you can find out who posted the hit on Dad on the Hit and Run website. Again, our tech team came up short on finding the identity behind the screen name. That is not acceptable to me. I need a name for my bullet."

He blinks twice but makes a note on his phone with no comment.

"And lastly, and this is a personal thing for me, and it's hard for me to ask, so bear with me." I stop and collect my thoughts, trying to tamp down on my embarrassment. "Is there any way you can find out who ensured that the video Stacey posted of me was removed and stayed removed?"

Colton shuffles in his chair before sighing loudly. "I already know that one. It was me."

I stare at the man in front of me as relief, confusion, and embarrassment all war inside me.

"Why would you do that? You didn't know me from a bar of soap back then," I ask him, and he shrugs.

"I would have done it for anyone. Nobody deserves to have their violation broadcasted to the world. It's bad enough she raped you like she did, and it was horrific for her to use it as a stepping stone to popularity. I can't believe people actually thought it was funny. There are some seriously disturbed people in the world who revel in a video like that."

"Wow, I'm not sure how I can thank you enough."

"If you want to take it to the police, I can restore it to the original," he offers, but I just shake my head.

"No, I will get even with Stacey. I'm going to let her crawl her way to the top at college, and then I'll destroy her. I'd like to say I'd put a bullet in her brain, but it's too quick. No, I'm going to make her suffer humiliation over and over again. Just when she thinks life is good again, kaboom." I mime something blowing up, and a smile creeps across his face.

"Sounds fun."

"You have no idea. So let's talk money. How long do you think this might take?"

"Maybe a week or two. I have to take classes in between, but I can focus everything on it when I'm not there."

"Excellent. Is a hundred thousand enough of a retainer, and then you charge me your hourly rate for everything you do?"

Colton's eyes bulge slightly at the amount. "Ah, yeah, that sounds reasonable."

"Good, I'll authorize the payment. Please give your bank details to my PA, Sally." I hand over her card. "She's based at the Lucky Diamond if you need to see her about anything. Gio can help, too, if you have any questions while we are away, and conveniently for you, he's right across the hall."

"Would you like me to get started now?" He points to the laptop on my desk, but I shake my head. "No, Colton, enjoy the rest of your weekend. You will be busy enough once college starts on Monday. I've waited this long, so another few days isn't going to matter, but I'd probably take Casey and get out of here. I'm not sure what kind of mood Gio will be in for the rest of the day. His temper can get the better of him sometimes."

Colton stands up and shoves his laptop back into his bag. "Do I have to worry about Casey?" he asks, holding my gaze.

I quickly shake my head. "No, he would never hurt her, I promise. He might say something thoughtless because he's mad, but he would eventually apologize. As for physically, not unless she betrayed him completely, so nothing you need to worry about."

Colton frowns, and I think I see a cloud of worry in his eyes, but when I look harder, it's gone. I must have imagined things.

"Should I be asking you to run background checks on yourselves? I guess there's no point, since you'd doctor any crap you didn't want me to see anyway," I ask him as we walk to the door, but he stops and puts his hand on my arm.

"I promise, Tori, that you can trust us, no matter how hard that might seem and no matter what happens," he assures me earnestly, but before I can respond, he's dropped his hand and is pulling open the door. We step out of my office just as Ben comes hurrying down the corridor.

"Tori, there are a couple of detectives at the front gate wanting to speak to you or Gio. I'm not sure where he is. I instructed the gate guard to let them in."

Ah, I was expecting a visit from them this morning.

I look down at myself, and because we are at home, I'm just wearing a pair of denim shorts and one of my favorite shirts with a unicorn with a knife for a horn, and it says, "I will cut you." It makes me look my age, and it's perfect for this scenario. They don't look at me and see the second person in the Russo crime family hierarchy, they just see teenage Tori. "Shall we go and see what they want?"

Chapter Nineteen

"Good morning, Ms. Russo. We're sorry to disturb you at home. I'm Detective Young, and this is my partner, Detective Simpson." The officer is probably in his mid-forties and has a pleasant smile. His partner is a little older and has the middle-aged spread happening, but he hides it well behind his cheap suit.

"Hi. Why are you here? Has something happened?" I ask, looking between them.

Detective Simpson frowns. "What would have happened? What do you know?" he demands, stepping forward.

"Whoa." I hold up my hands. "You're the ones knocking on my door, so I'm assuming something has happened. I would have thought you were too busy to be knocking on a random door for no reason."

Young puts his hand on his partner's arm and yanks him back. "I apologize for my partner. It's been a long night, and we are ready for our beds. Unfortunately, there has been an incident at a warehouse downtown. Property records show it belongs to the Russo Corporation."

"Incident? What kind of incident?" I ask, standing in the doorway while Detective Simpson tries to peer around me.

"Is your brother home? Maybe we could speak to him," the asshole asks, and I just roll my eyes.

Of course they consider him a suspect. "He's here somewhere, our butler is looking for him."

Just then, I hear a noise behind me, and Gio arrives, trailed by the others. The guys are sweaty, but neither Casey nor Vienna are. They must have been in the gym.

"May we come in?" Detective Young asks politely, and I step aside, but I don't show them in any farther than the foyer. Detective Simpson looks around, sneering at the opulence, but Young is the epitome of professionalism. "I'm sorry to have to advise you of this, but the warehouse in question burnt down last night."

"One of our warehouses burnt down?" Gio's surprise is genuine, and Casey gasps before putting a hand over her mouth, but Vienna eyes me suspiciously. I keep my face neutral.

"Do you know what happened?" I ask.

"You don't sound so surprised, Ms. Russo." Simpson rejoins the conversation, but I ignore his attempt at confrontation.

"Arson investigators are on scene, but it looks like a vagrant was making use of the space and they lit a fire, which seems to have spread to the inventory you kept there."

"What was in the warehouse, Tori?" Gio asks me, arching an eyebrow.

"Supplies for the Kitty Kat Club and the Lucky Diamond, as well as our other clubs throughout the state. Decks of cards, napkins, straws, glasses, and hand sanitizer." I rattle off the inventory, and Young nods.

"Yes, it seems like you had some industrial-sized containers of hand sanitizer, and I'm not sure if you're aware, but it's extremely flammable. The fire burned long and hot. It will take a couple of days for the arson report, but we will make sure you get a copy for your insurance claim."

"Thank you for coming and letting us know, Detective. Was anyone hurt in the blaze? Like, did the vagrant get out?" I ask with fake concern in my tone.

"We assume so, no bodies have been found," Young replies, and Simpson mutters, "Yet," under his breath.

Again, I ignore the deliberately belligerent asshole. "Is there anything we need to do?"

"No, but it seems like the fire alarm may have been damaged or malfunctioning, so I would suggest you have all of your buildings tested." He pulls out a couple of business cards. "This is mine, and this one is the head arson investigator's. If they haven't contacted you in a couple of days, I suggest you reach out.

Again, I apologize for the intrusion this morning." Young attempts to leave, but Simpson stands his ground.

"Where were you last night?" he asks, and I wave my hand at the house.

"We were here. We had a little party with guests, as you can see."

"Can anyone corroborate your whereabouts all night?"

Sage steps forward and wraps his arm around my waist. He's sweaty, and I wrinkle my nose as he nuzzles his face against my neck in a blatant attempt to suggest he's what kept me occupied all night, and it is the truth.

"Yes, Sage can," I tell the detective, leaning back against him.

He turns his lip up and switches to my brother. "What about you?"

Before he can answer, Casey steps forward with her hands on her hips. "I was with Gio all night," she states firmly, and the detective looks her over and starts to say something, but Young stops him and pulls him backward toward the door.

"Again, I'm sorry, Mr. and Ms. Russo. Have a lovely day." He sounds annoyed, and when they turn to head back out to their unmarked vehicle, he starts to lay into Simpson.

"What the fuck was that?" he asks as I start to close the door, but I pause with it cracked so I can hear Simpson's response.

"Those two are baby mobsters. I guarantee they did this, we just have to prove it."

"Fuck, Dave, you have no sense of self-preservation. Even if they did, there's no proof. Let it go. They may be mobsters, but at least they aren't warring in the streets, so be grateful for that."

Simpson's response is lost as they get into the car, and I close the door. Turning around, I find everyone watching me.

"Weed, huh, Tori?" Vienna is grinning, and I shrug.

"I don't know what you're talking about. It seems like my day just got busier. I'm going to have to call our insurance company and the one that does maintenance on our fire alarms, so I will wish you all a good week before I disappear to my office. Sage, we need to leave for the airport in an hour. Is that okay with you?"

"Yup, I'll grab a shower and pack a bag. I'll meet you at your car."

"Perfect. Just let Ben know when you guys want to leave, and he'll have the limo brought up. Have a great first week, and maybe we can hang out again soon. Colton, keep me updated on anything you find." I ignore my brother as I say goodbye to his friends. He owes me a pretty big apology, and I'm not willing to be the bigger person and let it go.

Actually, thinking about it now practically makes me feel stabby. I need the release I get from going to the club, so I will also give them a call and see if any of my subs are available for a session.

During the hour I was waiting for Sage and making my phone calls, what I learned about Lorenzo and Penny played over in my mind. I'd been kept too busy by Gio and his friends to really dwell on it too much, but now I need a plan of action. I shoot a text to Sam and Dean, who won't be coming with us today. I ask them to make sure that Penny's room at the hotel is bugged, as well as her car and our old home, then I tell them to bug Lorenzo's car and home as well. Hopefully both are too arrogant to assume we would do something like that and won't do sweeps. If they do, however, we will replace them as many times as we need to until we have all the evidence we require.

I remember the gun buy that went so very wrong. The cartel was tipped off to the location, and with what I know now, it's looking more and more like Lorenzo is the one who did that too. The fact that he's working with that same cartel now is all but a waving red flag. Was that his first attempt to get rid of Dad? Does this make him responsible for the bomb in the car?

But why? He had nothing to gain. Gio and I still stand in his way for gaining access to Russo leadership, but maybe we were supposed to be in the limo too. Maybe it went off prematurely. I shudder at the thought as we both duck our heads against the whirling blades of the helicopter. The pilot loads both our bags as Sage and I take a seat in the back and slip on our headphones. Dan has worked for our family as a pilot for years.

"Dan, we need to take a detour to the cabin please," I tell him when he climbs into his seat.

"Sure thing, Ms. Russo."

Sage raises a questioning eyebrow at me, and I shrug.

"What? You know what he's like. If I don't give him regular updates, he gets cranky, and that's not fair to Maeve. I'd also like his insight into everything that's happening."

Contrary to popular belief, Mickey is not in a hospice facility in a coma. He woke up a few days after we buried Dad and Carla, devastated when he learned that his wife and best friend were gone, and that he may never walk again. We perpetuated the lie to protect him from anyone coming after him again. He's been rehabbing in a cabin we own, hidden under ghost corporations, at June Mountain. Maeve is his nurse and caretaker. In the beginning, the only thing that kept him from taking his own life was the thought of revenge against whoever did this. He did his rehab in the hopes that he could be involved. Against all odds, he has been able to walk again, but he is nowhere near where he needs to be in order to be a soldier in our army anymore. He tires easily and needs to use a wheelchair on his bad days, so to keep him involved, I go to him for advice and send him regular reports. His help has been invaluable, and being able to use him as a sounding board has kept me sane and functioning.

His relationship with his nurse may have changed too, if the little touches and glances I noticed tell a tale, but who am I to deny him a little bit of happiness? I'd never seen any couple as happy as he and Carla had been. Her death destroyed something in him, so seeing him with a glimmer of his former happiness is a relief.

The flight to the cabin takes just over an hour and a half, and soon enough, we're touching down on the landing pad at the back of the house. As we duck down and run toward it, I can see Mickey waiting on the verandah for us in his chair.

"Ah, my beautiful girl, you are a wonderful sight for this old man," he says as I bend down to give him a hug and a kiss. "Sage, my boy. Good to see you." They exchange hugs and a handshake, and Mickey leads the way into the house and to the lounge. Maeve comes out, wiping her hand on a dish towel.

"Hey, guys, this is a nice surprise." She gives us both a hug and a kiss on the cheek. I really like Maeve. I think she's just what Mickey needs. She's Irish. I hired her after extensive background checks and interviews. Her uncle is an Irish mob leader and a longtime ally of the Russo family. When he heard what happened, he called me asking if there was anything he could do, and he's the one who recommended her. I didn't want anyone from the States, because I wanted to keep

Mickey a secret. It's worked up until now. We have had to thwart a couple of attempts at his body double's life in the hospice. There is an actual man in a coma staying in a room in his name to lessen any suspicion. He's horribly scarred from an accident and is the perfect substitute. So far, we've managed to stop any attempt to finish him off, but he is brain dead. His family is allowing us to use him for a tidy sum of money, but we will have to turn the life support off soon and announce Mickey's death. He will be safe until we have caught whoever was responsible for the bomb.

"Can I get you guys a coffee?" she asks us, and I shake my head, but Sage quickly agrees when she tells him she has some freshly baked shortbread for him to have with it.

The two of them go off to the kitchen to do that, leaving Mickey and me alone. He watches me as I wander around, touching things and generally being nosy because I don't know where to start.

"Come on, Tori, it's not like you to be at a loss for words. What's on your mind?" I knew Mickey would cave before I did. He's never been particularly patient.

"So something interesting happened to me this week." I don't turn to look at him, I just stare out the window at the little lake that is to one side of the cabin. It has a small dock, and Mickey spends plenty of time out there fishing. This used to be his and Dad's cabin where they escaped to whenever they wanted to unwind. Nobody knows about it except us and Dan. The helicopter is now silent, and I watch as Dan strolls down the dock with a fishing pole and chair in hand. It's what he always does when we come here, and he keeps one in the little shed next to the lake.

"Oh?" Mickey presses.

"Yeah, I ended up with a federal agent in my chair at the warehouse." I don't need to tell him what chair and which warehouse. I hear his shaky inhale.

"Fuck, did you kill him? We try not to kill feds, it attracts attention."

"Wow, thanks for the giant vote of confidence," I say sarcastically as I turn back to face him. "I'm not an idiot. But he had some interesting information to share once he sobered up."

"You cut a deal with a fed?" Both of Mickey's eyebrows jump in surprise.

I explain exactly what happened, giving him all the details about the cartel and Lorenzo and even my meeting with Penelope. I can see his knuckles whiten where he grips his chair as I get further into the story. When I get to the bit about Mario Maricuso being involved, it proves to be too much and he explodes. A volley of Italian curse words comes flying out of his mouth, and he picks up an empty ceramic vase that was on the table next to him and hurls it across the room with all of his strength.

The kitchen door swings open, and Sage and Maeve appear, both with guns in hand and on high alert.

"What the fuck was that?" Sage demands, peering around the room for an invisible enemy.

I wave a hand, telling them to lower their weapons. "I was just telling Mickey everything we've learned in the last few days."

"The Maricuso family has been looking for a way to muscle into the Russo empire for a very long time. Sure, we have an extremely tentative alliance, but it was contingent on something that your father wasn't willing to give. It was in the process of falling apart when the limo exploded. Lorenzo knows this. To hear that he and Penny are both involved with him now is almost complete proof that they are involved in the death of Stefano and Carla. I've long suspected that it was the Maricusos who planted the bomb. Without the tentative truce, it would have been war, and they almost certainly would have come out on the losing side."

Maeve and Sage put away their guns, and Maeve returns to the kitchen. She comes back carrying a tray with some cups and a teapot and a plate of shortbread cookies, but Mickey waves her off and points in the direction of the liquor cabinet.

"Pour me a whiskey, will you, Tori? And don't make me drink alone," he asks, so I grab two glasses and put ice in both before pouring us both a generous shot of the amber liquid.

"What was the treaty contingent on?" Sage asks as Maeve passes him his cup of tea. I always smother a smile when I see him holding dainty cups and saucers, but he loves the ritual of tea. Maeve has converted him from a coffee to a tea drinker when we're here.

Mickey sighs heavily as I pass him the glass of whiskey, closing his eyes and rubbing his free hand across his face. He opens them and looks at me. "A marriage between Tori and one of his children."

Chapter Twenty

"Whoa," Sage exclaims as they all look at me. "So he definitely has adult children then if he wanted a marriage between one of them and Tori."

"Of course Stefano knocked it back, even before he found out you were gay."

"Bi," I mutter as I consider what Mickey just told me.

"Huh?" Mickey looks confused for a moment but quickly shrugs it off. "He wanted more for you than just an alliance marriage. He knew you were destined for something greater, and look at you now, practically running the business."

"Yeah, because Gio is too busy playing college student," I grumble, taking a sip of my drink and savoring the smooth smoky flavor.

"Ah, yes, Gio. He's still planning on going to college?" Mickey sounds surprised. I guess it's been a few weeks since we last spoke.

"Yes, he moved back into the dorms yesterday. It's like a damn Banebridge school reunion there. Thank fuck I'm not going, since a lot of my old classmates are going too. Stacey included." I fill him in on everything, because he does like a bit of gossip and I'm not ready to unpack the whole marriage alliance thing right this second, especially since it wasn't going to happen anyway.

"Stacey, that bitch," Mickey spits out in English, followed by another tirade of Italian. Maeve stands up and puts her hands on her hips.

"Mickey, calm down now. It is not good for you to get so worked up. I won't let Tori tell you anything if you're going to be so dramatic."

"Damn you, woman," he snaps affectionately. "I'm Italian, we are dramatic. You Irish aren't much better." Still, he does as she says, and she sits back down.

"Yeah, I guess she was only friends with me because her family told her to be, or because she wanted to sleep with Gio. I'm not sure which one motivated her more," I say dryly, and Mickey's eyes light up.

"Stacey is part of the Maricuso family. Her father is Mario's cousin. Can we get Gio to seduce Stacey? We need to know more about what the Maricusos are up to," Mickey says thoughtfully, and I snort sarcastically.

"That would be a no. He's completely besotted with his chick, and to be honest, I'm not sure she would know anything. Her father is a misogynistic dick who wouldn't trust a woman with important information."

"No, but she might know more about Mario's line of succession and who the heir is. That would be good knowledge to have. He was very close-lipped when he was trying to broker the deal."

"Yeah, that's not going to happen," Sage agrees with my assessment. "But I could."

"No!" I shout and sit upright. "Over my dead fucking rotting corpse," I growl, and he smirks at my reaction. His eyes slide to Mickey, who also has a small smirk on his face and one eyebrow raised. Fuck. Oh well, it's not like we were going to hide it or anything.

"Is there something you'd like to share with us?" Maeve can't help her curiosity, and she's wearing a broad grin too.

"No," I tell them all flatly. "I'll get my tech guy to dig deeper into his background. Maybe he can find some birth records or something," I assure my uncle, and that seems to calm him down a bit. He also doesn't harp on my reaction to Sage's suggestion, which I appreciate, but I know he'll grill me at another time.

"Now tell me about Gio. Who is this chick?"

"It's the one Dad told him to stay away from. He disobeyed Dad and has been going behind our backs this whole time, sneaking off to spend time with her."

Mickey runs a hand through his hair and sighs before finishing his drink and holding out his glass. "I'll have another, Tori."

"Mickey," Maeve admonishes, but he just holds up his hand.

"Hush, woman, I am in need."

Maeve starts muttering under her breath, the words getting lost in her thick accent. Sage just grins, looking between them like it's some kind of soap opera.

I do as my uncle asks before returning to my seat on the sofa. "You know Stefano had high hopes for Giovanni when he was born, but even from the beginning, he proved to be a soft touch. There is so much of his mother inside the boy, soft and gentle and not really cut out for ruling a mafia family."

"Gio? Soft?" I snort, and Mickey nods.

"Yes. Unlike you, who took to this life like you had been made for it, Gio fought it for a long time. Yes, he puts on a good front, but it's all a performance. He does not have the balls to do this for a long time. It destroys a little bit of him every time he has to kill someone. You, though, don't even flinch," he explains. "Stefano knew that he would not stay away from this girl. He had been obsessed with stories of your father and mother's love for as long as I can remember, but Stefano had hoped the family first motto we live by would rule over his emotions. Sadly, it does not."

"So what should we do?" I ask, and he shrugs.

"Not much we can do. He is but a figure head, and you are the woman behind the iron mask, so to speak. Let him go to college and have his woman and pretend to hold the Russo family together, but us four here." He gestures between us all. "We know the truth. You are the Godmother, no?" His Italian accent gets thicker, and he starts to gesture with his hands, his whiskey sloshing slightly.

Maeve jumps up to take it from him, but when she does, he uses his now free hands to grab her by the waist and pull her into his lap. She shouts and smacks him with the hand not holding the glass. "Mickey, stop it," she protests, but she's struggling to hide her grin.

"So what should we do?" Sage asks, watching them with a smile on his face.

"Well, it is up to the two of you now. You will make the decisions that are right for this family. You have set this all into motion with your deal with the FBI agent. We are just going to have to watch it play out, and if it doesn't work, we'll put a bullet in each of their skulls and absorb the Maricuso family into ours. Easy-peasy."

Maeve settles on Mickey's lap, looking resigned, and he smacks a kiss onto her cheek.

"Now who is up for a game of poker?" He looks hopeful, and Sage and I quickly agree. I think he and Maeve both get lonely and bored up here. As soon as Colton can get me a name behind the hit and we take care of them, I'll move them back to the house. Their wing is empty and feels sad. It would be nice to have them both living with us. And who knows, they might have a family if things get more serious, or Maeve may go back to Ireland. I don't know, but I know I want to keep the remaining loved ones I have close.

———◆———

Later that evening, we land in San Jose. It's prime time for the Kitty Kat Club, so I decide that is our first stop on the way to the Lucky Diamond.

"So what are we doing? Just our usual check-in?" Sage asks as the limo that picked us up at the airport pulls in front of the strip club. There's a long line waiting to get in, which is pretty unusual. Maybe they have a drink special or there are an unusual number of bachelor parties tonight.

"Yes and no. We could have done this via Zoom, but Stella asked for a meeting. I guess she has some concerns that she wants to speak to me about." We only have the strip club and the Lucky Diamond Casino here in San Jose, and no other assets. Sterling, our hotel manager, runs a tight ship just like Bryce does, so I very rarely need to venture up this way.

"Did she give a hint as to what it could be?" he asks as the bouncer at the front door notices our arrival and stiffens slightly. I see him reach up to his earpiece and alert the staff inside that we're here.

He opens the door, nodding as we approach. Sage and I nod back, but I don't actually know his name, so I can't greet him by it.

"Is he new?" I ask Sage, and he tips his head.

"I don't recognize him, so I guess."

"I don't remember approving any new hires," I

muse out loud as we pass the hostess who takes the cover charge. I don't recognize her either, and she has the familiar, cracked out junky sheen in her eyes.

"Excuse me, it's ten dollars if you want to go inside," she says airily, but Sage and I both ignore her. There isn't another bouncer at the inner door of the coat room, which is strange, since there's supposed to be one.

Sage pushes the door, and it swings open, allowing us to enter the dark room. The lights are dimmed, and only the bar at the back of the club and the stage area is lit up at the moment. Loud music pumps out of the speakers, and smoke hangs in the air, bringing the familiar pungent aroma of both cigarettes and weed. There is an act on stage, and a group of men holler and shout as they watch her performance. They are closer to the stage than they are supposed to be, standing at the edge instead of sitting in the booths provided. We do this for the safety of the dancers. There is wait staff who can go around and collect dollar bills for the strippers, but it looks to me like this one is allowing them to stuff them in her thong.

I move a little closer to see if I can get a better look. Sage's warmth at my back tells me it's not unprotected, which is reassuring, because I have a funny feeling.

"Holy fuck." I feel Sage's breath wash across my face as he catches sight of the stripper on stage. "That's not stripping, that's a live sex show."

He's not wrong. The stripper on the stage has a suction cupped, giant dildo stuck to the stage, and she is riding it like a cowgirl. We watch as she bobs up and down on it, her hands on her breasts as the huge thing goes in and out of her cunt.

"Put it in your ass," someone calls, but thankfully she doesn't listen. No wonder the crowd is in a frenzy. They continue to yell and scream encouragement.

"We're going to lose our fucking license," I growl to Sage.

"What do you want me to do? Stop her?" he asks, and I whirl.

"I don't want you anywhere near her. Don't even look." I put my hand over his eyes, and he chuckles. I cringe in embarrassment before removing my hand.

"Ah, sorry, I kind of lost my shit for a moment, it's fine. I don't care."

He grabs my hand before I can drop it and places a quick kiss on the palm. "I low-key love jealous Tori," he says, smirking. "It gives me warm fuzzies."

My heart jumps at his use of the word "love," but I ignore it and stomp off to the employee only door, looking around for our usual security. I don't see any I recognize. I itch to grab my gun, but I refrain. I need to find Stella and get to the bottom of this. She's lost her ever-loving fucking mind, allowing a sex show to be performed on that stage. We may run whores, but it is all behind closed doors, with an exclusive escort service being the legitimate front. That way, we can claim that what the escorts choose to do on their off time is none of our business.

Like all of the Kitty Kat Clubs on the West Coast,

this one has a set of stairs that lead up to the dressing rooms on one side and the manager's office on the other. At the top of the stairs, I hear a commotion, so I up the pace, Sage close on my heels.

"I will not perform in front of that disgusting crowd. I was assured when I started work here that I would not have to whore myself out, and I will not be performing any sex acts on stage. I'm paid to take my clothes off, and I'm not paid to do anything else." The high-pitched voice is slightly hysterical, and I can hear someone else talking to her. A couple of someones, actually.

"No, Honey, you won't have to do anything but take your clothes off, that is fine." That's Stella trying to calm the stripper down.

"Like fuck she won't. You were all warned things were changing around here. You will do as you are told, or you can find somewhere else to work. Or maybe we will find you a job where you won't actually have a choice." I'm at the top of the stairs as the man, whose back is to me, threatens one of my girls, which gets my blood boiling.

"You and whose army?" I ask, reaching for my gun.

Stella's and Honey's eyes light up with relief. Stella reaches for Honey's hand and pulls her out of the way as the guy slowly turns around.

"Why don't you mind your fucking business, bitch? There's a new boss here now. Get your ass in the changing room and get your fucking clothes off." The guy's eyes widen just before the bullet from my gun makes a lovely, satisfying circle in the middle of his forehead. His body goes down hard, and blood starts to ooze out of the wound as his blank eyes stare up at the ceiling.

"Now, who the fuck wants to tell me what's going on around here?" I look between the two girls as they stare down at the asshole at my feet.

"I'll call in our cleanup crew." Sage brushes a kiss against my cheek and moves into the office to make the call. Stella lifts up a high-heeled foot and stomps the pointy end down on the crotch of the dead guy.

"I warned you, you dick. I told you that our boss wouldn't like it." She twists and bears down, and both Honey and I wince.

"Honey, go get changed. I'm closing the club down tonight. Let the strippers know we are having a staff meeting, but please don't let anyone leave." I send a message to Sterling, asking him to send over a couple of the bouncers from the casino and call in some replacements. I want to round up all the new staff, and I don't think it's something Sage and I can manage on our own.

Honey disappears, leaving Stella and me alone. "What the fuck, Stella? Do you know what is going on downstairs?" I stab my finger in the direction I just came from.

She sighs loudly and nods at the office. "Let's go in there where it's quieter." She gives the body another kick before stepping over it. I leave it where it is, since I know that Sage will have someone here to take care of it soon, but when he finishes his call, I ask him to go down and man the employee door. I don't want anyone to leave, but I also don't want any of those new bouncers coming up the stairs and finding the dead one.

He quickly agrees and disappears the way we came.

Stella flops down in the chair behind the desk and sighs. Now that the lighting is better, I can see she looks ragged. She's lost some weight, and there are strain lines around her eyes.

"Tell me," I demand.

"That is why I requested an in-person meeting. All of my Zoom calls were being monitored by that asshole, so I couldn't tell you during them."

"Who was he, and where did he come from?" I ask, feeling completely blindsided.

"The man is a part of the Maricuso family and was brought in along with all the other bouncers you saw tonight by Lorenzo. They bragged about it all the time, saying how it was time for a new family to take over, and that the Russos were done in the West Coast and it was just a matter of time before the Maricusos ruled. None of them cared that I heard."

I grind my teeth in anger, and the urge to go out and put another couple of bullets in the guy's head hits me hard, but I refrain. "Tell me everything starting from the beginning."

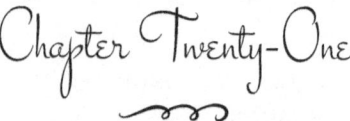

Chapter Twenty-One

The story that unfolds is almost unbelievable, and I want to kick my brother in the junk, because he dropped the ball. It's too much for me to handle on my own, but I certainly get a clearer picture of what is going on. I now need to ascertain if it's happening only here or in Seattle, Portland, and Vegas as well, not to mention Texas, New Mexico, and Arizona. Our whole entire network might be jeopardized, and dealing with Lorenzo will become even more critical as well as working out a way to take down Mario Maricuso.

"About two months ago, Lorenzo appeared in the club one night. He was with some other men, none that I recognized from the family." All our managers get a dossier on important people in our network, the ones they need to schmooze if they ever visit our establishments. "They had a few drinks and a couple of lap dances from the girls, and that was about it. I didn't think much of it."

"Okay, so what happened next?"

"Two days later, he rocks up early before the club had even opened. My bar staff was just setting up for the night, and the girls were sitting around gossiping. I was in a bit of a panic because none of my security staff had arrived yet. I was going to call Sterling and see if he could spare a couple from the casino." Our management staff knows that they can tap any of our other locations if they need help. "But Lorenzo announced that you had ordered a change of security rotation, and that my staff was heading down to one of the clubs in LA, and that the group of men he had with him was the new security staff for here. At the time, I didn't think anything of it. It's not unusual for that to happen, and I just thought I'd missed the memo."

She's right, we do it regularly.

"The dead guy outside was the man he placed in charge. He also announced there would be some changes to the lineup, and he brought in a couple of new dancers. You know how women are, they are catty and they fight, and I ended up losing a couple of my regulars, which was fine because with his new ones, the girls were complaining about stage time and losing tips."

"Okay, so how did this go from being a strip club to a live sex show?"

"For a week or two it was fine, it was business as usual, but then the girls started to show signs of drug use."

"Our girls? But they know they need to keep themselves clean. It's a condition of employment."

"Yeah, girls who I thought would never touch the stuff were doing meth and starting to turn tricks out of the club. The new security guards were helping facilitate it. They were providing the drugs and the patrons. I had to let five girls go."

"Did you send them to rehab?" I ask, because that's what we do with any addicts we fire.

"Yes, but none of them ever showed. In fact, they all seemed to disappear. Alessandro, the guy you just killed, assured me they were sent down to rehab in LA, but I got suspicious and called around, and I couldn't find any of them registered at any rehabs in LA County."

Fuck! I think I just discovered the supply chain for the sex trafficking.

"Then Alessandro turned up with another group of girls, and by then, I was kind of desperate. You can't run a strip club without strippers, so I took them on when he said Lorenzo okayed it. I was going to call you, but Alessandro has basically shadowed me or had my electronics monitored since then. I know because I tried to send you a text message, and it was intercepted. He broke two of my fingers and promised it wouldn't be the last." She holds out her hand where two of her fingers are bound together. "I was able to send that email to you when someone took pity on me while I was at the doctor's office. I told them it was an abusive husband who broke my fingers, and they allowed me to use their laptop. That was two weeks ago. The sex shows started the same day. They knew I wasn't going to be able to tell you, and most of the other staff members are hooked on meth or fentanyl, and Alessandro supplied them."

"Fucking hell." I sigh, leaning back in my chair and staring up at the ceiling. "How the fuck did we miss this?" I say to myself. I push out of my chair and stroll over to the two-way mirror that overlooks the club. The sex show appears to be finished, but there is a slimy, wet smear on the stage. All of the patrons have returned to their seats, and the lights are brighter now as our wait staff run around to serve them. I watch as one girl wobbles on her heels as she returns to the bar to place an order.

"They are all addicted?" I ask in disbelief.

"That, or there's something being held over them. They live in fear, and I think they are dealing drugs out of here. There's been a rush of fentanyl overdoses in the area recently."

Motherfucker, they are trying to muscle in on our trade again. A bullet is too good for Lorenzo.

I pull out my phone and make a call to Sam. "I need you and Dean and maybe six or seven of the guys in San Jose two hours ago. I'll have the jet on standby at the airport, and Sam, come prepared for a fight."

"Sure thing, boss," he replies before hanging up.

"What about the casino?" I ask, worry niggling away at my stomach.

"I haven't heard anything, but they have had me on lockdown, so I haven't been able to speak to Sterling."

"Okay, so I need to sort out this club first and then head over to the Lucky Diamond." I cross my fingers, hoping Lorenzo hasn't weaseled his way in there as well.

"Tori!" The door bursts open, and Sage rushes in. "A group of men just walked in, and they don't look like they are here for the show. At least two of them are carrying."

"Fuck. I guess the security guards must have let Lorenzo know that I'm here and they sent reinforcements." I chew on my lip and contemplate my options. Sure, we could have a fire fight, but there are a lot of drunk patrons downstairs who could get hit in the crossfire. I don't care about them, but I don't have time for an investigation.

"Quick, Stella, who do we have in our pocket here? The chief of police? Sage, shove that body into a closet and wipe up the blood. We don't have time to wait for the cleanup crew to arrive." He takes off to do what I asked. There's a janitor's closet that should work, and it also holds the supplies required to clean up the mess.

"The chief of police has proven to be a friend of the family in the past, but we haven't had any need for them recently, so I wouldn't know for sure. You should ask Sterling. He has some escorts who regularly use the facilities, so he may know more." Our whores get free use of our rooms if they get their clients to spend money in the casino.

I type out a quick message to Sterling, and his reply is quick and succinct. "He is on the books."

Well, that makes that decision easier. I didn't want to risk losing our license, but I need the place shut down for the night so I can take care of my own problems, so I'm going to call in an anonymous tip. If I have to grease a few palms or pay a few fines, so be it.

I grab a burner phone out of the bottom drawer of the desk and power it up. I dial nine-one-one and muffle my voice.

The operator answers within a few rings. "Nine-one-one, what is your emergency?"

"Oh my god, it's disgusting. We went to this strip club so we could have some fun for my friend's bachelorette party, but it wasn't strippers. I saw a girl fucking a dildo on stage. It was so gross." I accentuate a valley girl tone. "And there were drugs and some of the people had weapons, it was so scary. I don't think the girl doing the show wanted to be there, but the bouncer dudes kept pushing her back on the stage when she tried to leave. Do you think they are forcing her to do it?"

"Okay, sweetie, where did you say this was happening?" the operator asks, and I hear her tapping on a keyboard in the background.

"At the Kitty Kat Club on Main," I tell her before breaking the connection and hoping that was enough to send at least a patrol car out. I power down the phone and pull out the sim card, tossing both to Sage as he walks back in the door. He drops both to the ground and stomps on them, shattering them. He bends down and picks up the pieces before tossing them into the bin.

"Now we wait, and hopefully it doesn't take too long." I look down over the crowded strip club and instantly spot the men Sage was telling me about. They are completely obvious in a ridiculous way. Instead of blending in, they stand out in designer suits and ties, and none of them have a drink in hand.

"Fucking amateurs," I mutter as Sage joins me.

"Let's hope they don't get too impatient and come up here to search for us."

"Stella, go keep an eye on the girls. I don't want any of them disappearing early either. Act like nothing has changed, and tell the next act to get ready."

She wrinkles her nose but stands up. "The next act is gross. She has a snake, and she does lewd things with it."

"Fuck my life," I mutter and drop my head against Sage's chest as Stella leaves the room. He slides his arms around me and pulls me in tight. It feels nice, and I let out a sigh of relief. "How did things get so fucked up? If it's like this here, then what are the chances that they are worse in places farther away?"

"I'd say it would be a good chance. We get to the other cities less frequently than we do San Jose."

"It's all falling apart," I whisper to him, and he pulls away and holds me at arm's length.

"No, Tori, we had good teams in place, but

Lorenzo is sneaky. We should have outright disowned him, but they all see him as Stefano's big brother, and I guess he's throwing his weight around now that your dad is not here to yank him into place. He is disrespecting you and Gio. Gio needs to deal with him, and quickly."

"Yeah. We can't let him get away with this, and jail time is not enough. He has to die, but I still need to give the feds something."

"Let them have the cartel. Why don't you set Lorenzo up? Invite him to a private meeting, and tell him that you like what he's doing with the family business, that you think your brother is soft and not fit to run it. Stroke his ego, he's too blind to see the trap. Ask him to facilitate a meeting between you and the men backing him, and maybe come to some side arrangement."

"Betray my brother?" I ask, thinking it through.

"Well, it's not really betrayal, is it? It's just a setup. Once you have all the information, you can give it to the feds and kill Lorenzo and the cartel boss, and Mario Maricuso if we're really lucky, and absorb their operations into ours, just like Mickey suggested."

"All the fed really wants is his sister back. If we plug up the network, there's nothing left to poke at, and with all the people responsible dead, they can turn their attention to something else." I do my thinking out loud, and Sage nods enthusiastically.

"Yes, and we can go back to business as usual."

I flop down onto the sofa and heave out a sigh. "This is fucking exhausting," I tell him as he takes a seat next to me and puts his arm around me, hauling me into his side. He presses a kiss to my temple, and I melt into him. Sage is so touchy-feely. I thought I'd hate it, but it turns out I fucking love it. Not that I would admit it to anyone.

"Why don't you make a call to the Black Rose and ask them to set you up with your sub? You may feel a bit better if you release some of this tension."

I chuckle as he squeezes one of my shoulders with the arm he has around it. "I thought you'd suggest a different way of releasing our tension."

"Oh, I promise there will be a lot of that as well, but we all have our quirks. I smoke weed, and puttering around my plants is my zen time. You like to roll around on naked people covered in blood. Who am I to judge?"

"Shit, when you put it like that, it really is fucked up. Vienna and her guys are going to freak out, aren't they?"

"Maybe or maybe not. You can only ask."

A commotion at the door has us both tensing up. The main doors burst open, and a dozen cops enter with their guns raised. We watch on as the house lights are turned on and everyone is made to stand up and put their hands on their heads. Three of the police officers come up to the dressing room and office, and all the girls, Stella, Sage, and I are escorted down to join the rest. I identify myself as the owner, and after we are thoroughly frisked, we are allowed to sit on a bar stool and wait.

"I'm Officer Cockran. Police Chief Mason sends his regards." One of the officers comes over to speak to me as the rest of his men frisk our clients one by one before escorting them out of the building. If they are in possession of illegal substances, they are arrested, but most are just released. The five men who had arrived were all carrying concealed and were handcuffed and escorted outside. "You know you can't run a live sex show on the premises, right?" he asks, shoving his hands in his back pockets, looking adorably awkward.

"I know. There was a miscommunication from someone who thought they were management material. If you could leave all my employees here, I will address this once you have all taken your leave."

"Very good. We'll let you off with a warning this time, but if it happens again, we will have to charge you."

"No, I completely understand, and please take your boys off to the casino for a meal on me when you get a chance. I'll leave your name with the management of Aces High."

"Thank you very much, Ms. Russo. I'm sure they will enjoy that. Here's my card. Please give me a call if I can help you with anything else while you are in town." I take the offered card, and he nods his head and returns to the rest of the officers. It takes another half hour or so to sort through the mess, but eventually, they depart, leaving behind all the staff. The girls look dazed and confused, and the bouncers all have stubborn, belligerent expressions on their faces. The bar and wait staff just look tired.

I know how they feel. It's going to be a long night.

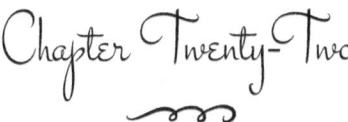

Chapter Twenty-Two

As soon as the police leave, three security guards from the casino arrive with Sterling in tow.

"Shit, Tori, we waited outside so we didn't get caught up in the raid. Is everything okay?" Sterling is the complete opposite of Bryce. He's big and brawny and has a well-groomed beard, but he's just as good at his job. All my managers are family men and completely trusted, but I did put their names at the top of Colton's list just to be sure. I'm going to be devastated if any of them come back as traitors.

He gives me a hard hug and then holds me at arm's length. "You look like shit."

"Wow, Sterling, thanks," I say sarcastically as he does a bro handshake with Sage. I always find the two of them getting into shit whenever we come up here to visit.

"What the fuck is going on? Stella, are you okay?" He leaves us in his dust and hurries over to the strip club manager. He swoops her into a hug too, but it looks a little more intimate than the one he just gave me. They are whispering quietly, so I leave them to their private moment and survey the sorry fucking crowd in front of me.

"Okay, here's what is going to happen. Anyone who was employed by Lorenzo, step over to the right side so we can have a chat." Over half the staff does exactly that, with the help of the three men Sterling brought with him, leaving me with only my two original bartenders, one waitress, Honey, and one other stripper apart from Stella.

"Fucking hell," I mutter as Sterling and Stella return to our side.

"Has Lorenzo been fucking with the Lucky Diamond too?" I ask him wearily, and he shakes his head.

"No, I think it's too big of an operation. Someone would have said something before now. The Kitty Kat Club was easier to manipulate." He still has his arm around Stella, and she nods her agreement.

"Yes, that was what I overheard them saying one evening. That Kitty Kat Clubs were prime targets because everyone thought strippers were junky whores anyway."

"Lorenzo has been running more cash across the tables recently though—I didn't really think anything of it until today—and he's been bringing shady looking people to play as well, but they haven't caused any trouble, so it's been business as usual."

"I'm pretty sure he's washing cartel money through our casinos, which I will not stand for." We charge a pretty penny for that service, and there are some people I refuse to do that for—specifically people who profit from the trade of skin and pedophiles. For the right fee, we'll even launder for a rival family. It's no skin off my nose, but we do have to draw the line somewhere, and that's mine. "But I have bigger problems than that at the moment. This is probably going to send him scrambling anyway. Now how the fuck am I going to deal with this?"

"Well, Lorenzo or whoever is pulling the strings obviously knows you're here because he sent men after you. I say we find out if these are contractors or the Maricuso family." Sage points to the rest of the security. "We only know for sure that Alessandro was. I bet these are all contractors, because then they can deny any involvement."

"Fuck, I wish I'd thought to have Colton on the plane with Sam and Dean. I bet he could have found all of that out within minutes."

"They probably haven't left yet. Want me to call him and ask?"

I bite my lip, unsure if I'm ready to trust him, but I really don't have any other options at the moment. I shake my head, tapping the business card the cop gave me against my thigh.

"No, leave him be. I'll give Officer Cockran a call and ask him to run their names through the police database. It should tell us whether they have any family ties. Even if they do, I can't go around killing them, because that would cause outright war between the Russos and the Maricusos."

"Aren't we already at war?" Sage crosses his arms stubbornly.

"Yes, but at the moment, it's covert ops. They make their moves, and we make ours. I would rather not start the killing portion for now. I want to clean up all the other Kitty Kat Clubs too. I'm hoping they think I'm too stupid to put two and two together and guess that they have done this to all my strip clubs."

I instruct the few loyal security guards to get photos of everyone's IDs. There's grumbling when they demand that people get them out, but anyone who argues is quickly shut down.

"At least we have a record of everyone here, but what are we going to do with them? If you fire them, I won't be able to open." Stella waves her hand at her minions, and I sigh again.

"Okay, let's work out who is here because they want to be and who is being forced, and if any of them want to get clean, we'll send them off to rehab and cut anyone else loose. Again, I'm not comfortable killing them, they are all just so pathetic."

"Can I let Honey and Macy leave?" Stella asks. "Those are my two remaining original girls, and I can vouch that neither of them are junkies. They still test clean weekly."

"Yes, of course," I agree.

The two girls look relieved when Stella gives them

their marching orders, but Honey stops as she passes me on the way out. "Please find our friends, the girls who went missing."

"I have a feeling that it's not going to be that easy, but I will try," I promise, and her eyes fill with tears, but she says, "Thank you," and the two girls leave.

"Hey, why are those bitches allowed to leave and we're not?" The girl who had been performing on stage when we arrived decides to grow a set of brass balls. She stands up with her hands on her hips. She's wearing a flowery robe, and it gapes at the top, but not enough for a nipple slip. Her eyes are mostly clear, and she looks pissed.

"Sit your ass down," I tell her, but she gets a stubborn glint in her eye.

"Who the fuck are you to tell me what to do?"

"Oh fuck," Sage mutters under his breath and puts his hand on my arm. "Remember we have witnesses, so you can't shoot her in front of all these people."

I look down at his hand on my arm and then pat his cheek. "It's okay, baby, I've got this." I almost smirk as I watch him melt at my small attempt at affection. I figure that kind of thing needs to go both ways, and I know how good it makes me feel.

"I am the woman who signs your paychecks," I reply calmly, and she scoffs.

"A woman? Hardly. That would be Lorenzo. He takes care of all of our needs." Eww, is she implying what I think she is? Man, there's no accounting for taste.

"Ah, no. Lorenzo is a tiny little fish swimming in a shark infested pond. Sit your ass down and let the adults handle this." I turn my back on her, and I hear her screech in annoyance.

"You have no right to barge in here and shut things down."

I turn back around slowly. "Excuse me, but I am motherfucking Victoria Russo, and I can do whatever the fuck I want, and no two-bit hooker is going to tell me I can't. Now sit down before I make you." The girl looks like she's about to blow up again, but one of the other dancers grabs her by the arm and whispers furiously to her. The girl still has a stubborn set to her jaw, but she does as she's told.

"You know what? I don't have time for this shit." I turn back to face the crowd. "If you were hired by Lorenzo, you are now fired, and if I see any of you poking around, I will make sure it's the last time you do. Once you've had your ID copied, get the fuck out of my club. Oh, and whoever owns the snake, make sure you take it with you, or it will lose its head." I shudder at the thought of the snake and using it to do dirty things. Maybe I should have just shot that girl. Disgusting whore.

Sage reaches over my shoulder and points to something. I follow the line and find a woman with a large python wrapped around her body. She's stroking its head and cooing to it quietly as the group looks at one another, trying to figure out if they should argue or cut their losses and make a run for it. I take my gun out and shoot a warning shot over their heads to make their decision easier. "Now."

That quickly makes their minds up, and there is a mass exodus, except for the one girl who was causing a fuss. She strolls back toward the stairs to the dressing room.

"What are you doing?" Stella crosses over and puts herself between the door and the girl.

"I'm going to grab my things. I'm not leaving Reggie behind."

"Who the fuck is Reggie?" I ask, and Stella rolls her eyes.

"That's what she calls that big-ass dong she was riding on stage earlier."

I wrinkle my nose in disgust. "Fucking hell, if you're that desperate, get it and be quick." I wave my hand, dismissing her, and she glares at me.

"You will pay for this. Wait until I tell Lorenzo." Her threats mean nothing to me, and I ignore her.

"Go with her," I instruct one of the casino security guards, who trails after her obediently. I wouldn't put it past her to do something destructive in revenge.

The doors to the club open again, and in comes the San Jose cleanup crew. "I'll show them what they need to do," Sage tells me and leads them up the stairs to retrieve Alessandro.

"Come on, you look like you could use a drink." Sterling grabs my arm and tows me over to the bar, helping me onto one of the stools before retreating behind it. Stella joins me as I consider the few remaining staff members.

"What about this group?" I ask her, and she shrugs.

"As far as I can tell, they are good. They just did things because they were threatened, just like I was."

I can see them listening in. "Is that true?"

"Yeah, they told us they'd break our legs if we stepped out of line," one of the bartenders says, pointing between himself and the other one.

"And you?" I ask the waitress, who bursts into tears.

"My sister is one of the missing girls, and they told me if I sold their product, I could see her again."

Fuck. I run a hand across my face, feeling exhausted. With everything that has happened in the last few days, I just need a break.

"Okay, well, I said we'd try and track down where they went. I'll get our tech guy on it." Another fucking job for Colton. With the rate we're going, I may as well induct him into the Russo family and employ him full time. I'm not sure if Vienna would be happy about that though.

"But you three take a couple of days off. If you feel unsafe at home, Sterling will put you up at the hotel. Actually, just grab some stuff and do that anyway." I turn to Stella. "It's probably a good idea for you to call Macy and Honey and tell them to do the same thing. You as well. Let's keep our loyal people safe and out of harm's way."

Her eyes widen, and she nods quickly, pulling out her cell. "Good thinking."

"My guys will escort you home so you can grab some things and then bring you to the hotel, okay?" Sterling tells the remaining three, who quickly agree, looking grateful.

I blow out a loud sigh as Sterling slides over a double shot of whiskey for me. I pick it up and take a large sip before putting it back down.

"Okay, well, that's a start."

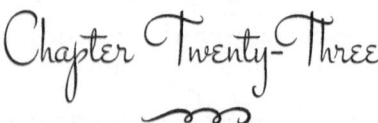

Chapter Twenty-Three

We don't hang around much longer after the cleanup crew has done their job. Sam and Dean and the rest of their crew will meet us at the Lucky Diamond, so we shut down the club and I tell the employees we will let them know what is happening in a week, then we make our way back to the hotel.

The ride has been quiet, all of us lost in our own thoughts. I've been going over my plan in my head, trying to figure out what to do next.

"What am I going to do about staff?" Stella asks from the back seat of our rental where she's sitting with Sterling. She decided she would grab her personal things tomorrow and would make use of the hotel gift shop tonight if she needed anything.

"Normally I would pull some staff from a couple of the other locations, but who knows how many have been compromised."

"Are we going to go and find out? You've called in the cavalry," Sage asks nonjudgmentally.

"I was going to," I muse thoughtfully. "But I think I've decided on something different."

"Care to share with the class?" Sterling asks, but before I can answer, there's a squeal of tires, and Sage shouts, "Fuck! Brace yourselves."

He yanks the wheel to one side as I grab hold of my door handle, trying to keep myself upright, but there's an almighty crash as we are T-boned. The back passenger side takes the most impact. My head smacks against the window, and I see stars as my ears register all the sounds of glass smashing and metal grinding as the car flips onto its side and slides along the road.

I must black out, because when I come to, the only thing keeping my body in place is my seat belt. I groan and try to look around, but my head hurts, and my neck aches.

"Sage!" I look for him and heave out a sigh of relief when he groans loudly.

"Fucking asshole. Our insurance premiums are going to go through the roof."

"It's a rental, it doesn't matter." I watch as he looks around, trying to figure out how to get out of the car. He's trapped by inflated airbags.

"Sterling, Stella, you good?" I call.

"Stella's hurt really badly. There's so much blood." Sterling's voice is shaky, and I wince at the thought of what the damage might be. Her side took the brunt of the impact. In the distance, I can hear the sound of sirens.

"It's okay, help is on the way. Are you carrying?" I ask him, and he scoffs.

"Of course."

"Keep an eye out until help arrives. We're sitting ducks, and we don't want anyone coming to finish the job before help can arrive for her."

"Will do, boss." He sounds a little more together now that I've given him something else to think about. It's a good trick I've learned over the last few months.

I assess my body, and apart from a few aches and pains and a nasty cut on my head, which keeps dripping blood into my eye, I'm not that injured. I pull the knife out of my bra and stab the airbags that protected me from the impact. They hadn't gone all the way down and were restricting my movement. "Watch out, Sage, I'm going to unstrap," I warn him.

"I've got you," he assures me, so I put my faith in him and undo my seat belt. Gravity takes hold, and I fall toward him. He puts his arms up to lessen the impact, and I find myself in his lap, a whoosh of air escaping my lungs. He grunts but holds tight as all my weight lands on him. "Kill those bags for me, will you, love? Then we can see about getting out of this car."

I ignore him and put my hands on his cheeks and kiss him hard. When I pull away, I sigh with relief. "I'm so glad you're okay," I tell him quietly, and a slow smile spreads across his mouth.

"I'm a lot harder to kill than that, don't you worry."

I roll my eyes and start taking care of his airbags before cutting his belt. It seems to be stuck, so it's the only way to release him. We do a little shuffle, and he stands up and tries to push out my door, giving us a way to get out of the car, but when we were hit, it must have buckled the frame, because the door isn't budging.

"Window it is," he says, holding out his hand for my knife. I pass it over reluctantly, and he chuckles quietly. "Don't worry, I'll give it back."

"See that you do," I grumble, shifting to take a look at our other two passengers. Sterling is hovering over Stella, who is still dangling in her seat belt. She has cuts all over her, and there's a large shard of glass protruding from her stomach. Thankfully, she's unconscious. Sterling was right, there is a lot of blood.

"Let's leave her there until the paramedics arrive. Moving her now will only cause more damage," I tell him. He's pulled off his jacket and is trying to staunch some of the blood flow from her stomach.

Red and blue flashing lights have me heaving out a sigh of relief, and the next half hour is filled with activity as rescue crews help extract us from the car.

Paramedics wrap blankets around Sage and me, but they concentrate on Stella and the driver of the other vehicle who hit us. You could have knocked me over with a feather when they told me that it looks like it was just a drunk driver. I thought for sure this had been an attempt on our lives.

We stand off to the side, staying out of the way like the police told us to. Once one of the ambulances leaves with Stella, Sterling going with them, they turn their attention to us.

"What about the driver?" I ask as they bring us over and sit us down to have a look at our injuries. Sage is fine except for a few bruises and scrapes, but my head requires stitches.

"I'm afraid he didn't make it," the paramedic giving me a numbing agent tells me. "It's an older vehicle, and there were no airbags."

I stare over at the broken windscreen. It's pushed out slightly and covered in blood, so his head must have hit it.

"Was he drunk?" Sage asks.

"It sure smells like it, but they'll do a tox screen just to be sure." I can feel the push and drag of the stitches, but no pain thanks to the numbing agent. My teeth start to chatter, though, and my body shakes.

"Ms. Russo, you seem to be going into shock. It really would be best if we observed you overnight." The other paramedic, who had been taking my vitals, frowns as he feels my pulse.

"No, I'm okay. I haven't eaten since breakfast. I just need some food and a good night's rest... and maybe a few decent painkillers. Everything is going to hurt tomorrow," I mutter, and Sage chimes in.

"Everything hurts now." He grunts as he shifts his

blanket from his shoulders to mine, giving me more warmth.

"Okay, but if you start to feel strange or anything, you need to call for an ambulance."

"The Lucky Diamond has a doctor on staff, so I'll be fine," I assure them, and they lay off.

Eventually, we're cleared to leave. We are given a lift to the hotel by Officer Cockran, who turned up at the scene not long after my stitches had been put in.

The ride is silent, both Sage and I feeling a little worse for wear.

"I hope this is the last time I see you this trip, Ms. Russo," Officer Cockran says with a wry smile as we thank him and get out.

"Me too, Officer Cockran, me too."

It's not until we're checked in and firmly ensconced in the owner's suite that we talk about what happened.

"What do you think about coincidences?" Sage asks, digging around in his bag. They were able to extract our things from the trunk of the rental before they took it away for investigation. When he straightens, he's holding a joint, and I just about cheer with glee. Neither of us have taken any painkillers yet, so we're good to go.

We hobble out onto the balcony, and Sage lights up as we both take a seat.

"I don't believe it was one at all. Somehow, that drunk driver was gunning for us."

Sage hands over the joint. "What are we going to do about Lorenzo?"

"I've been thinking about that. He's on alert now. He knows we know what he's been doing. I'm going to use it as my in. I'll tell him that I am impressed with his forward thinking and would like to speak to him about it."

"What about the other clubs?" he asks, watching me. I sit and smoke my joint for a moment longer before handing it back to Sage. I feel it start to work, and the tension I'd been holding for what feels like forever eases slightly.

"We're going to have to let it go for now. I will have to say I closed this one down because of the live sex shows. I'll warn him that we need to be more discreet, and maybe suggest he start his own underground sex club, giving him enough rope that he will take it and hang himself."

"You think he'll get greedy?"

"I think he's stupid and misogynistic enough to believe he's pulling one over on me. They may even traffic the girls they are sending to Mexico there first, as a testing ground. I may make some vague hints that will allow him to think it's his idea."

"Sounds plausible. What are we going to tell Gio?"

"Fuck Gio. This has all happened under his nose.

If he was as dedicated and disciplined as Dad, none of this would have happened."

"How were we to know that Lorenzo was the rat?"

"It's so glaringly obvious that I want to punch myself in the face. He has hated my and Gio's involvement from day one. I'm surprised there haven't been more attempts on our lives." I groan. Although the weed is helping me relax, it's doing nothing to relieve the pain.

Sage passes me the joint and goes back inside. I don't have the energy to follow him, so I stay exactly where I am. When he returns a few minutes later, he smells like a combination of lavender, peppermint, and eucalyptus.

"What have you been doing?" I ask as he holds out his hand, and I pass him back the mostly smoked joint. He stabs it out in the ashtray then holds out his hand again. I take it, and he helps me to my feet before dragging me back inside. We bypass the living area and head to the main bedroom, going straight to the en suite where I can hear running water. When we get in there, I see he is filling the huge tub, and it smells like he did.

"Come on, I used some of the oils they provided with this room. I googled it, and they are supposed to relieve muscle aches. Climb in, and I'll order you some room service. You need to eat."

I feel a goofy smile cross my lips as I realize he's done all this for me. "You're looking after me," I tease him, and he rolls his eyes playfully.

"Well, someone clearly has to, since you don't."

My smile drops. "No one has for a long time. I really appreciate it."

I lost my jacket somewhere when the paramedics were checking us over, but I struggle to reach my gun to remove it. Sage sighs and steps over, stilling my arms. He reaches in and pulls it out, placing it on the bathroom counter. Next, he helps me unzip the corset and slide it down my arms. I stifle a pained groan. My whole body feels like one giant bruise. He then undoes the clasp on my fitted pants and slides the zipper down before helping me out of them. I'm standing in just my panties, and I expect some flirty remark, but all he does is help me slide them off before he assists me into the bath.

I sigh as I slide down into the warm water, bubbles covering my body, and I close my eyes and rest my head on the ledge. I feel him lift it and place something beneath it. When he allows me to lower my head, there's a cushion of some kind underneath it.

"Ugh, you're a keeper," I murmur, leaving my eyes shut, and I feel him brush his lips across mine.

"I'll be back in a moment," he tells me, and I hear his footsteps as he leaves the room.

The weed is doing its job, and I allow my mind to float. I just need a moment where I don't have to think about a thing, a second to unwind and decompress from all the stress in my life.

I'm not sure how long Sage is gone, but when he returns, he has a glass of bubbly in his hand. "Here, you look like you could use this." He passes it to me and leans against the counter. "I ordered some food. Sam and Dean are here with their crew. I told them to grab rooms and we will debrief tomorrow."

I raise an eyebrow at him. "Well?"

"Well what?" He sounds confused, and he gets that adorable wrinkle between his eyebrows.

"Are you just going to stand there, or are you getting in?" It takes him a moment to compute what I said, but soon enough, he's stripping off his clothes. He has a big bruise on his chest from where the airbags saved him and a few scratches on his arms, but apart from that, there aren't any visible injuries. I breathe out a sigh of relief now that I have seen it with my own eyes.

"Victoria Russo, it's not polite to ogle a man like he's a piece of meat," Sage teases as he slides his briefs to the ground to join mine. My gaze moves to them, and I feel a sense of satisfaction. Seeing our underwear together on the bathroom floor makes me happy.

He quickly climbs in and hisses, cupping his balls as he lowers himself into the water. "Holy Satan's left testicle, woman, are you trying to cook us?"

"Oh hush, you big baby. You'll get used to it," I reply as he settles himself opposite me. I use my toe to reach up and press the button next to him, activating the jets. As I go to lower my leg, he grabs my foot in his hand and presses his thumbs into the arch.

"Oh my god." I moan at how good it feels, and when my eyes meet his, he's smirking.

"Don't you wish you hadn't held out so long? You could have been having nightly foot rubs for months."

I think about what he said, and I shake my head. "No, I disagree. If I had given into your advances at the start, you would have had your fill and gotten bored and moved on by now. I'm still worried that will happen," I tell him truthfully, and the smirk drops, and he shakes his head emphatically.

"No fucking way. You're it for me, Victoria Russo. I've been half in love with you since you grabbed my junk that first day. I'm in this for the long haul. You wait, on our fiftieth wedding anniversary, you are going to owe me a toothless blowy."

I wrinkle my nose but laugh at his words, kind of liking the sound of them. "If we're still together in fifty years, you've got yourself a deal."

Chapter Twenty-Four

After the bath and food, Sage and I went to bed and made gentle love. Neither of us were up for a vigorous fuck, so as he slid into me from behind, his body wrapped around mine, I marveled at how good something like this can be with the right person.

Sleep that night was solid, but when we woke up in the morning, we both decided to take the painkillers prescribed to us by the paramedics. We moved slowly and gingerly as we breakfasted on the balcony.

"So what's the plan?" Sage asks as he takes a sip of his coffee.

"I'm going to send Sam and Dean around to the addresses of the old security guards. I want to know if they were sacked or taken care of permanently. I want to reemploy them."

"That's a good start."

"And I need to call the hospital and see how Stella is. I didn't hear anything from them last night, which has me worried." I peer through the glass doors, looking around for my phone, but I can't see it anywhere.

"That's because I hid your phone and told reception not to disturb us."

I start to argue with him, but he holds up his hand, silencing me. I glare at him.

"I know you're worried for your staff, but there's nothing you could have done, and you were hurt too, bordering on shock, so you needed to be cared for, and I won't apologize for putting your needs above everything else."

My mouth drops open at the stubborn set to his jaw and his no nonsense ways.

"Even when you won't look after yourself, I will. It's also why I called the Black Rose and made a booking with one of your subs on your behalf. We will fly back to LA tonight, and the following night, you will go and rub yourself over someone's bloody body. I'm sure you will be back to normal in no time."

I blink once, twice, before surging out of my chair and launching myself at him, wrapping myself around him like a koala and hugging him tight. "I love you, Sage Russo," I whisper quietly into his ear, and his chest puffs up underneath me as he wraps his arms around me and holds me close.

"I know! I just needed to convince you. I love you too."

A knock on the door has me jolting, completely consumed within our little bubble. "Go away," I mutter into his chest. "Can't we just spend the day in bed?" I ask him, and I feel his body shake with laughter.

"I never thought I would see the day when Tori Russo would blow off work to play hooky." He lifts me and stands up, placing me back on the chair before answering the door after another rather loud and insistent knock. I sigh and follow slowly after him, still feeling my aches and pains. I find my phone powered down on the kitchen counter, so I press the button, turning it on as Sage opens the door to Sam and Dean. They come in, and I grab two more mugs and pour them both a coffee from the cart left by room service.

"Hey, guys, thanks for coming up here. I think I may have jumped the gun slightly." I pass them both a mug, and their eyes widen briefly at the sight of my bruised face before they quickly recover. Turns out that there was another reason. Sage kept me so distracted last night. While the airbag saved me, it also gave me a black eye and a nasty cheek bruise on the right side of my face. I look like shit, and I don't have any coverup here to conceal it.

"We spoke to Sterling at the hospital this morning. Stella made it through surgery, and she's going to be okay, but there's going to be a lengthy recovery period."

This is what I love about my guys. Instead of fussing, they get straight to the important stuff. My minions are well trained. A feeling of relief washes over me. I hadn't realized how tense I was from worrying about her.

"Okay, we need to arrange a caretaker for her, and we need a temporary manager for the Kitty Kat Club." I start making notes on my phone once it's powered up.

"A manager is not all you need," Sage points out as he returns from grabbing his breakfast plate from outside. He sits down at the kitchen table and finishes his food while he listens to us talk.

"I want you to head to the club and go through Stella's employment records. They should all be hard copies in the filing cabinet, so you don't need her computer passwords. Find the addresses of all the security guards who were working there the last time we were up here, and then use your guys and find out what happened to them. Offer them their jobs back and give them all a ten-thousand-dollar bonus if they accept. Apologize for any miscommunication or threats they might have suffered." I don't doubt, if they are still alive, threats were involved. "That takes care of everything but the dancers. What am I going to do about that? All the old ones disappeared."

"What about the Kitty Kat Club in Suncity? Do you think he was brazen enough to mess with that one?"

I scrunch up my nose. "No, but as far as I know, Candy still runs it."

Sage stops eating. "What do you mean as far as you

know? When was the last time you were there?" he asks, and I grimace.

I was there a month or two ago, when I knew that Candy had called in sick. "Look, don't judge, but after Dad's funeral, every time I went there, she seesawed between begging me to take her back and telling me I was the devil incarnate. She's fucked in the head, and I wanted to shoot her, but I can't go around shooting exes because they piss me off. It's not right."

The three of them chuckle, and I flip them all off.

"How about putting a flyer up at the local college? College girls aren't afraid to strip, and, well, if there's money involved, I'm sure they'll be even more enthusiastic." I eye Dean, trying to consider if he's serious or not, but with the way Sam and Sage are nodding their agreement, I guess he is.

"Really?" I ask, and Dean shrugs.

"College is expensive. Give them a signing bonus, a big one, and I'm sure you will have more than enough."

"That's actually pretty smart. Ten grand would go a long way in paying a lot of their bills or tuition, and it's not like the club doesn't make that kind of money," Sam agrees.

They are not wrong. The Kitty Kat Clubs are very lucrative, which is why we expanded from the original four. I bought established ones and rebranded and revamped, with much success. "Okay, one of you go and do that. How many colleges are here in San Jose? There must be a few."

Sam's phone is out, and his fingers fly across the screen. "Eighteen," he replies.

"Huh, that's more than I expected. Okay, maybe target the ones closest to the club. Girls aren't going to want to travel for ages to get to work. If we have no luck, we can expand out. When I return to LA, I'll take a trip to our club. I wonder if any of the girls there would like a promotion." All my managers started as strippers.

"Well, Lacey has been shadowing Candy, so she can cover for her when she's not there," Dean pipes up, and I remember the girl they are both so fond of.

"But how would you feel if she wasn't there anymore?"

Dean frowns like he hadn't thought that through.

"Why don't you transfer Candy and make Lacey the manager there? That would solve both your problems," Sage suggests as he puts his now empty plate back on the room service cart.

"Sage, you genius, I could kiss you." He puckers up and blows me one. "Okay, good, so we have a plan. I will go back and lull Lorenzo into a false sense of confidence and then deal with that fucker."

I feel lighter than I have in days. Having a plan and knowing what path to take is so much better than floundering around with no information. Hopefully in a day or two, Colton might have some solid information for me, and I'll have another name on my list to eliminate, but I have a funny feeling it's going to be the same name.

As much as I want to go and check out the other Kitty Kat locations, I have to leave them be for now. I want to weave the web that will trap Lorenzo and everyone else he's involved with, so if I go poking around, I'll just destroy their little network they have going and they'll go underground. I don't want that to happen, but I will add another task to Colton's list by having him discreetly check into the staff turnover at each of the clubs. I want to know if more girls have gone missing. Then I want him to do a wider search and see if a larger amount of girls than normal in the surrounding areas are also missing. I was going to call him, but I may stop in and see how Gio is settling in at college. I can ask him then, and if I get to see them all, then that's just a bonus.

I have my meetings with the relevant heads of the casino, and on the way to the helicopter, Sage and I stop at the hospital to see Stella, but as we park, my phone rings, and there's no ID on the screen.

"Victoria Russo," I answer and wait.

"Ms. Russo, it's Officer Cockran. I'm just calling to give you an update on the accident."

"Oh?"

"Turns out the driver wasn't drunk. There wasn't a drop of alcohol in his system. It was only poured on his clothes to make him smell like he was. And from the CCTV footage we've managed to gather, it looks like you were specifically targeted. If it wasn't for Mr. Russo's quick reactions and evasive maneuvers, that car would have completely T-boned yours, and you would have been just as injured as your friend, if not dead."

I sigh heavily. "Thank you for letting me know, Officer."

"Watch your back, Ms. Russo. It seems you've made an enemy." He hangs up, and I fill Sage in on what he said.

"So no coincidence?" he says, and I shake my head.

"Nope, but we didn't think it was. I guess we're going to have to be more careful until I can reach out to Lorenzo and set our plan in action."

"Yeah, I'm pretty sure we'll still have to watch our backs. We need to warn Gio, too, because he has to be careful. If they are gunning for you, I guarantee they are gunning for him."

"I'll go tomorrow and see if I can catch him between classes."

We get out and head into the hospital.

There's a soft, consistent beeping coming from her room. Sage and I pause in the doorway when we see that she's asleep. Sterling is on a chair next to her bed, his head resting on it with his eyes closed. He must hear us, because he sits up. One of his arms is in a sling, but he reaches for his gun with the other. Sterling relaxes when he sees it's us.

He gets up and comes over to us, ushering us

outside. "How is she?" I ask. "And what happened to you?" I nod at the sling, and he grimaces.

"It's fractured. I have to wait a day or two for the swelling to go down, and then they'll cast it. I must not have noticed with all the adrenaline running through me. Stella's okay. The shard of glass pierced her abdomen, and there was extensive blood loss. They need to do some repairs as well. The doctors have her on an antibiotic IV to ward off any chances of infections. She'll stay in for observation for a couple of days, and then she will return home. She will need help for a couple of weeks."

"I've organized for her to have the family suite at the Diamond, and a caretaker is ready for when they release her."

"Man, why don't you head home and get some rest? You look like shit," Sage suggests, and he's right. Sterling's still wearing the same clothes as last night, and they are covered in Stella's blood.

He looks back into the room. "I don't want to leave her alone."

"It looks like the accident was a hit on Tori, so Stella should be safe, but we'll get one of the guys over here to guard the door so you can go home," Sage assures him and pulls out his phone to message Sam and Dean the new instructions.

"Yeah, okay, that would be good. I could use a shower. Is it okay if I move into the suite with Stella until she's healed? I would feel a lot better if I could."

"Are you and Stella a couple?" I ask curiously, and he shrugs.

"Work keeps us pretty busy, but we do enjoy each other's company when we can."

I chuckle. "That's a nonanswer, but who am I to pry? You do you. Sure, go for it, and Sterling, take at least the week off, and let me know if you need more. Your assistant managers are more than capable of picking up the slack while you recover too."

We say our goodbyes and head back to the car. It's evening now, and I'm looking forward to being in my own bed. I'm hoping I can convince Sage to spend the night with me again.

"Hmm, Ms. Russo, you better be careful, or people will start calling you the mafia princess again if they see how much you care about some of your employees," Sage teases, and I flip him off. "Let's go home. You have that appointment at the Black Rose tomorrow. I don't want you to miss that."

I stare at him in horror. "I can't go in there looking like this." I wave at my face, and he winces.

"Just use the same concealer you use over your tattoos when you go. You wear a mask, so no one will even notice, and the lighting is dark."

"Oh, yeah, okay." I calm down, and he smiles.

"I just want you to have fun, blow off some steam, and enjoy yourself."

"Do you want to come and watch?" I ask him, and he takes his time considering it but slowly shakes his head.

"No, I don't want to mess with your thing. Though maybe just stick to rubbing yourself all over him and not going any further than you have before." I can hear the insecurity in his voice, so I reach out and grab his hand.

"I won't, I promise. Cutting and blood only. I'll leave all the touching and exploring for your body now that I've discovered your body is a wonderland." I jokingly sing the last part, and he smiles, losing the worry in his eyes.

"My body is a whole fucking theme park and the most thrilling ride ever," he boasts, and all is right with the world again.

"What are you going to do while I'm gone?" I ask him, and he smiles widely.

"I'm going to love on my plants. I need to top all my new crop. They are finally big enough to survive the process," he tells me, and I actually know what he's talking about.

I've paid attention over the last year because he's always been so enthusiastic about the whole process. Topping is when you remove the main part of the plant, encouraging bushier growth on the lower branches. I've watched him do it before, and he puts on music and basically skips through his field, singing and dancing and shaking his ass as he does his thing. It's so fucking cute. I'm torn now, I almost want to stay home and help him.

I bite my lip, and he must be able to see my indecision. "Babe, it's going to take a few days, so you can help the next day," he assures me, and I nod.

"Okay, it's a date."

"Oh, that sounds like my perfect date. I'll get Suzy to make us a picnic, and we can take it downstairs. I'll put out a blanket, and after we eat, I'll fuck you beneath my plants." He's practically dancing in his seat.

"They are not really big enough to fuck under," I tease, and he shakes his head.

"No, not those ones. The bigger crop down the back of the warehouse is the perfect size. We need to harvest next week."

Sage grows all his crops in stages, so that we're never without one that's almost ready for picking.

"Well, I can't wait. It will be my first date."

His head swivels to look at me, his mouth wide with surprise. "First date?"

"Yeah, I've never been on one. Before Stacey, I wasn't interested, and after Stacey, I definitely wasn't interested."

"But you had female lovers," he argues, and I shrug.

"Yeah, but we weren't exactly going on dates. I'd call them up, we'd fuck, and then I'd leave."

"Well, get ready to have your socks rocked, Victoria Russo. I am going to woo the crap out of you," he says with a light in his eyes that tells me he's making plans. I'm not worried, though, just excited for what is to come.

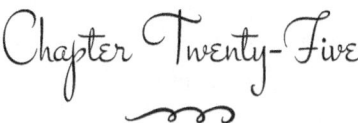

Chapter Twenty-Five

The following morning, I swear I hurt even more than I did when it originally happened. I swallow my morning coffee while Ben and Suzy fuss over both of us. Neither of them was awake when we returned, so they hadn't seen or heard what had happened.

"I knew I should have put my makeup on before breakfast," I grumble good-naturedly, but I'm secretly pleased that these two love me like my own parents did. I miss Dad so much today. I woke up wishing he was here to deal with all that was going on, and then I started to feel mad. I was angry that instead of just letting Gio live his life and making me the head of the family, he caved to stereotypes. Although we are a forward-thinking family, that would have been too much, even for us.

Sage and I fill them in on everything we've learned and what happened. I didn't get a chance to the other day, since Suzy was so distracted with preparing a meal for our guests.

Ben is pissed. "Just put a bullet in Lorenzo's skull and be done with it. Why play all these games?"

"Because I'm pretty sure he's not the one in charge, and if I kill him too quickly, then I won't have an inside man, so to speak."

"If Penny is fucking Mario Maricuso, though, that's your in," Suzy points out, and I shake my head.

"No, because men like Lorenzo and Mario only think women are good for one thing," I explain.

"Sucking their dick," Sage adds helpfully.

"No way would they have shared anything important with her. No, he lives for now."

"What are you going to tell Gio about everything?" Ben doesn't sound like he's being judgy, just curious.

"To be honest, nothing, and I'd appreciate it if you two kept it to yourselves as well." They both quickly agree. "Gio hasn't been helpful recently, and I've had to take over and delegate more and more. It's why I was so insistent on having our employees double-checked. I need to know they are loyal if I'm going to put them in places of importance."

"Surely he's going to ask questions when he sees your face." Suzy sounds skeptical, and I shrug.

"I have amazing concealer, and Gio is so far up his own ass, I doubt he will even notice."

"It would have to be amazing to cover that. I'm not sure all the concealer in the world is going to help," Ben comments as Suzy nods in agreement.

"Trust me, if it can cover my tattoos, it will cover my bruises."

"Go fix your face and then come back and show them. They are not going to believe it until they see," Sage encourages me, and I drain the rest of my coffee and hop up to do as he says.

"Oh, I won't be home for dinner tonight, and I'll be late, so don't bother leaving me anything in the oven. I'll just grab something while I'm out," I tell them as I leave the kitchen.

"Oh, that reminds me, I need a picnic," I hear Sage say to Suzy as the kitchen door swings closed behind me. I smile, knowing that he's in there organizing stuff for our date tomorrow night. I'm excited for it, and I plan on buying some sexy lingerie while I'm out today. I may even browse the sex shop at the club tonight before I leave. I want to see what kind of toys I can find for us.

Once I'm in my room, I gather up everything that I'll need for the day and my appointment tonight. I won't be coming back to Banebridge until after I've been to Black Rose. There's no point in driving back from Suncity when I can use the suite at the Lucky Diamond to get changed. Picking my favorite knife up off the bedside table, I flick it open and test the sharpness of the blade. It feels a little blunt. I may need to sharpen it. The sharper it is, the less strength I need to use to draw blood. Just a light touch gives me the desired results if the blade is honed to perfection. I close it up and stick it into my bra before moving to the bathroom and studying my face.

Most of the swelling is gone from my cheek, but the bruises are a nasty color. They are not actually wrong, it's going to take me a bit to cover it, but it's not that hard of a job. I do it for my tattoo when I go to the Black Rose to make myself anonymous—there aren't a lot of women with the Russo family motto on their ribs. It's just about getting the colors and layering right. The makeup itself doesn't wash off, so once it's on, it will stay there until I remove it. I can even swim and shower with it on.

I spend the next ten minutes concealing and covering it up, and when I'm done, you wouldn't even know I'd been in a car accident. I finish dressing for the day in one of my usual pantsuits, but when I try to get my corset holster on, it hurts, and I find I need some help to ease it up over my arms and shoulders.

"Sage?" I carry my corset to the door and stick my head out. Hopefully he's returned to his room to get dressed as well. When he comes out, he's in jeans and a band shirt, and his feet are bare, as usual. "You're not coming with me today?" I ask, and he shakes his head.

"No. Gio left a message and said that gun shipment needs to be shipped out today, and he's not going to be able to make it back to supervise it. He asked me to make sure everything is in the shipment." He eyes my naked torso like I'm the best thing since his weed farm.

"Fuck, it's literally the first day of college for him,

and he's already blowing off family stuff. Screw him!" I shout, and his eyes widen.

"Hey, don't shoot the messenger." He holds up his hands before coming toward me and pulling me into a hug. He coos sweet nonsense for a moment, rubbing his hands up and down my naked back until my erratic breathing settles.

"How about we go back into my room, and I give your pussy a tongue lashing? I bet an orgasm will make this Monday a little better."

I think about his offer so long he must take my silence as assent, because he drops his arms and tugs me into his bedroom. Before I can argue, he has me on my back on his bed and my pants and underwear are on the floor. He swipes his tongue through my pussy, making me gasp, before sucking my lips into his mouth then releasing them with a pop.

"Fuck, you are delicious, so sweet," he mutters before flicking his tongue against my clit. "This is going to be fast and dirty," he warns before sucking hard on my clit at the same time he shoves two fingers deep into my pussy. It's a tight fit, and my back arches off the bed as I shout at the overload of sensations. I wasn't really primed, but it only takes two pumps before his fingers are coated in my slick and I'm riding his digits, my head thrashing back and forth on the bed.

"That's it, my dirty girl. You're so responsive," Sage mutters. "So juicy and hot, your cunt grips my fingers so good. You want my cock, don't you? Your greedy pussy wants to feel my cock pounding into it."

Who would have guessed that dirty talk would push my buttons? Usually I'm the one who does all the dirty talk, but letting Sage be dominant is fun. I never thought I'd be submissive to anyone, but I've discovered I can easily switch between the two.

"Yes, Sage, fuck me," I beg, tugging at his head, trying to pull him away from my cunt. He comes up grinning and wipes his mouth with the back of his hand before dropping his jeans and coating his dick with my slick from his fingers.

"Quick and dirty, babe," he reminds me and flips me over onto my hands and knees before slamming home.

"Fuck!" I scream. Although he did the prep work, he's big, and I haven't taken enough penetration on a regular basis for it to be easy.

He pauses and whispers words of praise as his hands caress my ass. I feel his finger press against my asshole and tense slightly.

"Shh, baby, it's okay. I promise it will be good. But not today, we'll take it slow. I'll bring some lube to our date, and we can play. Both of us. Ready?" he asks as his fingers drift around to tweak my clit. I'm so fucking close, and I just want him to move.

"Yes please!" I beg, and he presses a kiss to the middle of my back.

"Oh, you said the magic words." He pulls back and thrusts forward again. With his fat cock hitting all the right places and his finger tapping my clit, I feel my body hurl itself off the orgasm cliff. My body explodes in waves of pleasure, and I'm not quiet about it.

"God, yes, Sage, fuck!" I shout, not caring if the whole house can hear us. "Faster, harder,"

I beg him as my pussy continues to ripple around his dick. He gets in a few more strokes before I feel him still and come. Thank fuck I have an implant. Neither of us have even thought about protection.

"Oh God, Tori, you feel so fucking good. I never had trouble lasting longer before, but maybe it's different when you're with the girl you love." He presses kisses up and down my spine as we both feel our orgasms start to subside. I collapse to my front, my arms no longer wanting to hold me up, and he comes with me with a grunt. "So fucking good." He smothers my face with kisses, and it's not long before I'm giggling. "Let's just stay here all day. Fuck the outside world."

"Ha, see, it's your turn to want to play hooky today," I tease him but pat his leg. "Let me up, I have to clean up," I tell him, and as he withdraws, I feel a gush of fluid follow his movement.

"Shit, I need to change my sheets now. Fuck, we didn't use protection." He rolls over onto his back as I climb off the bed. He's looking at me with concern, and I shrug.

"It's okay. I'm clean, and I have the implant. I'm okay with it."

His concern turns to relief. "I'm clean too, but I'll do a test if you want proof."

I shake my head. "It's okay, I'll just shoot you if you give me anything." I head to his bathroom, turning on the light and peeing before finding a cloth to clean up the mess. I don't have time for another shower, and I don't like the idea of walking around with cum-filled panties.

When I return, Sage is redressed and has grabbed my underwear and pants off the floor. "Did you need help with this?" he asks, holding up my corset, and I nod.

"Yes please, that's why I called you. As much fun as this was and an awesome way to start the day, I need to get going."

Gingerly, he helps me into the corset before I return to my room to grab my pair of Mary Jane pumps and suit jacket. Once I have them both on, I grab my phone and gun, and then we head back downstairs.

When we get down there, Suzy and Ben are still in the kitchen where we left them. "Wow, Tori, you did an amazing job covering that bruise," Suzy exclaims, "but your hair is a little messy."

I dump my phone and gun on the counter and hurry over to look at myself in the reflection of the oven. Sure enough, it's sticking out in all directions from me thrashing it back and forth on Sage's bed.

"Crap, I can't go out like this. Why didn't you say

anything?" I ask, whirling on Sage and putting my hands on my hips, but he just grins unrepentantly.

"Seeing the results of my hard work makes me happy," he says and winks as Ben hoots and Suzy claps in glee.

"Finally, you two have your act together. Thank goodness. All the repressed sexual tension was driving me mad," she tells us, and Ben grins.

"Yeah, but it was wonderful for me." He winks suggestively, and the two guys fist bump. Assholes!

"Here, Tori, just put it up in a messy bun and call it good today. No one will know any different." Suzy digs around in a drawer and passes me a hair tie.

I grab it and turn back to face the oven, doing as she suggested. When I'm happy with how it looks, I grab my phone and gun off the counter, shoving the latter into my holster and wincing as I overstretch my abused muscles.

"Did you take a painkiller this morning?" Sage asks, frowning with concern.

"No, they make me a little fuzzy, and if I have to drive, then I don't want to be distracted."

"I can run upstairs and get changed. Ben can go down and supervise the shipment," Sage offers, and Ben nods his agreement, but I wave them both off.

"No, I'll be fine. A few aches and pains never hurt anyone," I promise, giving him a kiss, and Suzy practically swoons. "I'll see you tonight?" I ask him hopefully, and he grins.

"If you don't come to my bed when you get home, I'll be tracking you down," he promises.

I wave goodbye to the other two and take off. I'm not sure what Gio's schedule is, but I have the Find My iPhone app on my phone, so tracking him down will be pretty easy. After that, I'm going to treat myself to a manicure and pedicure so that at least some of me looks pretty when I go to the Black Rose tonight. I wonder which sub I'll be seeing. I'm actually excited to be going, and I secretly hope it's my male sub. Even though I promised Sage I wouldn't do anything sexual with him, he gives me such delicious reactions. It's totally satisfying to me, making any orgasm I have that much sweeter.

Chapter Twenty-Six

The drive to Suncity is actually pleasant. I'm in a good mood despite my bruises and the news about Gio. Maybe an orgasm is the way I need to start every day. I have my own playlist blasting through the speakers for a change. Usually if Sage is with me, he insists on picking the tunes, so it's nice to be listening to my own for a change.

I take a detour to the warehouse before I go to the college, stopping the car in front and climbing out. I wrinkle my nose at the smell—wet and burnt—and examine what remains of the building. Most of it has caved in on itself, and there is caution tape all over the place. It is well and truly gone. That's a relief, and one less thing for me to worry about. I pull out my phone and snap a couple of pictures in case the insurance people require them before tucking it back into my pocket and heading on my way.

The Kitty Kat Club is not far from here, and I

consider stopping in and speaking to Lacey about moving up to San Jose temporarily until Stella is back on her feet, but I decide not to. Who wants to ruin a perfectly good orgasm buzz with a run-in with Candy? The more I think about it, the more I like Sam's suggestion, but it does mean I'm going to have to speak to her. Not today though, so I drive my car in the direction of the college.

It's midmorning by the time I get there, and classes must have just finished, because the campus is covered with people. I park my car and hop out. I couldn't get one close to Gio's dorms, so I'm going to have to take a walk through the campus. I lock my car and put my sunglasses on before pulling out my phone to locate Gio.

I find the appropriate app and almost throw my phone when I discover he has his location turned off. "Fucking asshole. Going to make my life difficult," I mutter as I start the trek across campus to his dorm. I may as well start there.

My mood plummets, and I decide today is the day we have this out. I'm done being walked on by my big brother. He either gets his priorities straight, or he can fuck off.

I must be putting off a don't fuck with me air, because people hurry to get out of my way, or maybe my reputation precedes me. A lot of Suncity U students frequent our nightclub in Banebridge. It is a Californian hot spot.

The trees open up, revealing a big square full of

socializing students. I consider going around, but I have shit to do, and this is already taking too long, so I march straight through the middle of it.

"Tori, Tori!"

I hear my name, so I stop and turn to find who's calling me. At a park bench off to the side, I find Vienna waving at me. She says goodbye to the girl she was talking to and hurries after me. She's wearing a cute pair of denim cutoff shorts and a Suncity U hoodie, with a pair of flip-flops on her feet. Her red hair is out and hanging almost to her waist. She's fresh faced and glowing, and I feel an irrational wave of jealousy that she was talking to another girl.

"Hi." She's breathless when she hurries up to me.

"New prospective bed partner?" I ask, peering over her shoulder, but I don't miss the way her face falls.

"Ah, no, just trying to make friends," she says quietly, but I don't miss her upset tone, and the jealousy turns to guilt.

"Fuck. Sorry, that wasn't fair. You can see whoever you want. I have to see Gio, and I'm pissy about it and taking it out on you."

"It's okay, I don't mind, and hearing that you might be a little bit jealous gives me hope."

I still haven't spoken to them about my kinks, and I'm reluctant to start anything with her before I do, but I take her hand, tucking it in mine, and start walking again.

"Do you have a class?" I ask her, and she shakes her head.

"No, I was just talking about the class outline with that girl. Colton didn't come today. He's busy back at the dorm, doing the work you asked him to do, and I wanted to make sure I had all the information so I didn't tell him anything wrong."

"Good, let me walk you back to your room. You can tell me about your class, and then I can see Colton. He was the other reason I came here, not just to see Gio."

"You couldn't have called either of them?" Vienna asks with a smirk on her lips.

"Fine, you caught me. It didn't hurt that maybe I would run into any of you."

She giggles and proceeds to tell me about her class as we walk to their dorm. When we get to the foyer, the elevator opens and Stacey steps out.

"Oh, there you are, Vienna. I was just telling Gio and your brothers that we should all have lunch together one day."

"You saw Gio?" I ask, and Stacey's peal of laughter echoes in the foyer.

"Oh, Tori, I told you it would be different this year. You're not here to gate keep, and Gio can recognize a worldly woman when he sees one. Men like it when a woman knows what they are doing in bed." She runs her hands over her body weirdly.

"Are you high?" I ask her, peering a little closer for bloodshot eyes.

"Worldly woman? Don't you mean skank or ho?" Vienna asks, laughing at her.

"Fuck the two of you. You'll see, I'll get them all, and the two of you will be left licking each other's pussies for the rest of your lives while I have all the men licking mine." With that psychotic rant, she pushes between the two of us and flounces off.

"Delusional much?" Vienna asks, and I scoff.

"Not even worth our time," I reply as we step onto the elevator and Vienna swipes her card to their floor.

When it stops, we get out, and I go to knock on Gio's door now that I know he's here, but Vienna stops me.

"Hey, come and have a drink with me. You said you wanted to see Colt too," she pleads, and I can't resist her fluttering eyelashes.

"Okay, hopefully Gio isn't going anywhere."

"Oh, I doubt it. Casey was in the same class as me, and she was heading back here after it. I'm almost certain Stacey was lying and the two of them are very occupied. Plus, I know Xavier and Tristan are both at the self-defense class X is running. Apparently they got a lot of students, and he asked Tris for help until he can get another instructor."

"Oh, I bet they did," I mutter, and she smirks.

"Yeah, every female student there is going to be so disappointed when every one of their advances gets shot down."

She pushes the door to her room open and steps in, and I follow after her. "You're that sure of their loyalty?" I ask, stripping off my jacket and putting it on the hook. I pull out my Glock and shove it into the jacket pocket so I won't have to worry about it. When I turn around, she's walked back toward me.

"Absolutely. Tris may flirt like a dirty dog, but the two of them are a hundred percent in with Colton and me, and we all discuss anyone we want to bring to our beds."

"Even me?" I ask her, and she nods, backing me up to the wall.

"Especially you." Her voice drops and gets seductive and husky, and I feel a shiver run down my spine. "And Sage. You know that night at your place? I came so hard thinking that maybe the two of you were getting yourselves off to the sounds of us fucking. Imagine my disappointment when I discovered you weren't even home." She pouts prettily, and I lean in and bite her bottom lip before sucking and releasing it. Her pupils dilate, and she moans in pleasure.

"Sage did," I admit, "and I probably would have if I didn't have an errand. I almost invited you to join Sage and me when we returned and I saw you watching us, but I decided to be selfish with my first time with a man."

"Hmm, was it good?" Vienna asks, her lids at half-mast as she runs her nose along my neck and nips my ear.

"Very good," I reply, putting my hands on her waist and tipping my head to give her better access.

"And have you given up on loving girls?" she asks, sucking a spot on my neck before biting down.

I shudder and groan. "God, no."

Her mouth smashes against mine, and she kisses me hard. She tastes like peaches and sin, and I can't get enough, so I pull her toward me. She's slightly shorter, so I have to bend a little to kiss her. I squeeze her round ass cheeks and let her grind on my leg as the two of us kiss for what seems like hours. When we pull apart, we're both breathing hard.

"Come on." She grabs my hand and tows me to a room that smells like both her and Colton. The bed's a mess, the sheets wrinkled and the covers tossed back. She winces.

"Sorry, I guess I forgot to make the bed this morning." It doesn't stop her from pushing me back on the bed and following me down. Her mouth comes back down on mine as the two of us roll around, each of us trying to be the one on top.

She wins, and I allow her to because it lets me pull her shirt off over her head. I toss it to the side and get my fill of her milky white globes, which are pushed up in the cups of her bra. I playfully nip each one, sucking up a pretty red spot on both of them.

"Oh, Colton's going to take that as a challenge," she says, writhing on top of me, her pussy rubbing against mine.

Her words stop me dead. "Shit, Colton. I didn't see him on the way past. Is he going to be okay with this?" I ask her, and she smirks.

"I'm not sure where he went, but he's going to be pissed that he missed this." She shuffles so that she's sitting up and straddling my body. She reaches up and grabs the zipper of my corset and slowly lowers it. My breasts pop out like a jack-in-the-box once the zipper gets below them. "Oh, I like this." She unzips it all the way before taking my breasts in her hands and giving them a gentle squeeze before pushing them together. She leans in and tongues each of my nipples, laving first one, and then the other, until they are both bright pink and peaked.

"Hmm, just like raspberries." She shuffles her backwards, and I allow her to take the lead. Sage has mellowed me, and I'm enjoying being on the receiving end of pleasure. That's not to say I'm not going to give as good as I get, but I'm trying to learn to be more patient. She pulls off both of my shoes, glancing down at one. "These are gorgeous, and we are the same size. You know what that means, don't you?" she asks, tossing one over her head.

I shake my head in confusion, and she grins playfully. "We just doubled our shoe wardrobe." I chuckle as she continues to strip my clothes off of me. Once I'm completely naked, she pauses for a moment to soak it all in.

"You're gorgeous, Tori," she says sweetly before crawling up the bed and pushing my legs apart. I remember what I've already done today, and I freak and slam them shut. She frowns at me.

"What's wrong?" she asks.

"Ah, I had sex with Sage this morning," I tell her sheepishly, and she grins.

"Good for you, but there's nothing stopping us,

unless he doesn't want to share you." She sits back on her heels with a frown.

"No, it's not that. He's fine with us all doing whatever. He's excited about it actually, but, um, we didn't use a condom."

Her confusion turns to understanding, and she laughs. "I'm not afraid of a bit of man spunk, Tori. I have three boyfriends."

I wrinkle my nose, blushing a little, and her eyes fill with understanding. "You haven't given a blow job before, have you?" I shake my head, and she smiles gently. "No problem, I'll talk you through it if you want. I'm sure Colton would be happy to volunteer."

I squirm at the thought of giving her boyfriend oral sex, and I can practically feel my pussy weep with excitement.

"Oh, you like that idea?" She reaches out and pushes my thighs apart again, staring at my pussy. "Oh, you dirty girl, you are a mess down there. I'll just have to help you out." She settles between my thighs and runs her tongue through my folds. We both groan at the same time.

"Fuck, that's hot," I mutter and reach down, pulling her up toward me. "Let me return the favor," I suggest, and she nods, jumping off the bed and stripping off the rest of her clothes.

I get my first look at a completely naked Vienna. Her skin is pale and milky white, with only a smattering of freckles. She has gorgeous, dark brown nipples, and her pussy is bare, which I'm a little disappointed to see—I wanted to know if the carpet matched the drapes.

"Come here." I grab her, and she climbs back on me, settling her pussy above my mouth.

I grip both of her ass cheeks and pull her down so I can really get my lips on her. I lick her clit a couple of times before thrusting my tongue in and out of her pussy. She murmurs her encouragement as she rides my face, taking her pleasure. It's hot and fucking sexy. So many women are scared to get into a sixty-nine position, worried about their weight or smothering you or whatever, but Vienna is confident in herself, and she revels in the pleasure. She tastes musky and sweet, and I can't get enough. I love eating pussy and hearing the noises girls make when I bring them pleasure.

She leans down, and her breasts press against my stomach as she flicks her tongue across my clit. I groan at how good it feels as she dives in, not afraid to enjoy it herself. Sucking on two fingers, I slide them into her pussy, and it flutters around them. She moans against my cunt as I pump them in and out, her pussy slowly tightening with every flick of my tongue on her clit.

"Oh God, Tori, yes, that's it right there," she chants, sliding her own fingers into my pussy. It's hard to concentrate on what I'm doing because it feels so good, but we manage. It's messy and uncoordinated, but soon enough, the two of us fall over the edge into bliss. She comes so hard it shoots into my mouth, and I lick up every drop. She returns the favor, but I soon push her away, becoming oversensitive to her touch.

She rolls off of me, and we lie top to tail, panting. "God," I mutter, pushing the hair that escaped my tie back off my face. "That was not what I had planned when I came to campus today."

She chuckles, rolling onto her side, and wraps herself around my leg, stroking my naked hip. "But wasn't it fun? And it distracted you from what had you so pissed off."

She's right, the head of steam I'd built up about Gio is gone, replaced with resignation. "Ugh, I don't want to ruin my glow with mad thoughts."

"Okay, I'll be quiet," she promises and mimes zipping her lips.

"Is anyone home? Vienna?" Colton calls out, and I feel a moment of panic. As I go to move, Vienna clings to me like a little monkey, not allowing me to escape.

"No, Tori, we're not hiding this," she scolds, so I settle back and wait to be caught.

Within seconds, Colton's at the door, taking in the scene in front of him. A slow smile spreads across his mouth, and he leans against the doorframe. "She finally wore you down, did she?" he asks me, crossing his arms.

I shrug. "What can I say, she's very persuasive."

He chuckles. "I got some subs if you're hungry. Why don't you two get dressed and come out, and we'll eat together."

"Sounds great, thanks, babe." Vienna blows him a kiss and rolls over, stretching. Both Colton and I watch as she stretches her body like a cat before jumping off and grabbing a robe from the back of a chair.

"Come on, I'm starving, even though I just ate." She winks before picking up my clothes and tossing them to me. I realize I'm still in my corset, so thankfully, I don't have to shrug my arms back into it, but I still grunt with pain as I sit up.

Vienna freezes, and Colton pushes off of the door-frame. "What's wrong?" he demands, coming over and looking down at me. There are some bruises on my chest, and I'm not sure how Vienna missed them. I guess she was titillated.

"Oh my god, what happened?" Vienna asks, lightly running a finger over the marks.

"Why don't we finish getting dressed, and I'll tell you over lunch?" I suggest, and the two of them back off.

"Fine, but we want the truth," Colton demands and whirls around, stomping out of the bedroom, and Vienna chuckles.

"Now you've done it. Daddy Colton is in the house. He's going to nag you until you tell him."

Chapter Twenty-Seven

I slowly sink down onto the couch. Now that I'm no longer distracted by Vienna, my aches and pains have come back with a vengeance. "Here, Tori, have this. It might make you feel better." Colton lit up a joint, and he holds it out for me.

"Are we allowed to do this in your room?" I ask, reaching over to take it, and he shrugs nonchalantly.

"I doubt it, but what are they going to do?"

"Kick you out," I tell him, and Vienna snorts.

"We could only wish," she mutters cryptically before going to the fridge as Colton pulls some subs from a bag.

"Help yourself, Tori. I got extra because I thought the guys might be here."

"What do you want to drink, babe?" she calls, and Colton asks for a soda.

"Not you, I was talking to Tori," she scolds him,

and he grins at me when my mouth drops open in shock.

"Oh, ah, I'll just have a water if you have one, thanks."

"Sure thing, sweetie," she calls back, bending over and grabbing the drinks. Her robe rides up, and the bottom of her ass cheeks show.

"Tori, you have a little something here." Colton points to the corner of his mouth, and I reach up before I realize what he's doing. I flip him the bird as Vienna returns to the seat and hands us both our beverages.

"Now tell us what happened," she demands, searching through the bag of subs and handing one to each of us before taking one for herself. I leave mine on the coffee table as I continue to smoke the joint Colton gave me. It does help ease the pain, which I'm grateful for.

"Sage and I were in a car accident in San Jose yesterday," I tell them, and Vienna sits up straight.

"What? Gio never said anything. Did you know about this?" she questions Colton, who shakes his head and pats her knee.

"Calm down, love. Let Tori explain."

"Gio doesn't know, and I'd appreciate it if you didn't tell him. There's a whole heap of things going on at the moment that I can't talk about, and with him being so busy with college, he's next to useless to me."

Colton frowns, and Vienna looks between the two of us.

"What? No, we need to know more." She sounds upset, so I reach over and take her hand.

"Vienna. There are always going to be things I can't tell you. It's the nature of my life. If you can't deal with that, then we should stop this right now."

"But that's not fair." I see tears well in her eyes, and she looks to Colton for support, but it's obvious he understands.

"No, Vienna, you need to make a decision. Tori is not telling you things for your safety. Don't put her in this position," Colton says gently but firmly, and she pouts.

"Fine, but I need to know when you're hurt. Who is going to look after you if I can't?"

"I promise Sage did a very good job of looking after me last night."

Colton grins, but she crosses her arms, looking put out.

"Oh, I bet he did," she grumbles.

I take one last drag of the joint before handing it back to Colton and standing up. "Look, I'll leave you to think things over. Just know I really enjoyed what happened, and I'm open to exploring more, but you need to be happy with the limitations," I tell Vienna before turning to Colton. "You all do." He nods. "Listen, can I have a quick word? And then I really do need to speak to Gio."

He stands up. "Come into my office, we can talk there."

I lean in and give Vienna a gentle kiss on the lips,

293

which stay stubbornly set. "Bye, Vienna. Let me know what you decide," I tell her before following Colton to his office. I hear her screech, and then there's a thud behind me as we leave the room. Colton starts to chuckle.

"She doesn't like to be told no, and we have indulged her too much. It's good for her not to always get her way. Now what can I do for you?"

I explain the things I need added to the job, and he takes a few notes but promises some results by the end of the week. I get up to leave, and he follows me out. The drinks and food are still on the table, but Vienna is nowhere to be seen. "Don't worry." He sees me looking at their closed bedroom door. "Vienna's temper runs hot and fast. She will be texting you before you even get back to your car," he assures me, and I grab my jacket and my Glock, shoving it back into the holster and wincing with the movement.

"Do you think maybe you should be taking it a little easy today?" he asks, frowning, and I smile at his concern.

"Sure thing, and I promise I will, I just need to speak to Gio, and then I'm off to the Lucky Diamond for some pampering before an appointment I have tonight."

"Ah, well, that's good. Now how about you give me a kiss goodbye before you leave? In that office, you're the boss, but I kind of like to get my own way in the bedroom." He backs me up against their dorm room door much like his girlfriend had not all that long ago. I feel my nipples pebble and goosebumps break out across my flesh. He runs a finger over my bruised cheek like someone who knows exactly what is below the makeup.

"You know how to cover your bruises well," he mutters. "But in the right light, there's still a little bit of swelling."

"Shit. I thought it had all gone down."

"Don't worry, no one who isn't looking for it will notice." Before I can respond, his mouth is on mine. Again, it's so different from my other two recent kisses. Vienna's lips were so soft, and Sage kisses me like I'm the air he needs to breathe, but Colton's mouth is firm and commanding, and I melt into him, enjoying it thoroughly. It doesn't last long, and when he pulls away, I'm a little befuddled.

"See you soon, Tori," he murmurs before stepping out of the way and letting me leave.

I stumble out of the door, dazed and confused, but I soon come to my senses.

Shit, girl, pull yourself together. A little afternoon delight should not be turning the Angel of Death into a sap.

Fuck, I need to kill someone.

I look carefully at my brother's door and turn toward the elevator. He might be the one I kill if I go in there now and he brushes me off once again. Nope, I'm going to get my pampering on and go see my sub. Once I shed some blood, I should be in the right frame of mind to deal with my brother.

—◆—

Colton was right, and Vienna sent me a text before I got to the car, but I let her hang until I reached the hotel. By then, I had ten more texts, each one sorrier than the last, so I decided to put her out of her misery and send one back.

And that's how I spend my afternoon, acting like a normal eighteen-year-old texting back and forth with my lovers, Sage and Vienna. Eventually, the two of them catch on, and it becomes a flirty three-way message group. I'm smiling broadly when it's time for me to get ready for the Black Rose.

I let them know that I'll be radio silent for a while. Sage responds with a, "Have fun." When I power down my phone, Vienna is nagging Sage to tell her where I'm going. I wonder how long it will take for him to cave or if he'll hold strong.

I'd sent my knife out to be sharpened, and the concierge returned it in immaculate condition. I think it had even been taken apart and cleaned. I dip it in bleach after I use it every time so any dried blood they found would be useless in case they thought to black-mail me.

I dress in a cute new lingerie set that I'd bought. It's all black, with leather straps crisscrossing my body in a delightful pattern. The bra cups have cutouts, and my nipples are poking out. At least my sub will have a nice view, even if he can't touch. I wrap my fur coat around me like I always do, and shove my mask into one pocket and my knife into the other. I leave my Glock behind in the room's safe and slip my feet into my heels. Wiggling my toes, I smile at the pretty pink color that the beautician put on them.

My hair is up in a high ponytail, and my makeup is on point. I am more than ready to go. I called the limo, so it's waiting for me when I get downstairs. Bryce waves and winks at me from the front desk—he knows I go to the Black Rose, but he doesn't know my pseudonym—so I wave back and climb into the vehicle.

We don't trust anyone anymore, and I know this one has been checked thoroughly by the guards at the house. We don't park them anywhere they might be tampered with either. They will drop me at the Black Rose and then return to the fortress and wait for me to call them. We use more fuel, but it's safer this way.

The crowd is quieter than normal, but it is a Monday night, so I guess that's not unexpected. I already donned my mask in the limo, and after a quick drink at the bar, I'm escorted to my usual room. I'm thrilled to find Romeo there, waiting for me exactly how I like them—bound and cuffed and stretched out on display in the middle of the room.

My heels click on the concrete as I stride over to stand in front of him. He gasps when he sees me. "Mistress V. I've missed you. I've been waiting for your summons." He sounds strung out and desperate, and I reach up and stroke his face.

"Oh, Romeo, have you missed me?" I ask quietly, and he nods vigorously.

"Do you need me to make you bleed?" I coo, running my finger across both of his naked pecs. Again, he's wearing only a pair of black boxer briefs. The rest of his body is free from adornment, just waiting for me to run my blade across it.

"Yes please, I need it."

"Is your life particularly chaotic?" I ask him, pulling away and removing my long fur coat. I step away, letting him look his fill at my thong-clad ass, before draping the coat over a chair. During our first session, he explained why he likes to be cut. It helps ground him and silence all the chaos that runs through his mind much of the time. Romeo is a genius, and his photographic memory sometimes becomes too much for him to handle. Cutting him gives it a release.

"Yes. I have a new job, and it's very big, and there's a lot of information. There are also some new people in my life who are giving me mixed feelings."

I blink momentarily, stunned at his outburst. Wow, that was a lot. After our first conversation where I learned why he comes here, we haven't talked about personal stuff. It's only ever been about the moment.

"Shall we get started?" I ask him, removing the knife from the coat pocket and turning to face him. His eyes lock on my nipples as I move back to him, and then his eyes drift lower, and they widen.

"Tori?" he asks, and I stop dead.

"What the fuck?" How does he know? I follow his

gaze and freeze. Fuck, I didn't cover my tattoo. Hang on. Only Sage and Gio know my tattoo is there, but then I remember my afternoon.

"Colton?" I ask, and I reach up and tear off his mask. Sure enough, standing there tied up in my chamber is Vienna's gorgeous blond boyfriend. "Oh my god."

We stare at each other, and I look down at the knife in my hand before screeching and launching it across the room.

"Fuck!" I reach up to untie him, and he flinches back.

"Please don't, please, I need it. You have no idea how much."

"Oh, believe me, I know. I need it too, but I can't send you back to Vienna with cuts all over your body. Does she know about this?"

"Yes, I promise they all do. They are out there. Xavier is the one who looks after me when you're done."

"But they don't know it's me?" I ask, and he shakes his head.

"No, I didn't either. It was only your tattoo that tipped me off."

Before I can think of how to respond, the door bursts open.

I hear the staff member who guards the room shout, "You can't go in there! The room is occupied," but it sounds like he's struggling.

"I'm sorry, but Romeo is needed." The intruder's

body is hidden behind Colton's, but I recognize the voice.

"Tristan?" I peer around the still hanging Colton.

"Tori?" He looks confused for a moment before he starts nodding. "That actually makes sense."

"What do you want?" Colton asks, and Tristan shakes his head, remembering why he just barged into a private session—something that can get him evicted from the club.

"Fuck, man, Casey just called. There's an emergency. We need to go."

"You're not allowed to have phones in the club," I say absently, still confused by all this.

"She called the club, and they came and got us. We have to go, our dorm room is on fire."

THE END

Afterword

Phew that's done. I had trouble getting back into Tori's head, but I'm really happy with the way it turned out.

Thank you all for reading Lies Untold I can't tell you how much it means to me. I hope you enjoyed the book. It would be super awesome if you could leave a review wherever you bought it, because I love to hear what you thought of the story.

Don't worry it won't be too long before we return to find out what happens next. Keep an eye on may Facebook group for all things Lexie.

In the mean time why don't you check out one of my other series. You can find everything on my website at www.lexiewinston.com

Acknowledgments

To my cover designer Ashley, of Breakout Designs these covers are so beautiful.

Thank you to Jess at Elemental Editing to being the flexible wonderful person that you are. My book is pretty and readable thanks to you

And lastly to you guys the readers. I love what I do, and probably would do it regardless if anyone read them or not, but you guys make it that much sweeter so thank you.

Broken Promises is a little darker than I usually write but I'm having fun and looking forward to everything that is planned in the next book. While you wait why don't you check out Spies Like Me, a new offering, which is up fro preorder and scheduled for the start of March.

Until next time, happy reading

Lexie